A CONTEST TO KILL FOR

A HOPGOOD HALL MYSTERY

E.V. HUNTER

Boldwood

First published in Great Britain in 2023 by Boldwood Books Ltd.

Copyright © E.V. Hunter, 2023

Cover Photography: iStock and Dreamstime

The moral right of E.V. Hunter to be identified as the author of this work has been asserted in accordance with the Copyright, Designs and Patents Act 1988.

Every effort has been made to obtain the necessary permissions with reference to copyright material, both illustrative and quoted. We apologise for any omissions in this respect and will be pleased to make the appropriate acknowledgements in any future edition.

A CIP catalogue record for this book is available from the British Library.

Paperback ISBN 978-1-80483-575-3

Large Print ISBN 978-1-80483-576-0

Hardback ISBN 978-1-80483-578-4

Ebook ISBN 978-1-80483-573-9

Kindle ISBN 978-1-80483-574-6

Audio CD ISBN 978-1-80483-582-1

MP3 CD ISBN 978-1-80483-581-4

Digital audio download ISBN 978-1-80483-577-7

Boldwood Books Ltd
23 Bowerdean Street
London SW6 3TN
www.boldwoodbooks.com

'Why is it so damned cold?' Alexi stamped her UGG-booted feet on the frosty ground and thrust her hands deeper into the pockets of her sheepskin jacket. 'It never got this arctic in London.'

'Stop being such a baby,' Cheryl chided. 'It's only November. Give it a few weeks and then you'll really have something to complain about.'

'It gets worse than this?' Alexi shuddered at the prospect.

'It only seems warmer in London because of all that pollution.'

'Can't beat an unhealthy dose of carbon monoxide to keep the mercury above freezing.' Alexi caught Cheryl's elbow to prevent her from slipping on a patch of ice. 'Point proven, I believe.'

'Go on, admit it; you like it here.' Cheryl nodded towards Alexi's cat. 'He certainly does.'

'Only because there's more wildlife for him to terrorise.'

'Given some of the sights I saw the last time I was in London, I'd have to disagree.'

Alexi's breath clouded in front of her face when she chuckled. 'I guess you have a point.'

Cosmo, Alexi's cat, trotted ahead of the two friends while

Cheryl's little terrier Toby danced ecstatically around his feline friend.

'You'd think they hadn't seen each other for weeks rather than a couple of days,' Cheryl said with an indulgent smile.

Cosmo was twice Toby's size and weight, his paw prints in the frost double the size of the dog's. Alexi had been a reporter on the trail of a story that only the derelicts sleeping rough beneath Waterloo arches could help her to break. Cosmo, a feral cat who also resided beneath the arches, had taken a liking to Alexi and allowed her to adopt him. They'd been a double act ever since.

'You okay?' Alexi slowed her pace when she noticed that Cheryl had to scurry to keep up with her. 'You should have stayed inside with your little bundle of joy.'

Cheryl grinned at this reference to her two-month-old daughter. 'What, and deprive Drew of an excuse to pamper her?'

'Since when did he need an excuse?'

Cheryl rolled her eyes. 'Very true.'

Alexi laughed, thinking of Cheryl's larger than life husband and his total absorption with baby Verity. As a first-time father, he was duty bound to be terrified of dropping her, or somehow screwing things up. And yet Drew had yet to put a foot wrong as he dealt with her needs like a seasoned professional.

'That baby is definitely going to be a daddy's girl,' Alexi predicted.

'Don't I just know it!' Cheryl grinned. 'He even has me...'

'Oh no!' Alexi dropped Cheryl's arm and raced ahead. 'Cosmo, stop that at once!'

The film crew guy setting up to record the first session of a reality cooking programme at Hopgood Hall had caught Cosmo's attention and he'd decided to amuse himself by terrorising him. The man had dropped his equipment – probably something expensive and irreplaceable – and legged it for the nearest door. At the sound of Alexi's voice, Cosmo gave up pursuing him and morphed into a sleek black purring picture of innocence as he twined himself around Alexi's legs.

'Bad boy! You know better than that.'

'What the hell is that thing?' the crew member asked from behind the safety of a closed door. 'Looks like something out of Africa! Doesn't he... well, frighten the horses?'

'Sorry about that. He's actually quite harmless,' Alexi said, crossing her fingers behind her back. 'And, despite what you might have heard, he's not a black panther. He just looks like one and thinks he ought to live up to the rep.'

'Yeah well.' The guy poked his head cautiously around the door and eyed Cosmo dubiously, trying to look as though he hadn't just let a cat freak him out. 'If he's harmless, I'll put a tenner on the outside in the one-thirty at Kempton Park.'

Alexi rolled her eyes. This was a horseracing town and everyone talked the talk. The guy retrieved his equipment, uttered a few more expletives and disappeared inside the improvised studio. With Cosmo under control again, Alexi returned to Cheryl.

'Don't be too hard on him,' Cheryl said, tears of laughter pouring down her face. 'It's been a while since he exerted his authority.'

'He'll be the death of me yet.'

'He's only amusing himself. He's like a teenager who gets bored and acts up to get attention.'

'I can see I'll have to keep him clear of this lot.'

'No need.' Cheryl flapped a hand. 'I'll tell them to man up. This is the country. Who could possibly be afraid of a sweet little pussy cat?' Cheryl dropped a hand to stroke Cosmo's large head. He pushed against her hand and purred like the innocent he most decidedly was not.

'Brat!' Alexi said, failing to keep the affection out of her voice.

Alexi cast a critical eye over the building that the film guy had just taken refuge in, still astonished at the speed with which so many changes had taken place in seven short months. Hopgood Hall was situated in Lambourn, the valley of the racehorse. It was a boutique hotel owned by Cheryl and Drew. Alexi and Cheryl had been friends since their university days, but Cheryl had married Drew almost as soon as she graduated with a degree in hotel management while Alexi headed for a career in journalism. The career that she had put every waking hour into excelling at had come to a spectacular end in the spring when her paper, the *Sunday Sentinel*, downsized – make that dumbed down – and as a serious investigative journalist, she was a casualty of the cutbacks.

She and Cosmo came down to Lambourn so she could lick her wounds and decide where to go from there, only to become involved in a missing persons case when a friend of Cheryl's had disappeared. It later transpired that she had been murdered by a local trainer: a man who many around these parts considered to be on a par with God. Alexi broke the case with the help of a rather attractive local PI, Jack Maddox.

Alexi had subsequently received a hefty advance from a publishing house to write a book about the case. She had taken a cottage in Lambourn and settled into village life, a very quiet location in which to get the book written and decide where to go next. A city girl by nature, she was surprised how easily she had slotted into the whole country scene, and how readily the locals had accepted her. Given that she'd unmasked one of their own as a murderer, she'd half expected to be ostracised.

Cheryl and Drew's hotel had been failing when Alexi arrived. The building they were looking at now – constructed from aged brick to match the facade of the lovely old Georgian house – had been an ugly extension of prefabricated buildings to house the grooms working at the yard of the disgraced trainer. At Alexi's suggestion, they turned it into a proper extension with conference facilities and more accommodation. Alexi had gone into partnership with Cheryl and Drew and financed the extension. Drew used his influence to push planning consent through and the structure had been completed less than a month previously.

'I can't wait until spring to see how all the little courtyards and landscaping look,' Cheryl said. 'It was clever of you to suggest that Fay did the designs.'

'It gave her a purpose,' Alexi replied, referring to the mother of the murder victim, who now lived in her daughter's cottage locally.

'Come on, let's go inside. I'm dying to see how it all works. Not you,' Alexi said, holding up a hand to Cosmo, who meowed indignantly. 'You've already blotted your copybook. And no nipping at anyone's ankles, okay?' Cosmo peered up at Alexi through astute eyes. 'We won't be long.'

There had been a big rush in getting the extension finished so quickly and now its future hung in the balance. If it was to pay for itself then this television series would have to show it in a good light and be a success. There was a lot riding on it and Alexi prayed on a daily basis that she hadn't persuaded Drew and Cheryl to overextend themselves. Following the murder investigation, the hotel's business picked up dramatically for a while. All the ghouls wanting to say they'd seen the scene of the crime, Drew figured, taking advantage of their... well, ghoulishness by upping his prices. Alexi took the opportunity to promote the conference facilities, intending to use them for journalism and writing retreats, weddings and just about anything else they could charge top dollar for.

What she didn't make allowance for was her old boss and former lover, Patrick Vaughan, Political Editor on the *Sentinel*, coming up trumps. Desperate to get Alexi back, he wasn't taking no for an answer. She agreed to write the odd freelance article for the paper, but made sure she offered pieces to the competition as well. She had a point to make. Patrick kept offering her more and more enticing deals if she'd return to the *Sentinel*, to London and to his bed.

Alexi wasn't going anywhere.

The *Sentinel* was owned by a mogul who also had interests in a big cable television channel: one that was giving serious competition to the national stations. The channel was filming fly-on-the-wall cookery programmes from five different locations in the country: one per weekday night from each location for six weeks. The regional winners would cook-off against one another for the star prize. Patrick heard that one location had problems with the Health and Safety people, knew of the extension to Hopgood Hall and sold Alexi on the idea, if the building could be completed on time. Anything was possible, with the incentive of six whole weeks of near full occupancy to spur a hotelier on. Alexi didn't like the idea of being indebted to Patrick but knew he would be doing it as much for the kudos it would earn him with the boss – pulling the series out of the mire – as to curry favour with her. Patrick always had his eye on the bigger picture.

Much as she hated to admit it, Patrick had been right to suggest Cheryl's hotel, and more especially her temperamental chef Marcel, to star in the production. The hotel was situated in one of the most picturesque villages in the country, where racehorses outnumbered people. The house itself, furnished with lovingly preserved antiques, made a beautiful backdrop. As for Marcel, he could give Gordon Ramsey a run for his money when it came to effing and blinding, except he did it with a French accent that somehow made the profanities sound more exotic. His moodiness and dark good looks made him a natural for the small screen. The camera loved him and he played up to it like the prima donna that he was.

'Do you think they've done their homework on Marcel?' Cheryl asked. 'I mean, he looks, sounds and acts French but you and I both know his roots are in the East End of London and he's actually a bona fide cockney.'

Alexi took a moment to consider the question. 'I don't think he's ever actually claimed to *be* French, just that he grew up in France and trained there, which is true. Everyone just assumes—'

'And he doesn't put them right.'

'Well, in fairness, competition in his sphere is brutal. Anything to gain an edge.'

'I suppose.'

Cheryl opened the door to the reception area and wiped her feet. Alexi followed suit, knowing it was a waste of time and that their pristine new wood floors would soon be filthy from all the comings and goings. Alexi thought about the obscene amount of money they were being paid to allow the facilities to be abused by the film crew and immediately felt better.

'The four contestants should be here soon,' Alexi said, nodding to the harried producer who was conducting a conversation on his mobile and talking to a man in a suit at the same time. 'I can't wait to see what masochistic types would be willing to have every aspect of their lives under scrutiny twenty-four seven for the next six weeks.'

'They do it on *Big Brother*.'

'Yes, but none of our lot will be voted off. They are committed to staying the course, being bullied by our pseudo-French chef and living with cameras everywhere except in the bathrooms.' Alexi shrugged. 'I guess you've really got to want to make it as a chef to put up with having no privacy.'

'Think of our bank balance,' Cheryl said, grinning. 'And be grateful that we don't have to appear on camera.'

'Oh, trust me, I am!'

The friends entered a small reception room where, in front of the television cameras, the contestants would be introduced to Marcel for the first time. Alexi and Cheryl took chairs out of range of the cameras. Alexi nodded to the guy Cosmo had terrorised and again apologised.

'No sweat,' he replied, sticking out a hand. 'I'm Gerry Salter, sound engineer.'

'Alexi Ellis, co-owner.' She shook his hand. 'And Cheryl Hopgood, the real owner.'

'Welcome to our little piece of paradise,' Cheryl said, taking her turn to shake his hand.

'Did I miss it?' Drew came dashing in carrying Verity across his body in a hooded, thickly quilted pink papoose. She was sleeping peacefully. 'Real men aren't afraid to wear pink,' he added, grinning when he saw Alexi's shocked look.

'How does he do that?' Cheryl demanded to know, cooing over her sleeping child. 'She's never this quiet for me.'

'It's a gift,' Drew replied, kissing the end of his wife's nose. 'Well, actually, I sing to her. Works every time.'

Cheryl gaped at him. 'You couldn't carry a tune in a bucket.'

He grinned. 'Verity makes allowances.'

'She would have to.'

'No, the show hasn't started yet,' Alexi said, answering Drew's original question.

'No sign of Jack then,' Drew said. 'I thought he might show his face.'

Alexi shrugged, unprepared to say she'd hoped the same thing. She hadn't seen much of him since they'd tied up Natalie Parker's murder. Not that there was any reason why she should have. There had been a spark between them when they first met, but it had failed to ignite. They'd been out to dinner a few times during the ensuing months, but nothing more. Perhaps Alexi had misread the signs or someone else had a prior claim on Jack's affections. The possessiveness of his attractive business partner sprang to mind. Probably just as well if nothing came of it, she thought. Since getting her fingers burned with Patrick, she wasn't ready to play the love game again quite yet, even if Jack did tick all the right boxes.

'Last time I spoke to him he was tied up on some big investigation in Newbury,' Alexi replied.

'Ah, shame.'

'Hey, gorgeous.'

'What are you doing here?' Alexi demanded to know when Patrick stole up to one side of her, slid an arm around her waist and kissed her cheek. She balked at his presumption and pulled away from him. She absolutely didn't need these public displays of affection that made her feel as though he was making some sort of obscure point.

'Don't you mean, thank you for organising all this and making the hotel a fortune?'

'No, I mean, what are you doing here? You run a paper, not a TV show.'

'Thought I might write a piece on the meet-and-greet stuff myself.'

Alexi sent him a disbelieving look. That was junior reporter stuff. 'How the mighty have fallen,' she said. 'Anyway, I'm surprised you got past Cosmo.'

'Ah, I tricked him.'

Alexi shook off the arm that had worked its way around her waist and waved a finger at him. 'If you hurt my cat then you're a dead man, Vaughan.'

The producer, Evan Southgate, climbed onto the stage and everyone fell quiet. He introduced Marcel to the programme's host, a man by the name of Paul Dakin. He sported a fake tan, heavily lacquered, bouffanted hair and dazzling white dental implants.

Alexi had already had the dubious pleasure of meeting him and disliked him on sight. His plastic charm didn't impress her any more than the smile that failed to reach his eyes. Paul Dakin was his own number one fan, no question. She actually yawned when he spoke almost entirely about himself for ten minutes and then failed to interest her in writing a piece on him for the *Sentinel*.

Alexi smiled as Marcel hammed it up for the cameras, banging on about how passionate he was about all things in life, food being just one of them.

'He'll get all the ladies tuning in, even the ones who hate cooking,' Cheryl whispered. 'The camera really does love him and the French accent is the perfect touch. I can see why the producers were so keen to have him. Good job you had the sense to tie him into a contract with us, otherwise...'

'Here come the contestants,' Alexi said, sitting forward, keen to see what they were like. Details had been closely guarded and all she knew was that there were two men and two women.

A hush fell over the audience. It was made up of an assortment of crew, suits from Far Reach – the production company Patrick was so keen to make an impression upon – and an array of local bigwigs, including the mayor.

'Bloody hell!' Drew breathed as the first victim, a lady by the name of Juliette Hammond, tottered onto the stage in four-inch heels and a skirt that could have doubled as a belt, leaving precious little to the imagination. She was hotter than the temperatures generated in Marcel's kitchen and judging by her confident air, she knew it. There was an audible gasp of appreciation from the entire male audience. Alexi could understand why the men had all sat up and taken notice. The woman was short, stacked and feminine to her well-manicured fingertips. She had a waterfall of long, blonde hair artfully cascading over one shoulder and suspiciously green eyes. Odds on she was wearing coloured contacts. Oh hell, even Alexi was starting to think like a bookie.

Alexi forgave Ms Hammond the heavy-handed makeup which was probably necessary for appearing before the cameras. Did that mean the contestants would have to wear makeup all the time, even when they weren't 'performing'? So much for being caught in their downtime looking natural. Juliette's figure was slender yet curvy and everything about her screamed sex appeal. Even Marcel seemed momentarily speechless which, in Alexi's experience, was unheard of.

'Wonder if she can cook,' Cheryl murmured.

'Who cares,' one of the crew replied.

Greta Reid was Juliette's polar opposite: tall, overweight and totally unremarkable. The two male contestants, John Shelton and Anton Heston, were different species as well. Anton had the caramel-coloured skin of a West Indian, with a fine head of dreadlocks and laidback attitude to go with it. John was short, balding and on the ugly side of forty. They each did their spiel for the camera, talking about their backgrounds in the catering trade, their love of all things to do with food and what it would mean to them if they won this leg of the competition.

'Heaven help the winner,' Drew muttered, aware that he or she was guaranteed a year in Marcel's kitchen, if they could take his temper for that long, learning the trade under his not-so-tender tutelage. The winner of the entire competition would get a big cash reward and an opportunity to feature in a regular TV cooking show.

When asked by Dakin what he thought of the competitors, Marcel gave them a contemptuous look, including a preening Juliette in his disdain, and said he would reserve judgement until he found out if any of them could actually cook. If Juliette expected the preferential treatment her looks probably guaranteed her with men then Alexi reckoned she was in for a disappointment. In her

experience, good looking, charismatic people like Marcel didn't
need the competition. Time would tell.

Paul reminded them that from now on, they would all be on
camera. Everything they said and did would be recorded for poster-
ity... or, more precisely, the edification of the viewing public. With
those words ringing in their ears the producer called 'cut' to the live
segment. The contestants didn't seem too sure what to do with
themselves after that. They milled around, drinking champagne,
making small talk, looking apprehensive.

'The gloss is already wearing off,' Drew muttered.

'Don't say that,' Cheryl replied. 'I'll throttle Marcel if he screws
this up for us by being too... well, Marcelish.'

'He needs this opportunity as much as they do,' Alexi said,
hoping she was right about that.

Alexi's party were about to leave them to it when a screech of
protest erupted from the contestants, more specifically from
Juliette.

'You did that on purpose, you bitch!' she cried, dabbing split
champagne from her bust.

'Sorry,' said Greta insincerely. 'It was an accident.'

'Well, just keep away from me. God knows what you're doing
here anyway. The camera will make you look like a lump of lard.
Don't you have any self-respect?'

'Blimey,' Cheryl said as she turned with the others towards the
main part of the hotel. Cosmo and Toby materialised and escorted
them back. 'Talk about over-reacting. She really seems to love
herself. There was absolutely no reason for her to respond so
violently to what was obviously an accident.'

'She likes to be the centre of attention, is my guess,' Alexi
replied. She had taken a dislike to Juliette. 'I'm thinking everything
has to be about her. I've met her type more times than enough in
my line of work.'

'At least that lot will be confined in there for the duration,' Drew said, jerking a thumb over his shoulder in the direction of the annex, 'and we can keep our distance. If Juliette wants to throw a wobbly and insult her fellow contestants, at least we won't have to hear it.'

'Except it will be caught on camera, I dare say,' Cheryl replied.

Alexi suspected that with four such diverse contestants, living and working at close quarters, there were bound to be fireworks. That, of course, was what the television station was counting on to boost their ratings.

'Who gets to jump Juliette's bones?' Patrick asked. 'Anyone running a book?'

'You won't get odds on that,' Drew replied. 'Marcel decides who wins so she'll have him in her sights.'

'Actually, I think she'll go for Paul,' Alexi said musingly. 'As presenter he has more influence with Far Reach Productions. Or Evan, the actual producer, of course. There again, perhaps we're doing her a disservice and she really is here to prove herself as a cook. The skirt and heels might have been the station's way of vamping up interest.'

'And my baby might sleep through the night,' Cheryl replied, rolling her eyes.

'Will you let me buy you lunch?' Patrick asked Alexi in a quiet aside.

Alexi hesitated. 'Why?' she asked. She had absolutely no desire to have lunch with Patrick but wondered if there was more to the invitation than a simple desire to get back into her good books.

'We need to talk a bit about your upcoming feature,' he reminded her.

Alexi nodded. The idea for the story came about due to the Natalie Parker case. It transpired that Natalie had been abused by her adoptive father, which had ultimately led to her murder and

had inspired Alexi to delve more deeply into the whole minefield of
parental abuse. The article, she thought, was one of her finest
pieces and Patrick agreed with her. The paper's lawyers, though,
had reservations. When didn't they?

'It would be a business lunch then and you can put it on your
generous expense account?'

'Sure it's business,' he replied, looking smug.

Jack Maddox popped the tab on a can of beer, kicked off his shoes, settled back in his recliner and took a long swallow of his drink. He chuckled as the opening credits rolled and the second week's episode of *What's for Dinner?* filled the screens on primetime cable TV. In spite of the lame name, the programme was already topping the ratings and he couldn't seem to switch on the telly or open a paper without hearing or reading some fascinating new fact about one of the contestants.

He was glad for Cheryl and Drew's sake, and especially Alexi's, even if it galled him to admit that Alexi's ex was responsible for getting Hopgood Hall the lucrative gig. Personal animosities aside, he was at a loss to understand what it was about fly-on-the-wall TV that gripped the nation.

Marcel was, Jack conceded, a top-notch chef. He also had charisma by the bucket load and the camera was his best friend. He shared his disdain for the contestants' efforts equally amongst the four of them – no favouritism in his kitchen. But the scenes featuring him and the sexy blonde outside the workplace were another matter. You could literally sense the chemistry between them. There were lots of touchy-feely moments, and Jack figured the nation had to be taking bets on whether Marcel would be caught sneaking into her bedroom for a private tasting.

Marcel's biting criticisms bordered on being downright offensive and he had almost reduced the other female contestant to tears on several occasions. Why would people put themselves through that much humiliation just for their fifteen minutes of fame? They either wanted to make it in the world of culinary excellence really badly or had their sights set on the celebrity Z list.

In the case of the blonde, it was hard for Jack to decide which.

The fact was that Marcel hadn't had to up his game much for the benefit of the cameras. Jack happened to know he treated everyone who worked for him with the same withering contempt. And still all the wannabe chefs in the area flocked to his door every time he had a vacancy to fill. Go figure.

When Alexi had got involved with the business side of Cheryl's hotel, Jack had advised her against offering Marcel a contract that included a percentage of the profits. He hadn't been able to give her a valid reason for his doubts, other than that prima donnas were always a pain in the backside to control. He was an inspired chef, no question about that. But he was also temperamental, rude and arrogant.

Jealousy? Jack didn't think so. As far as he was aware, Marcel hadn't tried to hit on Alexi. Not that it was any of Jack's business. He had tried his luck, tentatively, but her response had been lukewarm. He figured that was because Alexi was still hung up on her former boss and smarting from the way he'd treated her. She was newly unemployed, had moved away from everything she knew and promptly stumbled across a murder case that made headlines and shocked the nation. It was enough to unsettle anyone.

Jack also wasn't sure if he was in the market for a serious relationship so had backed off to give her the space that she needed.

More space than he had intended. He hadn't seen much of her the past few months. A big industrial espionage case had kept him fully involved before he'd cracked it, but he intended to give her a call when he'd wrapped it up, see if she fancied going out to dinner. Then this latest damned case had reared its head and for the past two weeks he'd been acting as a glorified sales clerk in a jewellery and pawnbroker's shop in central Newbury. He now knew more about earrings, bangles, and the gold price than he'd realised there *was* to know.

The credits rolled at the end of the show, just as his mobile rang. He checked the caller ID and took the call.

'Hey, Cas, what's up?' he asked his business partner.

'How's my favourite sales assistant?'

'What's the difference between a princess and a pear diamond?'

'I give up. What's the difference?'

'Several hundred quid.'

'Blimey, just because of the shape?'

'Apparently.' Jack sighed. 'Please tell me that you've found something that just might prevent me from dying of boredom.'

'Very possibly.'

'Have I told you lately that I love you?'

Jack wished the words back the moment they slipped out. Cassie had been a friend to Jack's former wife but when their marriage fell apart she had wanted to lend Jack more than just a shoulder to cry on. Jack had been happy to join her fledgling PI agency but wasn't interested in anything other than a business arrangement. Newly single, he was looking for a fresh beginning, having just left his position as a detective with the Met under something of a cloud. On paper, he and Cassie made a good partnership. She was a geek, could hack into just about anything. Jack was a great detective, good at reading people and with a highly tuned bullshit detector.

But Cassie's jealousy had come to the fore when Jack and Alexi worked together on the Natalie Parker case. Jack had told Cassie that he wouldn't be dictated to when it came to his personal life and they'd had a frank exchange of views on the subject. They now trod on eggshells around one another, studiously avoiding talking about what they did in their downtime.

Not that Jack had had too much of that lately. This latest case involved a company that specialised in pay day loans, with a head office in Newbury. It was a small organisation trying to make an impression in Berkshire, up against the big boys. The senior partner, Mick Bailey, had called Jack in, complaining that they'd had to cover a lot of bogus loans recently. They'd taken the hit in preference to admitting they'd been conned but Mick thought that one of the country-wide companies might be screwing with them. Jack doubted that. Cash Out was too small to bother the guys who advertised their questionable practices on national TV.

When someone wanted a loan for the first time, they could call into any one of the twenty Cash Out outlets in and around Newbury. They had to supply ID, employment history and so forth, which was sent electronically to Mick's office. They ran a credit check and within ten minutes the outlet had a yay or nay. The client was then provided with a laminated photo ID card to encourage repeat custom and it was game on. The problem was, as Cassie soon discovered because she did it herself, someone had hacked into Mick's database and copied various IDs. People were now popping up at various Cash Out facilities, presenting their bogus credentials and getting their loans. Mick had had to cover nearly twenty grand's worth of such loans over a two-month period.

Whoever was doing it was clever, and not too greedy. Just a few hundred pounds each time. Nothing to raise red flags. They'd also chosen winter to pull the scam, when youngish people wearing hoodies and muffled up against the cold didn't look too much like the pictures on their IDs. Did anyone ever? Jack thought of his own passport photo and how little it actually resembled him, thank God.

When it became apparent that something was definitely up, Mick's people put out an email alert to all their outlets, warning them to be extra vigilant. Jack shook his head as he thought about how stupid that had been. If the scammers had hacked into the database, it was kind of obvious that they'd read any email alerts and change their game accordingly. One of the first things that Jack had imposed was an embargo on any online mention of the scam. All future communication with the managers of the outlets would be made by a company rep in person, on the telephone or, better yet, not at all. Businesses loved having meetings which were often unnecessary and frequently counterproductive but if word leaked out about Cash Out's problems, they could lose customer confidence.

'If we want to catch the perpetrators,' he'd told Mick, 'we need to let them think we're not on to them.'

Jack took an in-depth look at the bogus transactions and found that the majority had taken place in the shop he was now working in. Most loans were made at the busiest part of the day and almost all of them were dealt with by one particular clerk, a guy by the name of Dean Davis. He had been taken on three years ago, straight from school, lived with his mother in a modest house locally and had no criminal record. He was friendly enough and didn't show any of the nervousness Jack would expect from someone ripping off his employers. He said little about his private life to the other clerks, never mentioned hobbies, a girlfriend, holiday plans: any of the normal stuff the others talked about when it was quiet. He never went for an after-work drink with his colleagues either, always having a handy excuse. No law about being private, but it also seemed a little odd. There again, perhaps Jack had a suspicious mind.

Make that definitely.

Davis had followed the rules to the letter and the loans had been made to a raft of different people, none of whom looked suspicious, Jack acknowledged, as he trawled through hours' worth of CCTV footage. Davis couldn't be blamed for not smelling a rat. They all had identification that looked kosher – Davis had photocopied them each time he made a loan, which was part of the company's procedure – and there was no way to point the finger at him. Yet.

'Unfortunately my progress, such as it is, will be insufficient to earn your undying love,' Cassie said. 'All I actually called to say is that I've managed to take a look at Davis's bank account. He spends two weeks of each month banking with his local branch and the other two having them bank with him.'

Jack grinned, amused at Cassie's way of describing the guy's overdraft. 'So, if he is involved, he's too clever to bank his ill-gotten gains.'

'Looks that way and, if it isn't him, I'm all out of suggestions. No one else working in that shop throws up any alarm signals and I've looked into them all. Even so, Davis has dealt with most of the bogus claims, and that can't be a coincidence, can it?'

'I did notice on CCTV that a couple of the people waiting for loans hung back, looking in display cabinets and stuff, until Davis was free to serve them. Most people looking for a loan don't have the cash to shop for jewellery and just want to do the transaction as quickly as possible.'

'Then Davis definitely deserves a closer look,' Cassie said.

Jack sighed. 'I guess that means I'm going out tonight.'

'Hot date?' she asked, sounding a little too casual.

'Yeah, tailing Davis, and it's frigging freezing out.'

'Don't be such a baby. Put your thermals on and you'll be fine. Where are you headed, anyway?'

'No idea. I overheard Davis on his mobile in the break room today, arranging to meet someone at nine this evening. He ended the call when he heard me coming, so I have no idea where or who. Might just be a girlfriend.'

'Take care on that motorbike.'

A bike wasn't an attractive option in such arctic conditions but it was the best way to get about and, interestingly, a good vehicle on which to tail a person. It was surprising how little notice people took of anonymous bikes. Jack's helmet was a great disguise, the bike nippy in traffic and easy to park.

'The things I do to earn a crust.'

'Take care and let me know how it goes.'

'Will do.'

Sighing, Jack took Cassie's advice and pulled on thermals and biking leathers. You had to take the rough with the smooth in this game but he had no intention of freezing his nuts off if it turned out to be a long wait.

He knew where Davis lived and pulled the bike into an alleyway opposite, killing the engine. There was a light on in the front room. Hopefully he wasn't meeting the mystery person in his own place. When the front door opened twenty minutes later, Jack felt vindicated. Davis appeared, climbed into his ten-year-old Vauxhall and drove off without looking to see if anyone was loitering and without seeming the least bit furtive. The lights remained on inside the house and Jack noticed a figure moving around behind the thin curtains. The mother, presumably.

Davis's living arrangements were not Jack's concern, but where he was off to now could be. Jack gave him a head start, then fired up the bike and followed a safe distance behind. Davis negotiated his

way around Newbury's one way system and turned off in the direction of Lambourn.

'Where are you going?' Jack muttered to himself.

The roads were getting quieter, and it was necessary for Jack to
hold back. Fortunately there were few street lights and it was easy
to keep Davis's tail lights in sight. Nine p.m. was the equivalent of
midnight around these parts. People in horse country got up before
dawn to see to the animals so they ran on a different time clock.

After about fifteen minutes, Davis indicated and pulled into the
driveway of a large house. Jack rode on and found a place to stop a
bit further on. He doubled back on foot and read the name of the
house on the brick gatepost: Smithfield. From the outside lights at
the front of the house, it was obvious that it was a big place, but
then most of the private houses in this part of the world came with
telephone number price tags. It would be easy enough to find out
who it belonged to but why a lowly paid shop assistant would be
visiting at this time of night was less clear.

Davis left again after twenty minutes, heading back towards
Newbury. On a whim, Jack reclaimed his bike and headed for
Alexi's cottage. Chances are she would still be up and, if there were
no strange cars outside, he'd pay her a surprise call. After all, he
could honestly say he'd been in the area. She might even know who
owned the house Davis had just visited.

Disappointed to find her cottage in darkness and no sign of her
car, Jack decided to call it a night. His route home would take him
past Hopgood Hall. Might as well drop in for a swift half and listen
to Drew wax lyrical about his baby daughter's myriad attributes.
Jack smiled as he thought about the Christening he'd attended a
couple of weeks ago: the last time he'd seen Alexi. He'd seen some
proud parents in his time but Drew and Cheryl were in a class of
their own. He envied them their contentment and felt a moment's
regret for all that domestic harmony he'd never got to experience.

Even when Hopgood Hall was in danger of going under, as far as Jack had been able to tell, Drew and Cheryl never let the financial strain impinge upon their relationship. That was unusual. In his line of work, Jack had seen a good many marriages fold under such pressure. He was glad that Alexi had come up with ideas to help them survive.

Jack sensed something was wrong even before he saw all the flashing lights and emergency vehicles blocking the road outside Hopgood Hall.

'What the...'

He parked the bike up and covered the rest of the distance on foot. Alexi's distinctive Mini with its garish pink roof was in the car park and he immediately worried that something might have happened to her, or to Cheryl or Drew. A uniformed constable was standing guard at the main door and there were all sorts of human comings and goings. He recognised a detective he knew from Reading nick and... oh hell, the coroner's van.

'Can't let you in,' the uniform on the door said when Jack tried to walk past him like he owned the place. 'Unless you're a resident, of course,' he added, consulting a clipboard.

'I'm with Ms Ellis,' Jack said.

'Oh, she didn't say to—'

'Jack?' Alexi ran down the steps and threw her arms around him. 'I thought I heard your voice. Am I glad to see you!'

'What's happened?' he asked, catching hold of her.

'Oh, I figured you must already know.' She blinked up at Jack and he could see she was freaked out, not thinking straight. 'Why else would you be here?'

Now wasn't the time for his *I was just passing* routine. The stark porch light shone on Alexi's face. It was ghostly white and she was trembling; nothing like the tough, independent journalist he'd come to know and admire during the Natalie Parker case. Nothing had seemed to faze her then. Not even being almost strangled by the guy who'd killed Natalie.

'Tell me,' he said, closing his arms protectively around her. 'It'll be all right.'

'Not for one of the contestants in the show it won't,' she said, her voice trembling almost as much as her body. 'Cheryl called me and I came right over. Got here at the same time as the police.' She paused, looking up at Jack through eyes luminous with shock. 'She's been murdered.'

3

'It's okay.'

Jack's capable hands spanned Alexi's back and held her firmly against him until she stopped trembling. She closed her eyes and rested her head on his shoulder, aware that things were far from okay. It made her tired just thinking about all the hoops they'd now have to jump through, to say nothing of having a murderer on the loose. Even so, having Jack there – a timely arrival he had yet to explain – somehow made it feel as though the whole terrible mess wouldn't spiral completely out of control.

God, she was being selfish! A girl had lost her life and Alexi was thinking about damage control for the hotel.

'Let's go inside and you can tell me about it.'

Jack slid an arm around her waist. He signed the duty copper's clipboard and was allowed past the cordon. Alexi didn't look into the bar where the remaining contestants, a couple of guys from Far Reach Productions, and Marcel were gathered, waiting to be questioned. Instead, she took Jack's hand and led the way to Cheryl's private kitchen.

'I was at home,' she said, unable to remember if she'd already told him that. 'Cheryl called me in a dreadful state so I came straight over.'

'You should have called me.'

'Why?' She shot him a bemused look. 'Anyway, it doesn't matter. You're here now. You must have a nose for bad news. We haven't seen much of you for weeks and then, out of the blue...'

Realising that she sounded accusatory, Alexi abruptly shut her mouth. Cheryl and Drew were sitting at the table when they walked into the kitchen. Cheryl looked as shocked as Alexi felt. Drew was trying to comfort her.

'Jack,' they said together. 'What are you doing here?'

Cosmo and Toby were in the dog's basket. Cosmo looked up, saw Jack and made a sound like a cross between a meow and a purr. He leapt with feline grace straight into Jack's arms and Alexi could have sworn the traitorous beast actually bared his teeth in a smile. Cosmo was at his curmudgeonly best whenever he came to the hotel and found it buzzing with film people, all of whom he'd taken a dislike to. At the producer's request, Cosmo was banned from going anywhere near the annex. Everyone was terrified of him. Juliette had even tried to kick him. Cosmo's reaction to Jack was a much-needed lighter moment in an otherwise fraught evening.

'Hey, big guy,' he said, rubbing the purring cat's head. 'I missed you too.'

He put Cosmo down, pulled out a chair for Alexi and took the one next to her.

'Believe it or not,' Jack said, 'I was in the area on another job. I thought I'd call in for a swift half, then saw all the commotion so had to know what was going on.'

'We're well and truly screwed, is what's going on,' Drew replied despondently. 'The star of the show has only gone and been killed. First Natalie Parker connected to us, now this. No one will risk coming here after the news gets out.'

'Marcel?' Jack shook his head. 'But I just saw him—'

'No, not Marcel. Juliette, the blonde.'

Jack shook his head. 'I just saw her, too. In tonight's episode.'

'That was filmed two days ago,' Cheryl said.

'I sounded a bit harsh just now,' Drew said, 'thinking about the hotel when Juliette has lost her life. Ignore me, it's the shock. She wasn't always easy to get along with; her tantrums on screen weren't just for show. She had tunnel vision with regard to winning the contest and didn't care whose toes she trampled on in order to get herself noticed. It didn't make her popular but none of us would have wished her dead.'

'Too right we should think about the hotel,' Alexi said. 'And, call me a cynic, or a horrible, heartless person, but it'll be good for business.'

'And ratings,' Jack added. 'Perhaps one of the film crew did it.'

'There's only one or two of them around unless it's filming day,' Cheryl explained. 'There's a go-to person if a contestant has something to complain about, and one of them almost always does.'

'Usually Juliette,' Drew added.

'Yeah well, not any more,' Cheryl said sadly. 'Then there's a guy who monitors the cameras and deals with any technical stuff. That's about it. The day before they put the episode together, a ton of people descend on us, and all hell breaks loose.'

'They look at the footage from the cameras remotely,' Alexi added, 'and pretty much decide what bits will go in the week's episode. You know, the stuff when the contestants are bitching amongst themselves, or about each other. Marcel chilling out with them. He's contracted to spend an hour a day with them outside of the kitchen. Anyway, it's a pretty slick operation.'

'It was the technical guy who found the body,' Drew said. 'The other three were enjoying some down time, but Juliette was in a strop about something and stomped off to her room. Nothing unusual about that. She's acted up that way since day one. Anyway, as far as we can gather, Gerry Salter, the techie on duty, noticed the camera in Juliette's room was out. He thought she'd hung a piece of clothing to block it to get some privacy while she recovered from her mood. She's done it before.'

Cheryl sighed. 'But not this time.'

Drew covered his wife's hand. 'Gerry found her lying naked on her bed with a chef's knife buried in her chest.'

'Ouch!' Jack shuddered.

'Right.' Drew nodded, his expression dour. 'We called the cavalry, they arrived mob-handed and we've been told to sit tight. And that,' he added, 'was over an hour ago.'

'Who would want to kill her?' Jack asked. 'Any initial thoughts?'

'Well, she wasn't popular, like we already explained,' Alexi replied for them all. 'I could cheerfully have murdered her myself when she attempted to kick my cat. I cannot abide animal cruelty. We had words about it. I told her I'd get her thrown off the show if she pulled a stunt like that again and she backed off immediately; even apologised. Said she'd always been afraid of animals. She came across as almost human when she wasn't acting up for the cameras.'

'Who's in charge of the investigation?' Jack asked.

'Not sure,' Alexi replied. 'Does it matter?'

'It will help if it's someone I know, that's all. A friendly face is more likely to tell me what's going on.'

Alexi's mobile rang. 'Oh God,' she said, glancing at the display. 'It's Patrick. Talk about bad news travelling fast.'

Jack rolled his eyes. 'Don't take it.'

'I'd best see what he wants, otherwise he'll turn up in person.' She took the call. 'Patrick.'

'What the hell's going on?' he asked.

'I'm fine, thanks. How are you?'

'Sorry, babe. That's what I was asking. I was beside myself when I heard a female had been found dead at the hotel. I thought it might... that it could be—'

'It's Juliette.'

'Hell, are you okay? You didn't find her, did you? What are you doing there anyway?'

'How did you hear?' she asked, ignoring his barrage of questions. 'It hasn't hit the news yet or we'd be inundated with press.'

'The station heard something was up and asked me what I knew.'

Ah, Jack thought, able to hear Patrick's voice even though Alexi hadn't put the call on speaker. The studio would have been the tech guy's first call. 'We haven't been told anything yet.'

'I wanted to be sure you were okay.'

'I guess this means the show will be cancelled.' She sent Jack a quizzical glance when he made a scoffing sound.

'Too soon to know,' Patrick replied evasively. 'They're sending down a couple of their legal people to protect their interests. They'll want to sit in on any interviews the contestants have with the police.'

'I think they're being questioned now.'

'Tell them not to say anything.'

'I doubt if they know anything, Patrick. Anyway, they won't let me near them. I wasn't even here when the body was found. Cheryl called me and I came right over.'

'I'm going to come down as soon as I can get away.'

'What for?'

'I don't like to think of you getting involved in a murder.' He paused. 'Again. You were safer here in the city, where you belong.'

'That was a cheap shot, Vaughan, and not helpful.'

'Sorry, but you have to admit... hell, that's my other line and I need to take it. I have to go. Call me if you need anything.'

Alexi cut the call and threw her phone on the table. 'You don't think the station will cancel, do you?' she asked, turning towards Jack. 'I know it looks bad, but none of this is our fault. And poor Juliette, for all her faults, didn't deserve to die.'

'Amen,' said Cheryl, dipping her head.

'I doubt very much if they'll call it off,' Jack replied. 'The show was already topping the ratings. Far as I could tell, the audience was equally divided between loving and hating Juliette. And I'm not talking about her ability to make a soufflé rise.'

'She made a few other things rise around here,' Drew said, 'and I don't just mean tempers.'

'Is that all you men can ever think about?' Cheryl asked. 'Even now, when the poor girl's dead before her life had properly began, your minds are still in the gutter.'

Drew raised his hands in a gesture of surrender. 'Just telling it like it is.' His expression sobered. 'Or was.'

'Well, whatever the attraction was before, you'll get odds on that the ratings will go through the stratosphere while the great unwashed try to decide who did it. It'll go viral.' Jack grimaced. 'Trust me on this. Nothing sells better than bad news, especially, sorry Cheryl, when the victim of a brutal murder is a bombshell with attitude.'

'Christ,' Drew said, standing up and grabbing a bottle of brandy from the cabinet. 'That is so depressing.'

He poured healthy measures for three of them. Cheryl was breast feeding so still off the booze but Drew forced a small measure on her as well. 'Won't hurt to have just a taste,' he told her. 'And it'll help with the shock.'

She'd barely drunk it before wails came through the baby monitor.

'She needs feeding,' Cheryl said, standing.

'I'll come and keep you company,' Drew said. 'Excuse us for a while.'

'Sure.'

'Hey, how are you?' Jack asked into the ensuing silence, reaching for Alexi's hand. 'I've missed you.'

Alexi nodded, wanting to ask if he'd heard of that new-fangled thing called the telephone. She refrained. Jack's defection had seemed like a big deal, even if she wasn't prepared to admit it, until an hour ago. Set against Juliette's brutal slaying, it now seemed inconsequential. She hadn't much liked Juliette – she was too up front in all respects for Alexi's taste – but she didn't wish her dead, either.

'What actually happened here tonight?'

As the shock began to wear off, Alexi found she was in the type of combative mood that would make Cosmo drool with envy. Now that she was thinking more coherently, it occurred to her that by trying to help Drew and Cheryl, encouraging them to expand and providing the financial support they needed to do it, she might well have sounded the death knell for their hotel. *Nice going, Alexi.* She subsided into a simmering silence.

'How was it going with the show before tragedy struck?'

Alexi sighed. The silent treatment wasn't working, mainly because if Jack had even noticed, it wasn't getting to him. Quite right too. She was no longer ten years old and her own petty grievances had no place here, especially given that a young woman had lost her life under tragic and brutal circumstances.

'Honest truth,' she said. 'You could cut the atmosphere with a knife. I thought the contestants were selected because they were polar opposites but what I didn't realise at first is that they're all fiercely competitive. The one thing they do have in common is their love of cooking. There was no faking it there. They all really wanted to make it big time in the culinary world—'

'It struck me as a viewer that Juliette just wanted to make it.'

Alexi conceded the point with a nod. 'True. Did you know that she'd got an agent?'

Jack gaped at her. 'She what?'

'Yeah, after the first episode aired and she got so much attention, the agents came to her.'

'A chef has an agent?'

Alexi smiled. 'Marcel now has one, too.'

'Give me strength!'

'A lot of the sniping you see on the screen is taken out of context. Most of the time the contestants, on their downtime, either ignore one another or get along okay, differences in temperaments notwithstanding. Juliette did blow up over the slightest thing but everyone ignored her, which is why she kept stomping off to her room to sulk. Anyway, the studio guys come along every so often, throw out a few contentious questions, and you get to see the results. It's not at all typical of the way things really were.'

'How it really is would most likely bore people rigid. Watching paint dry springs to mind.'

'Right.'

'What was Juliette really like?' Jack asked.

'Very self-centred, very self-assured and, according to Marcel, a half-reasonable chef. But, like I say, they all are. I've tasted some of their culinary efforts so I know about what I speak. She did have a softer side, like we all do, but she didn't show it very often. I think her agent encouraged her to play up her sassy attitude.'

'Any fallings out amongst the chefs?'

'Not so far as I know. Marcel's the only one allowed to throw his toys out of the pram in the professional kitchen.'

Jack smiled at her. 'No change there then.'

As though he'd heard his name being mentioned, Marcel pushed his way into the kitchen, looking pale, his hair dishevelled, a day's designer stubble covering the lower half of his face; nothing like the autocratic television chef the country had grown to either hate or lust after.

'Jack. I heard you were here.'

'Blimey,' Jack muttered and Alexi knew why. Marcel was back to his normal Cockney self – a side of him he showed to very few people and one which Jack hadn't seen before. It demonstrated, Jack thought, how rattled he actually was, and had good reason to be.

'Sit down before you fall down, Marcel,' Alexi said, pointing to Cheryl's vacated chair. 'Have the police spoken to you yet?'

'Yeah, they just finished grilling me.' His expression was set in granite. 'Or should that be roasting in hot oil?'

Jack nodded sympathetically, well able to imagine how it had been for Marcel because he used to be the one doing the grilling. Suspicious by nature, trusting no one, Jack knew that the first few hours after a murder was the time when he was most likely to find useful clues. Before people got over the shock and learned to keep their mouths shut.

'That bad, huh?' he asked.

'They don't seriously suspect you, surely?' Alexi asked at the same time. 'I know they have to suspect everyone but why would you sabotage your opportunity for prime-time fame?'

'Yeah, well...' Marcel rubbed his face in his hands and peered at them through bloodshot eyes, a shadow of his bombastic self. 'Seeing as how it was my knife stuck in Juliette's chest, I suppose you can't blame 'em for being suspicious.'

'Shit!' Alexi breathed.

'My thoughts precisely. I didn't even know it was missing until the police asked me to check.'

'You made a big thing of it on the show that no one touches another chef's knives,' Alexi reminded him. 'They're more jealously guarded than your grandmother's recipe for fudge cake... your words.'

'And no one would dare to touch mine if they wanted to keep all their fingers.' He sighed. 'But someone did.'

'Where are they kept?' Jack asked.

'Mine are on a magnet on the kitchen wall, where anyone could get to them. My regular help and the contestants all keep theirs in pouches at their stations so they can't fall and can't be misplaced.'

'There are cameras in the kitchen, running all the time,' Alexi pointed out gently. 'If someone took the knife, the police will find it on the tapes.'

'Not necessarily,' Marcel said gloomily. He reached for the brandy bottle that Drew had left on the table, poured a generous measure into Cheryl's glass and downed it in one swallow. 'It was chaotic in there this afternoon. We had two full sittings for lunch, and people buzzing all over the place. Anyone could have taken it without being seen by the camera. Can't remember when I last saw it but I suspect it was taken towards the end of service when I wouldn't need it again.' He shot Alexi the ghost of his trademark killer smile. 'Thanks for implying that you think I didn't kill her.'

Jack nodded, clearly aware that the restaurant had started serving lunch again, which it hadn't found profitable before. The contestants acted as chefs beneath Marcel's aggressive supervision, along with his regular help to do the donkey work. The full-time chefs were seen in the background but no focus was put on them. Perhaps they were peeved about this and one of them had killed Juliette in a fit of professional jealousy. Presumably the police would think of that. Anyway, the restaurant was now packed at lunchtimes because the sittings were filmed and everyone wanted to be on TV. Alexi had thought it was such a brilliant way to see a return on her investment.

Ha, much she knew!

'I know you didn't kill her.' Alexi reached across the table to touch his hand. 'Well, if you did, you wouldn't have used your own knife. Besides, the only thing you're any good at assassinating is aspiring chefs' reputations.'

'Thanks.' Marcel snorted. 'I think.' He sighed. 'It's all an act. I mean, Gordon Ramsey set the bar and now the rest of us have to try and jump that little bit higher. All I want to do is cook, but it isn't that easy in this day and age. There are loads of decent chefs out there. If you want to make a mark for yourself you have to come up with an angle that will get you noticed. I play up my Frenchness and stay prominent by being outrageous.'

'Why do they think you might want to kill her?' Jack asked. 'What's your motive?'

'Hell if I know, mate.' Marcel shrugged. 'Ratings? Attention seeking?'

'A rather drastic way to go about it,' Alexi muttered.

'A lover's tiff?' Jack asked.

'What?' Marcel's head shot up. Worry lines creased his forehead and he looked more frightened than defensive. 'How did you know?'

Jack lifted his shoulders. 'Lucky guess. I sensed the chemistry when the two of you were hanging out in the residents' lounge. A lot of the stuff they filmed was clearly faked but the way you two were into each other set the small screen on fire.'

'Yeah well, that's what I didn't tell the cops, but they'll know soon enough.'

Alexi's jaw almost hit the floor. 'You were actually having an affair with her?'

'Tonight, for the first time,' Marcel said, not making eye contact with them. 'She came to my room over the kitchen. No cameras in there.'

'How could you have been such an idiot?' Alexi was furious.

'Did you really think no one would find out and that the future of the entire show wouldn't be in jeopardy because you were no longer impartial? Besides, bedding Juliette and putting your professional judgement at her mercy is a pretty damned good motive for murder. The police will certainly think so and your not having 'fessed up will look very suspicious to them.'

'I didn't exactly plan it. It just kind of happened,' Marcel replied defensively.

'Oh, for God's sake! Do you realise what you've done...' Alexi had found an outlet for her rage but the feel of Jack's fingers touching her arm halted her in mid-rant.

'Please tell me you used a condom,' Jack said.

Alexi clasped a hand over her mouth. 'Oh, shit!' she said, suspecting by the stricken look on Marcel's face that they hadn't.

'She said she had birth control covered,' he said defensively, scrubbing a hand down his face as the seriousness of his situation belatedly struck a chord. 'How was I to know she was about to be murdered?'

'You should have told them,' Alexi said. 'It would be better if you volunteered the information instead of waiting for them to find out. Which they will if your semen is inside her.'

'What time do they think she was killed?' Jack asked. 'And what time was she in your rooms?'

'The restaurant was closed this evening; our one night of the week off. She came over around six, said there was something she needed to ask me.'

'Do you think it was an excuse to get the inside edge with you, so to speak?' Alexi asked.

Marcel shrugged. 'I told her I had no favourites in the kitchen.'

Alexi shook her head. Was he really that naïve? 'And you think she wouldn't have used your relationship to make sure she came out on top? No pun intended.'

'It's too late to tell Marcel what an idiot he's been,' Jack said. 'I think he gets that part. Better to concentrate on keeping him clear of suspicion.'

Alexi could see the sense in that. Provided the hotel still had Marcel, and providing, of course, that he didn't actually do it, there was hope. 'You think we can do that?'

'You said Juliette came over. You didn't invite her by phone or text, anything like that?'

Marcel shook his head.

'You sure, because if you've been in contact that way, the police will soon find out.'

'No, God's truth, I wasn't expecting her.'

'Okay, so she came over, presumably invented a reason and you finished up in the sack.'

Marcel nodded.

'How long did she stay?'

'About an hour, and she was alive and well when she left my place. I swear it on my grandmother's recipe for bouillabaisse.'

Jack raised a brow. 'Seriously?'

'That's Marcel's equivalent of the Holy Grail,' Alexi explained with another eye roll.

'Best not speak to the police in those terms,' Jack advised. 'They'll think you're being flippant and won't appreciate it. Anyway, did you and Juliette split on good terms? No fights, nothing we need to know about? No disagreements that might have been overheard and will look bad for you?'

'Nah, we were good.'

'But?' Alexi asked, sensing there was more.

'Well, everything with Juliette was a bit of a drama. She could be fun but she was also a spoiled little rich girl.'

'Really?' Jack looked surprised. 'A rich girl who liked to cook?'

'Yeah, she really did. Okay, so she was in it for the celebrity status, but she wanted to cook as well. Trouble is, she was used to having everything come easy and wasn't too particular what she did to make sure it kept right on coming.'

'She thought because you'd taken her to bed, the title was hers?' Jack asked.

'Pretty much, but I set her straight on that score. She wasn't happy about it but we didn't get into a screaming match, or anything. She just pouted, like she didn't believe I was serious and that she'd get her way in the end.' Marcel shrugged. 'Of course, she might well have won on merit. She had the capability.'

'You were probably one of the few men who's ever stood up to her,' Alexi said, screwing up her nose. 'I'm surprised it isn't you who finished up dead.'

Marcel harrumphed, refilled his glass and took another swig of brandy.

'Have you ever been in her room, where she was killed?' Jack asked.

'No, never.' Marcel answered without hesitation.

'Then they won't find your prints in there?' he asked for clarity.

'No. They could still be on my knife, though.'

'Like you'd be stupid enough to kill her with your own knife and leave it for the police to find,' Alexi said, shaking her head as she repeated Marcel's earlier thoughts on that particular subject.

'I think that's the only reason why they didn't take me in and apply the thumbscrews.' Marcel scowled. 'The moment they know I slept with her, that situation will change.'

'If she was alive at seven, found dead at nine, and you haven't left the premises,' Alexi mused, 'where are your bloody clothes? There's always loads of blood when you see stabbings on CSI.'

'Ah, I didn't tell you the best bit. She wasn't killed in her room, apparently. She was killed elsewhere, the body dumped on her bed with my knife in her chest.'

'Shit!' Jack said.

'Yeah, I think I need a lawyer. My agent's already been on the phone, offering to find me one. She's on her way down here now.'

Marcel screwed up his features, clearly struggling to maintain his cool, as well he might, Alexi thought. If he was telling the truth and Juliette did leave him alive and well, it wouldn't prevent the police from making him their number one suspect. All the evidence they knew about pointed to him and Marcel would be an idiot if that fact hadn't already occurred to him. This was real, not reality TV, and his celebrity status would cut no ice with the police. Quite the reverse, in fact. It could well work against him. His star was, or had been, in the ascendency. What would he do to protect his new-found status if Juliette had threatened to reveal details of their roll in the hay? Those are the questions that Alexi would be asking if she was investigating the case.

'The station is sending its lawyers down,' Alexi said. 'You might be better dealing with them.'

'You need to tell the police about having sex with her now. Right away,' Jack said. 'I'll sit with you while you talk to the officer in charge, if you like. Who is it, by the way?'

'A guy called Vickery from Reading Serious Crimes Squad,' Marcel replied. 'Do you know him?'

'Yeah. He'll play it by the book. But don't underestimate him. He's a shrewd cookie.'

4

Inspector Mark Vickery was a tall man of about forty, fighting ongoing battles with an expanding waist and receding hairline. Jack had worked with him before and was glad that he'd be calling the shots on this one. You'd pass him in a crowd but he had a sharp mind and didn't cut corners in order to get a quick result. He probably already knew Marcel hadn't been completely forthcoming in their previous interview. Jack hadn't seen him for a while, but he'd always liked him and respected his professional attitude to his job. He wouldn't take the easy option of fitting the evidence to a suspect, which was something.

Vickery and a female officer came into the kitchen in response to Marcel's message that he had something to add to his statement. He saw Jack, made a sound that could have been anything from a grunt to a sigh, and nodded. Cosmo protested vehemently at the arrival of the police officers. His constant hissing and growling forced Alexi to shut him in the scullery. Jack thought it interesting that Cosmo hadn't protested when Marcel had joined them. Then again, he had yet to figure out how Cosmo decided if he liked a person or not. He usually instinctively liked the good guys, which was a point in Marcel's favour, or would be if Jack was in charge of the case.

'Christ, what was that?' the female officer breathed. 'This place is seriously weird.'

Jack tried not to smile when he noticed Alexi's offended expression. 'Cosmo is somewhat protective and not keen on strangers but, actually, he's... well, a pussy cat.'

The officer shuddered. 'I'll take your word for that.'

'Thought I might see you here,' Vickery said. 'Never did know when to keep your nose out.'

'Good to see you, too,' Jack said, taking Vickery's hand rather than offence because he knew none had been intended. Jack wasn't sure he'd have been quite so accepting of a former officer showing up at a crime scene of his and didn't want to do anything to rock the boat.

'This is Detective Constable Hogan,' he said, referring to the attractive female DC trailing in his wake. 'Patti, this is Jack Maddox, one of ours, or used to be.'

'I know that name,' Patti said, sizing Jack up and appearing to like what she saw. 'You were involved with the Parker case, weren't you? Nice work that.'

'Thanks.' Jack indicated Alexi. 'This is Alexi Ellis, investor in this establishment.'

Both officers shook Alexi's hand.

'Investor and journalist, I think. You shouldn't be here, Ms Ellis,' Vickery said. 'We need to speak with you all separately.'

'So we don't collude on our stories.' Alexi said, a wry twist to her lips. Jack suspected she was about to blow a fuse. He'd sensed her simmering away for the past half-hour and understood why she was getting so worked up. She'd invested a lot of time and effort into getting Hopgood Hall back on the map and now its future had been thrown into uncertainty. He gave her a nudge. Getting antsy with Vickery wouldn't help matters. 'Don't worry, Inspector. I arrived at the same time as the emergency vehicles. I didn't see anything.'

'Even so, you're here as a courtesy and because I respect Jack. If I see a single word of what's said here repeated in print, I shall know who to blame. And, trust me, I'm not a good person to get on the wrong side of.'

'I hear you, Inspector. I'm not interested in a scoop. All I care about is protecting the interests of this hotel and, of course, finding out who killed Juliette, and why.'

'Fair enough.' They all took seats around the table. 'You had something to add to your statement, Mr Gasquet?'

'Just so you know, Marcel's lawyer will be here soon,' Jack said. 'I'm watching his back until he gets here.'

Vickery looked mildly surprised which, Jack knew, was all for effect. 'He needs a lawyer? Got something to hide, Mr Gasquet?'

'Come on, Mark,' Jack said. 'You know better than that. The television station wants to protect its assets, obviously, which is why they're sending suits down from London.'

'Of course they do.' Vickery looked amused. DC Hogan sat down and opened her notebook, pen poised. 'We're all ears, Mr Gasquet.'

'Yeah well, the thing is—'

'What happened to the French accent?' Vickery asked suspiciously.

Marcel briefly explained. 'My mother's French but can't boil an egg.' He shrugged. 'My dad's a Cockney and has forgotten more about cooking than I'll ever know. I was born in London but grew up in the suburbs of Paris, went to a French school.'

'So the French thing you do on screen isn't a complete act?'

'Not in the least, inspector,' Marcel replied, not rising to the bait. 'I grew up speaking French to my mother and at school, but I spent hours in the kitchen with my dad, which is where I got my Cockney from.' He shrugged. 'It's no secret but I don't shout about it, either.'

'Your Cockney father is called Gasquet?'

'That's my mother's maiden name. I took it when I decided to play up my French roots.'

'Won't that make for good ratings when word gets out,' Vickery said, almost to himself. 'Okay, what did you want to add to your statement, sir?'

'Juliette.' He cleared his throat. 'Ms Hammond came to see me in my flat over the kitchen at about six this evening.' Both detectives sat a little straighter. 'She... er, stayed and we talked for an hour.'

'I see. And what did you *talk* about for that hour?'

'We had sex,' Marcel said abruptly. 'But she was fine when she left.'

'That would have been at about seven?'

'Yeah, about then.'

Jack knew they would be able to confirm that from the cameras in the annexe, always assuming Juliette went straight back to her room.

'Will the medical examiner find evidence of your liaison with Ms Hammond?'

'Why should that matter?' Alexi asked. 'Marcel has already admitted having sex with her.'

'At the risk of painting the victim in a poor light, she could conceivably have been with someone else, too,' Vickery replied in a mild tone. 'It would be useful to know.'

'We didn't use a condom, if that's what you're asking.' Marcel ran a hand through his hair and looked, to Jack's suspicious mind, as guilty as sin.

'What made you do it?' Vickery asked.

A brief smirk broke through Marcel's dejected expression. 'Did you see what she looked like?'

'But you were adjudicating the competition. Didn't you stop to think about the difficult position you were putting yourself in?'

'I made it clear to Juliette that I wouldn't let it sway me.' Marcel leaned forward on his elbows, looking more confident now they had returned to the subject of the contest. 'And I wouldn't have. A lot of the stuff on the screen is playing up for the cameras but I'm deadly serious... sorry, poor choice of words,' he said, paling. 'But the point I'm trying to make is that I take the contest very seriously. I have a lot invested in making a success of it.'

'Which makes taking one of the contestants to bed that much harder to fathom,' Vickery pointed out.

'I thought I could deal with it. I wouldn't have had a problem marking her down if one of the others did better than her. I made that clear to her.'

'Before or after you had sex with her?' DC Hogan asked.

Marcel merely shot her a sour look and Vickery didn't press him for an answer.

'If the others found out you were sleeping with her, they'd have the upper hand,' he pointed out instead. 'They could have used that knowledge to coerce you into cutting them some slack. Otherwise, and I'm guessing here, they could have let something leak to the press and you and Juliette would both have lost credibility.'

'There's nothing in the rules that says personal relationships are a no-no.'

'Come on, Mr Gasquet.' Vickery shook his head. 'Does there need to be? Surely you can see the need to remain professional?'

Marcel sighed. 'It was stupid, I know, but I wasn't thinking with my brain. I wouldn't have let it happen again.' He paused and shook his head. 'Probably not, anyway.'

'It also gives Marcel no reason to want Juliette dead. Not if they were having sex and she didn't expect any favours in return,' Alexi pointed out.

Vickery sent her a look that said *you have to be joking*, saving Jack the trouble. 'Please leave the reasoning to me, Ms Ellis. You are here as a courtesy, not to help me do my job.'

'Sorry,' Alexi replied meekly.

'And anyway, from where I'm sitting, it gives Mr Gasquet a very good motive. He had his fun, then realised what he'd done, Ms Hammond threatened to call foul if he didn't make sure she won and... well—'

'He killed her with his own knife.' Alexi shook her head. 'Come on, Inspector, Marcel is many things, but stupid isn't one of them.'

'The jury's still out on that one,' Jack muttered.

They talked around in circles for a while longer but Jack refused to let Vickery draw Marcel out on other aspects of his life and work at Hopgood Hall.

'All the contestants have been told, by text message I gather, not to say anything to you until legal representation arrives,' Jack explained. 'I persuaded Marcel to tell you about having sex with the victim because I knew it was important.'

'And that we would find out about it sooner rather than later.'

'You would have found out she'd had sex,' Jack agreed, 'but not with whom. At least, not immediately.'

'Is it true that she wasn't killed in her room?' Alexi asked.

'Almost certainly not,' Vickery replied. 'Not enough blood.'

Jack frowned. 'Why move her *into* a place that was full of cameras? It's one hell of a risk to take.'

'If I was a cynic,' Vickery replied, with a hint of sarcasm, 'I'd say someone was trying to boost the ratings.'

'How did that someone carry a bloody corpse through the recreational room that's full of working cameras *and* possibly the other contestants to get to Juliette's room without anyone noticing?' Jack mused pensively.

'All the rooms have individual doors that lead directly to the

courtyard as well as access from the communal lounge,' Alexi
replied. 'If the killer wanted to have Juliette found in her room it
makes sense that he disabled the camera—'

'He?' Vickery asked.

'Well, I'm assuming the killer carried her. Juliette wasn't that tall
but still a fair weight. I doubt any woman could have managed it. I
know I couldn't and I'm taller than average.'

'She could have been wheeled in something?' Jack suggested.

'A lot of trouble and a big risk to take,' Alexi replied, subsiding
into thought. 'I assume you've checked outside that door for foot-
prints, drag marks and so on. She has to have been brought in that
way.'

Vickery sent her a look.

'Sorry.' But Alexi clearly was in no mood to keep quiet. 'Using
Marcel's knife is just plain dumb. Even if Marcel wanted her
dead, and I believe him when he says that he didn't... but even if
he did, anyone who watches the show would know he treasures
his precious knives. Chefs get very territorial about such things.'
She shrugged. 'I'm pretty sure he wouldn't use one to kill a
person.'

'People do out of character things in the heat of the moment,
especially when it comes to crimes of passion,' Vickery replied.

'Oh God!' Marcel buried his face in his hands. 'You actually
think I did this.'

'It's early days and we're keeping an open mind,' Vickery
assured him. 'We haven't spoken to everyone yet.'

'You told us earlier that you had two of your regular chefs
working the lunch sitting,' DC Hogan said, flipping back through
her notebook.

'Yes, but they signed out at the end of service.'

'We shall have to speak to them anyway,' Vickery said, almost to
himself. 'Check their whereabouts.'

'They won't have done it,' Marcel said. 'They would have been noticed in the private part of the hotel if they came back—'

'But they know how to access it,' Vickery remarked. 'Which means we have to satisfy ourselves that they didn't. I should have thought you'd be glad to know we are being so thorough.'

'Sure, but I can't see why they would go to the trouble of killing Juliette. They had nothing to do with the contest.'

'No, but they put up with your tantrums day in and day out and get no recognition for it. Whereas the contestants, whom they probably think aren't as talented as them, take the limelight.' Vickery shrugged. 'Just a thought.'

'Sure.' Marcel replied. 'You have their contact details. And just for the record, I am not a child and don't have tantrums. I just have a short fuse when I'm faced with stupidity in my kitchen, which happens a lot.'

Jack made a shushing motion with his hand and Marcel belatedly shut his mouth.

'Thank you. Oh, and one more thing, Mr Gasquet. I assume you won't object to our taking a look inside your apartment.'

Marcel glanced at Jack, who nodded. It would look better if he allowed the search. If there was something incriminating to find, Marcel had lost the opportunity to dispose of it and they'd find it anyway.

'Be my guest.' Marcel reached into his pocket and tossed them the keys.

'We appreciate your co-operation.'

'Do either of you know why anyone would want to see Ms Hammond dead?' asked Vickery, looking at Marcel and Alexi.

'She wasn't popular,' Alexi replied. 'Too much of a prima donna. Most of the guys on the crew fancied her at first but I think they soon realised that she would be trouble, to say nothing of high maintenance.'

Marcel's head shot up. 'Have you spoken to Paul Dakin?'

'The show's host?'

Marcel nodded. 'He was all over her off camera.'

Vickery sent him a look that implied it took one to know one. DC Hogan made yet another note in her book.

'Look, inspector.' Marcel spread his hands. 'She *was* a stroppy little madam but she was also focused on winning this competition by whatever means necessary, not all of them within the spirit of the rules. She came on to me because she thought it would give her an edge over the opposition. I'm a red-blooded male with a pulse and... what can I say? I gave in to temptation. But who's to say who else she tried to manipulate? Did I fancy her? Hell, yeah, course I did, otherwise I wouldn't have taken her to bed. Did I like her? No, I don't like her sort. Everything came too easy for her. She hadn't really had to work for anything and that pisses me off but she also had a vulnerable side that she seldom showed but which I saw in private. If you ask me, everything she did, she did for parental approval, which was never forthcoming, but I can't tell you anything more about that. It was just an impression I got, reading between the lines. Did I kill her?'

'Did you?' Vickery asked, meeting Marcel's hostile gaze and holding it.

'No.' The fight appeared to drain out of Marcel and he looked bone weary. 'I had no reason to. What we did might not have been in the best of taste but it wouldn't have got either of us thrown off the show. We were both single, not in relationships... well, I'm not and she assured me she wasn't, so if anything, it would have boosted the ratings.'

'But what about afterwards?' DC Hogan said, her voice introducing a melodious note to the heavy silence, 'when you made it clear that you wouldn't show her favouritism in the contest, despite what passed between you. That must have made her angry. Did you argue about it? Perhaps it got out of hand. You didn't mean to kill her.'

'Don't answer that, Marcel,' Jack said. 'Wait for the station's lawyers to get here.'

'I don't mind answering. I've got nothing to—'

There was a tap at the door and a uniformed constable put his head around it. 'The victim's father is here, sir. He insisted on coming down immediately after he was told about his daughter.'

'Juliette was a local girl?' Alexi looked surprised. 'I didn't know that.'

'Yes, she was born and brought up not three miles from here,' Vickery replied, standing. 'Right, that will be all for now, Mr Gasquet. We will return your keys later but you will have to sleep elsewhere tonight. Oh, and we shall want to speak with you at the station tomorrow, take DNA samples and so forth.'

Marcel nodded.

'Right, Hogan,' he said. 'Let's go and find out why Mr Hammond felt the need to come here. Our people have already been to him at Smithfield.'

'Smithfield?' Jack repeated. 'You mean that big house on the Newbury Road?'

The surprised edge to Jack's voice had Vickery turning from the doorway with mild suspicion in his expression. 'Yes, that's where Juliette Hammond grew up. Do you know the place?'

'No, but I've seen it.' Jack cursed his blunder. He wasn't ready to tell Vickery that the case he'd been working on had led him to that address less than two hours ago and was the reason why he'd been in the area. 'I've driven past it a few times and wondered who it belonged to.'

It was a lame explanation and Vickery clearly wasn't buying it.

'Of course you did.' Vickery did not look happy. 'Don't hold out on me, Maddox. If you have information germane to this enquiry then I need to know what it is. If you don't share, then ex-copper or not, I'll do you for withholding.'

Jack turned his hands palms up. 'I honestly don't have anything.'

Vickery studied him for a moment, then nodded. 'Good enough.'

Cheryl and Drew joined them the moment the police left the kitchen. Alexi liberated Cosmo and they all sat at the table, Cosmo weaving his way between their legs, reasserting himself after the ignominy of being relegated to the scullery.

'Have the police spoken to you yet?' Alexi asked her friends.

'Yes, a couple of uniforms cornered us as soon as we left Verity's room.' Cheryl appeared visibly distressed, as though she was only just appreciating the enormity of what had happened. 'Not that we could tell them much that they didn't already know. They seemed interested in how Juliette got on with people. Was there anyone in particular she'd fallen out with, stuff like that.'

'Yes, they asked us the same sorts of questions,' Alexi said.

'What's been happening here?'

Jack brought Cheryl and Drew up to date on Marcel's revelations. Jack wasn't surprised when both of them accepted Marcel's explanation without equivocation.

'You're a bloody fool, Marcel,' Drew said, while Cheryl gave their chef a supportive hug. 'But Juliette was enough to tempt a Trappist monk. She knew it, flaunted it and you've never laid claim to celibacy. Even so, I hope to Christ your little liaison had nothing to do with her death, directly or otherwise. She might have had an agenda but she sure as hell didn't deserve to die for it.'

'Her dad's here now,' Cheryl said, wiping away a tear. 'I feel so bad for him. I had a brief chat with Juliette once, when she wasn't playing up for the cameras. We sat at this very table together. She was all over Verity. Said she loved kids and it showed. I saw a very different side to her that day. Anyway, she told me she and her dad used to be joined at the hip. He gave her everything her heart desired. "Spoiled little rich girl" is how she described herself. But apparently, they fell out over her wanting to cook for a living.'

'What does he do?' Alexi asked. 'Her father, that is.'

'Some sort of investment banker, I think. Pots of money, anyway. Divorced from Juliette's mum when Juliette was still young. She lived with her dad. Lost touch with her mum and didn't remember much about her.' Cheryl grew pensive. 'I get the impression that her father was controlling and actively discouraged her from contacting her mum.'

'Did her dad remarry?' Jack asked.

'A whole succession of live-in girlfriends but he never tied the knot again. None of them lasted long, according to Juliette—'

'That was quite a chat you had,' Alexi remarked. 'Sounds like she told you her life story. Did you tell Vickery any of this?'

'He didn't ask. Should I have done?' She directed the question to Jack.

'I expect Vickery will speak to you again tomorrow. Wouldn't hurt to mention it. You never know how it might tie in with other aspects of the enquiry.'

'Okay, I will then.' Cheryl tilted her head, clearly thinking about Juliette. 'I did rather like Juliette when she stopped pretending to be something she wasn't,' she said. 'Beneath all that sex appeal and bratty attitude, she was a lonely kid who missed a woman's influence in her life.' Cheryl flashed a droll smile. 'What with me being a new mum, my maternal instincts are on high alert right now, so I could read between the lines.'

'You say they fell out, her and her dad,' Jack said. 'How recently was that?'

'Just before she signed up to do the trials for this show, I think. Her dad was appalled at the thought of her flaunting herself in front of the cameras. He implied she would be selected for her looks rather than her ability to cook and would be exploited.'

'Which she was,' Drew pointed out. 'She made sure of it and lapped up the attention. I know the producer encouraged her to vamp it up but she was more than happy to oblige *and* she came on to Marcel because she thought it would give her an edge.'

'Has it occurred to you that it might have been my Gallic charm that attracted her?' Marcel asked, a flash of his brash attitude breaking through his morose mood.

'Nope!' they all said in unison.

'Her dad wasn't into celebrity at any price, I take it?' Jack asked when the laughter subsided.

'Evidently not. He told Juliette it was tacky and she was better than that. He was willing to set her up in her own restaurant, apparently, so she didn't need to enter competitions.'

'Blimey,' Drew said. 'She was Daddy's little princess, wasn't she?'

'Well anyway,' Cheryl said, yawning. 'We need to concentrate on making sure this doesn't get pinned on Marcel.'

'The studio's lawyers are on their way,' Jack reminded them. 'But I won't pretend that everything'll be fine. You are their prime suspect right now, Marcel. You've admitted to having sex with her and they only have your word for it that she didn't want anything from you in return.'

'So I killed her with my own knife?'

'To make it look like you're being framed.' Jack flashed an apologetic smile. 'Sorry, just thinking with my detective's brain.'

'Yeah, I know.'

'Ah well, at least we'll fill all the rooms for a while,' Drew said, earning himself a punch on the arm from his wife.

'Talking of which,' Marcel said. 'Can I use a room tonight? The police are searching mine.'

'Sure. We have one free.'

'Thanks.' Marcel stood and stretched his arms above his head. 'Thanks for your help, Jack,' he said, offering him his hand.

'No problem. Just remember not to say anything else without legal representation. I know you have nothing to hide but you can't be too careful. This will be a high-profile case, what with the TV coverage and the victim's father having so much influence. Vickery will be under pressure to get a quick result and right now, you're it. So you might want to think about who has it in for you and would risk setting you up. If you come up with any names, run them past me first.'

'The list could be a long one. The jealousies in this business are legion and it's no secret that I have a bit of a short fuse. But none of the enemies I've made are in this part of the world.' He paused. 'Well, not so far as I know, but the show, my being such a big part of it might have ignited old jealousies. Even so, setting up such an elaborate murder just to pin it on me and settle an old score is a bit of a stretch, to put it mildly.'

'That's what I was thinking,' Jack responded. 'But someone clearly has.'

Alexi was more concerned that there could be a homicidal maniac on the loose, intent upon wrecking the show and the hotel's reputation. Feelings were still running high following Natalie Parker's murder and Graham Fuller's conviction for it. The fact that he was as guilty as sin didn't prevent local opinion being partially on his side. And the owners and investors in Hopgood Hall were all to blame for exposing him. Ridiculous, but there it was.

In spite of that, Alexi found it hard to imagine that a Fuller fan would have gone so far as to commit murder, just to make a point. Besides, how would they have got into the private part of the hotel?

Marcel rolled his eyes. 'Tell me about it,' he said in response to Jack's remark as he sauntered towards the door. 'Okay. Night, everyone.'

'Night, Marcel.'

'I need to head home,' Alexi said, standing. Cosmo stirred himself from Toby's basket and was at her side in a flash. Damned cat always seemed to know when it was time to go. 'I take it you're going back to Newbury, Jack?'

'Actually, I thought I'd hang around. You might need my expert help,' he said with a self-deprecating grin. 'No chance I can camp out on your couch, I suppose, seeing as how the hotel's full?'

Alexi paused, looking anything but delighted by the suggestion, and he thought at first that she would refuse. Then she shrugged in a why-not casual type of gesture. 'Sure. You want to ride with me or risk life and limb on that bike?' she asked, eyeing his biking leathers with distaste.

'I'll ride with you and Cosmo.'

'Behave yourselves, children,' Cheryl said as she hugged them both.

5

Alexi wasn't sure how she felt about having a house guest, especially the specific house guest currently occupying the passenger seat of her Mini. His legs looked cramped, even though he'd pushed the seat back as far as it would go. Cosmo had no such reservations and had already wrapped himself around Jack's neck, purring like a traction engine.

Traitor!

Despite her personal conflict though, there was no one she would prefer to have help find out what happened to Juliette, if that was his reason for staying. Alexi chose to believe that it was, vindicating her decision to let him share her cottage. He knew how the police worked but no longer being an officer meant he could short-circuit the system and didn't have to jump through all the hoops that serving officers were obliged to negotiate. He'd proved his ability to think outside the box on the Parker case and saw angles that didn't occur to anyone else.

Keep telling yourself that, Alexi.

Why she was already thinking about conducting her own investigation, she couldn't have said. Vickery seemed proficient, but would be under pressure to get a result – the wrong result. Besides, there would be a story in this. She was in the right place to get the inside scoop, just as she'd been on the Parker case. She wanted to ensure it was told right and that Hopgood Hall came out of it in the best possible light. That gave her a legitimate excuse to talk to the other contestants and members of the production team.

You could take the journalist out of London...

'You okay?' Jack asked as she fired up the engine and negotiated her way around all the emergency vehicles still clustered in the parking area and on the verges of the narrow road. 'Sorry, stupid question. Of course you're not.'

A uniformed policeman held up his hand to stop Alexi while two police cars, still with lights flashing, moved out of her way. She didn't answer Jack until she was waved on.

'I feel angry and physically sick, since you ask,' she said, changing into third and taking the road too fast for the conditions. She slowed fractionally when she narrowly avoided skidding. 'Who would want to do this to Juliette? Why us and why now? I don't mean to sound hard hearted,' she added, sighing, 'but I can't help thinking about Cheryl and Drew's livelihood. I really thought we'd got the hotel moving in the right direction. Now we're going to get a ton of negative publicity, the Parker case will be dragged up again and questions will be asked about the likelihood of lightening striking in the same place twice. Doubts will be cast on our credibility and cancellations are bound to follow. I expect the series will have to be cancelled too if they don't catch the killer right away.' She inhaled sharply. 'Or if the killer does turn out to be Marcel.'

'Let's wait and see. Being a cynic, I'd say the station will publicly mourn Juliette's loss but privately revel in all the publicity, which equates to viewing figures, which equates to sponsorship. The studio will make Juliette into some sort of martyr and the viewing public will lap it up. Whatever, they won't rush into cancelling and probably hope the police will find the killer quickly, making it unnecessary. Either way, I don't envy Vickery all that pressure.'

'Well, I suppose...' Alexi tilted her head as she considered what they had learned so far. 'If she was killed by someone who has nothing to do with Lambourn then I guess it won't harm us too much.'

'What are the chances of a local being involved? I know you're thinking Marcel, and hating that you are because you don't want to believe it's him. But you can't entirely ignore that the evidence all points his way, either. Still, let's not jump to conclusions.'

'Hmm.'

She didn't say anything more until they arrived at her cottage. She didn't understand why he'd suddenly appeared back in her life tonight of all nights and was surprised by just how much she wanted him to stick around, which annoyed her. Alexi had always been self-sufficient and this newly discovered needy side didn't sit well with her.

'Got anything stronger than tea?' Jack asked when she'd parked up, unlocked the front door and switched on the lights.

'I'll find alcohol, you bank up the fire.'

'Deal.'

'Might as well carry on the way we started,' she said, returning to the small living room a short time later clutching a bottle of brandy and two glasses.

'When did you start doing log fires?' he asked, adding fuel to the dwindling blaze.

'I'm a local girl now. Have to follow the country code.'

'So I see.' He glanced down at her UGG boots and raised a brow.

'Hey, when in Rome. It's too bloody cold to care about fashion. Anyway, regarding the fire, I have a neighbour who delivers logs to the door. I said I'd give it a try and find I like having open fires. I enjoy the smell.' She poured the drinks and handed him one. 'Never thought I'd want to bother with the mess. Just goes to show.'

Why was she blathering on about fires when a young girl had just lost her life? She threw herself into the corner of the couch, still nursing her drink, kicked off her boots and tucked her feet beneath her backside. He took the chair across from her, stretched his long legs out and smiled that infuriatingly sexy smile of his. Cosmo jostled with him for space in front of the fire but didn't attack Jack's legs to get the best spot.

Definitely a traitor.

'Cheers,' he said, raising his glass.

'To Juliette,' she replied. 'I wonder what the hell she got herself into that cost her her life. I find it hard to believe that anyone would actually kill her and try to frame Marcel. All to win a silly contest or top the ratings.'

'You don't believe what you just said. Not really. And certainly not after all you've seen and heard in your years as a journalist.'

'No, I suppose I don't.' She sighed. 'The extremes people are prepared to go to for the most nefarious of reasons never fails to astonish me.'

'Anyway, finding out the who, how and why is Vickery's problem.'

'It could be ours. If he's decided that Marcel's the villain, it will take the pressure off him. But I know Marcel and all his faults and the only things that boy is guilty of is bad judgement and a worse temper.' Alexi frowned. 'Do I think he's capable of killing someone?' She wavered her hand from side to side. 'Possibly, in the heat of the moment. Do I think he would be daft enough to off someone and then frame himself?' This time she shook her head decisively. 'Not a snowball's chance in hell. Marcel is many things, but he's nobody's fool. I've never been his greatest fan, in spite of his brilliance with food, but putting personal prejudices aside, I don't think he did this.'

'Vickery won't jump to conclusions and neither should we.' Jack took a sip of his drink, watching her over the rim of his glass as the fiery liquid warmed his oesophagus. 'Tell me what it's really been like with the filming going on.'

'Tense. Juliette might have had a vulnerable side, like Cheryl suggested, but none of the rest of us ever saw it. She made no effort to play nice with the other contestants on or off camera and was at pains to set everyone at loggerheads.'

'The sort of person who thrives on conflict?'

Alexi screwed up her nose. 'And being the centre of attention. I didn't like her much and the feeling was mutual.'

'Careful.' Jack wagged a finger at her. 'Don't let Vickery hear you say that or he'll add you to his suspect list.'

'Ha. I wasn't even there and Cosmo can vouch for that.'

'Good to know.' Jack put his glass aside and laced his hands behind his head. 'Marcel mentioned that she was arguing with Paul Dakin earlier tonight. I didn't see him anywhere.'

'Oh yes.' She frowned. 'You'd think he would have mentioned something that important to Vickery.'

'I think he already did.'

'Right, well I had no idea Dakin was hanging about.' Alexi frowned. 'He's not usually there unless it's a filming day but at least now we have another suspect. That ought to make Marcel happy.' Alexi's frown morphed into a grin. 'Now Dakin I can see murdering someone to protect his own interests.'

Jack laughed. 'Okay, so you don't like him. Does he live locally?'

'No idea. But even if he lives in London, it's not that far to come, especially after rush hour when the motorways are clear.'

Jack stretched as though easing the tension in his shoulders. 'If Juliette was busy covering all the bases to give herself an edge in the competition, she was probably getting close with Paul as well. Or at least giving off all the right vibes. It would explain why he was at the hotel when he wasn't supposed to be.'

'And if he saw her leaving Marcel's private apartment, it wouldn't take a rocket scientist to figure out what she'd been doing there.' Alexi brightened. 'It would explain their argument. He'd come down especially to see her and she was having it off with another man. Jealousy is a main motivator for crimes of passion, isn't it?'

'If their fight got out of hand and say, for the sake of argument, he hit her, she fell, cracked her head and died, why not just leave her there and leg it?' Jack pondered his own question for a moment. 'Why take the risk of returning her to her room and using Marcel's knife on her? The post mortem will tell us if she was moved, of course, but Vickery already implied that she wasn't killed in her room.'

Alexi returned her feet to the floor and sat forward, elbows resting on her knees. 'Are you saying she wasn't killed by the knife?'

'Hard to know for sure because I haven't seen the crime scene. Hell, if she wasn't killed in her room then they probably haven't found the crime scene yet. That's why they were so keen to see Marcel's apartment. So, we know she was killed somewhere else and then moved back to her room. What we don't know yet is whether it was that knife that killed her.'

'Good point.'

'None of the other contestants heard or saw anything out of the ordinary and the camera in her room was conveniently out of action. Makes me wonder if there was something premeditated about her murder, or whether that's just a coincidence and it was perhaps an argument that got out of hand.' He expelled a mirthless chuckle. 'I have a suspicious mind.'

'Presumably the killer knew she'd just had sex with Marcel and that it would come to light, so using his knife to implicate him further would make more sense.'

'Bloody stupid killer to imagine Marcel would use his own knife.' Jack shook his head. 'No, that knife was definitely symbolic because the killer would have had to take the trouble to filch it from the kitchen without being seen. That was one hell of a risk so must have been important to him or her.'

'What's symbolic about it, then?'

He shot her one of his lethal grins. 'Damned if I know, but it's as good a place to start as any. Question everything and take nothing at face value. That's what Vickery will be doing and we should, too. If you want to do what you can to protect the hotel and make sure Marcel doesn't become... well, a sacrificial lamb.'

Alexi rolled her eyes. 'I thought you said Vickery wouldn't jump to conclusions.'

'He won't, but it won't have escaped his attention that Marcel hasn't told us everything he knows.'

'Really?' She blinked. 'What makes you say that?'

'He held something back. I could tell and Vickery would have noticed it, too. It doesn't help that he didn't admit straight out that he'd slept with Juliette and I had to talk him into 'fessing up.'

'You told me once that everyone lies to the police. That you expect it.'

'Yeah, but this is a murder case.'

'All the more reason.'

'Talking of reasons, I suspect Marcel hasn't yet been hauled in for more questioning because that knife is too obvious, and because they can't put him in her room. When they know her actual time of death, they'll subject his alibi to microscopic scrutiny. He didn't actually tell us where he was once Juliette left him, or if anyone saw him. I hope to God they did, for his sake.'

'Well, at least he's never been in her room. He was definite about that.'

'Hmm, it's also in his favour that he had no signs of injury that I could see. If they fought, Juliette had long nails, didn't she?'

Alexi nodded.

'Well, she would have scratched him. I'm betting the police took pictures of his torso and the pathologist will take scrapings from under her nails. If there's nothing there, that'll help.'

'We ought to talk to the others once the police have finished with them, see if they know anything. Or rather I should. Sorry, I know this is nothing to do with you.' Alexi sent him a probing look. 'What *are* you doing here, by the way? You never said.'

'Can't I drop in on an old friend?'

Better late than never. 'You didn't drop in on me. You stopped at the hotel.'

'I came here first.' He stroked Cosmo's long body with the toe of his boot. Alexi expected her cat to violently object. She was the only person whose feet Cosmo tolerated. But once again he surprised her by rolling on his back and exposing his belly for more in-depth scratching. Alexi watched, filled with a ridiculous desire to change places with her cat. Well, she told herself, in her own defence, she'd been a man-free zone since dumping Patrick months back. 'No one was home,' he added, watching her closely, a slight smile playing about his lips.

'Okay, now tell me the real reason.'

'I've been working a job in Newbury. A lead brought me down to this neck of the woods.'

'Tonight? In these conditions? On a motorbike?'

'Yes, yes and yes. And, here's the best bit. That lead took me to Smithfield.'

Alexi gasped when the penny dropped. 'Juliette's dad's place?'

'Right. Now I don't need to find out who it belongs to.'

'No, but you do need to tell Vickery.'

'Why? My case doesn't have anything to do with Juliette's killing.'

'Come on, Maddox. You don't believe in coincidences any more than I do. There *has* to be a connection. And it might take the spotlight off Marcel.'

'Trust me, it won't, and my client expects confidentiality. That's why he hired the best.'

'So modest,' she muttered, leaning forward and treating him to a sexy smile. He'd been doing it to her. All was fair in love and posturing. 'But you can tell me. You know I won't blab.'

'Talk to a journalist?' He shook his head, his eyes doing the smiling this time. 'You know what I think of that breed.'

'I'm not a journalist any more.'

'Really? I still see your name, mostly in the *Sentinel*, all the time.'

'Yeah, but only because Patrick pays me well. Guilt money. But I freelance too.'

Jack sent her a sceptical look. 'I'll just bet he does.'

'What's that supposed to mean?'

'You two back together?'

'Not that it's any of your business, but no, we're not.' She tilted her head, ready to give as good as she got. 'How about you and Cassie?'

'Nope, just friends and business partners.'

'Patrick and I are friends... well, kind of, and he still wants me to go back to the paper but, unlikely though it seems, life in the country is growing on me. I've made more real friends here in a few months than I ever did after years in London. Oh, I had plenty of colleagues and acquaintances, but that isn't the same thing. I never had anyone, I realise now, that I could drop in on any time I felt like it and have a good natter. Never realised I needed to because I was always too busy building my career, watching my back and jealously guarding my stories. No time for friendships then but I know better now.'

'Then I'm glad you've seen the light. It was that way for me when I left the force. I was so damned mad at them for hanging me out to dry, at your lot for making me a fall guy and... well, it cost me my marriage and started a long association with a bottle. I wasn't an alcoholic but was going down that route. I realised it, or had it pointed out to me, and I have it under control now. But you know all that. Anyway, it would have been easy to fall into a deep depression and I have Cassie to thank for kicking me up the backside and offering me a way out. Now I almost feel the press did me a favour by driving me out of the force.'

'Glad to oblige, even if I had nothing to do with it.'

'So Patrick won't tempt you back, either professionally or personally?'

'No.' Alexi shook her head emphatically. 'I can't get past the fact that he destroyed my career. People don't do that to people they're supposed to love. Besides, I can see now that I didn't love him, not really.'

'I'm so very glad,' he said softly. 'But I don't think he'll give up on you. I suspect he persuaded his boss to film the show in your hotel in an effort to impress you and make you feel like you owed him something.'

'I consider myself duly impressed but I don't owe him diddly squat.'

'That's my girl!'

They both laughed and suddenly the tension was no longer there.

Jack then told her all about the case he'd been working on that led him to Hammond's door. Alexi threw back her head and laughed.

'What's so funny?'

'Sorry. It's just that I find it hard to imagine you working behind a shop counter, being polite to people and persuading them to part with their hard-earned cash.'

'I'll have you know that I'm a natural. All the ladies ask for me by name.'

Alexi shook her head. 'Do you actually *know* anything about jewellery?'

'Enough to get by. Anyway, I'm convinced Davis is part of the scam so when I overheard him on his mobile, making furtive arrangements to meet someone tonight, I figured I ought to tag along.'

'And this man took you to Smithfield?'

'Right, and I aim to find out why. Once I do, if there's even the remotest possibility of a connection between the loan scam and Juliette's death, then I'll let Vickery know. But let me do some digging first.'

'Okay. Does that mean you'll be hanging around?' Alexi could have bitten her tongue off. She hadn't meant to ask, to sound as if she cared about his answer or to let the conversation get that personal.

'Sure, if you don't mind me cluttering up your cottage for a while. Cheryl's hotel will be booked out.'

'You can have the spare room.'

'That'll do.' His eyes made sizzling contact with hers. 'For now.'

'Don't get ideas. I haven't seen or heard from you for weeks.' Oh damn, there she went again!

'I deliberately gave you some space.' He reached across and took her hand. 'I knew you were trying to sort your life out, decide what you wanted and where you wanted to put down roots. You were at a crossroads and didn't need pressure from me.' Frustration shimmered in his eyes. 'It wasn't easy to stay away; trust me on this.

But I give you due warning, your time's up. I want to get to know you better, Alexi Ellis.' His challenging smile, pure predatory male, sent shivers of awareness trickling down her spine. 'A whole lot better, but only if you're interested and ready to commit.'

Alexi swallowed. An intelligent man with sensitivity who knew what he wanted, all wrapped up in a sexy package that turned heads. 'How does anyone know when they're ready?'

'Now isn't the time to get into this,' Jack replied, releasing her hand. 'I came looking for you tonight with the intention of having this conversation, but when I saw what was going down at the hotel... well, obviously my timing sucks. All you need to know is that I'm hooked on you but I don't share. You need to be absolutely sure you're over Patrick before we do anything about... about the vibes that have always been there between us.'

'Patrick being history is the one thing I'm totally sure about.'

'Good.'

Cosmo stirred, took a look around the room as though he might have missed something significant, then jumped agilely into Jack's lap.

'I don't believe that cat,' Alexi said indignantly. 'He doesn't ever do that to anyone except me.'

Jack looked smug as he stroked Cosmo's back and the cat purred up a storm. 'He likes me. He's a good judge of character and is telling you it's okay for us to get involved. You should be guided by him.'

Alexi laughed. 'He's the star of the show, you know. He's been banned from the set because he entertains himself by terrorising the film crew. He thinks it's amusing to attack all their cables. He brought a whole lighting unit down once, which is what finally got him evicted. Even so, they've taken footage of him in the grounds, playing with Toby, and it's gone viral. He gets more fan mail than any of the contestants.'

'I'm surprised *he* didn't get bumped off, then.'

'Ha, I'd like to see anyone try that!' She laughed. 'Honestly, Jack, he's such a poser. He seems to know when the camera's on him and goes from devil to angel in the blink of an eye. He could have given Juliette a few lessons in stealing the show.'

'He knows his worth, is all.' Jack continued to stroke Cosmo's back. 'Can anyone else get into the annexe? Anyone not connected to the show, I mean?'

'You think an outsider could have done this? A deranged fan, perhaps?'

Jack shrugged. 'I don't think we can discount the possibility, unlikely though it seems. Juliette's been making the headlines. People get seriously involved with these programmes, live vicariously through them, and what goes on matters to them.'

Alexi nodded. 'Sad, but true.'

'I hear people have been coming to cyber-blows, arguing the case for and against the way Juliette's been behaving. Some say she uses her sexuality to make an impression; others say she can't help the way she looks and should be judged on her cooking abilities alone.' Jack looked perplexed, as though he couldn't understand why these fans didn't have something better to do with their time. Good question. 'The debate has not been civilized.'

'Yes, I know. But the hotel's booked out by the production company. The rooms aren't full all the time, only when the hotshots come down to shoot the week's episode, but they don't want hangers-on trying to crash the party.'

'The bar and restaurant are open to all-comers, though?'

'Yeah, but punters can't get anywhere near the annexe. All entrances are locked and access is through a numerical keypad.'

'That would make it tougher but wouldn't discourage someone determined to get in.'

'They'd be caught on camera if they tried to crash the residents' lounge in the annexe.'

Jack shook his head. 'We both know how effective the cameras have proven to be.'

'Whoever killed Juliette knew where they are and how to avoid them, which rather disproves your outsider theory.'

'Just being thorough.'

'Right, so what's our next move?' Alexi asked after a short pause. 'Since you've decided to stay, I assume you'll want to get involved in this business, even though it isn't connected to the case that brought you down here.'

'We need some deep background information on all the main suspects; mine and yours. Vickery will be doing that with regard to everyone at Hopgood Hall but there's nothing to stop us working the same angle. I can get Cassie on it first thing. Davis's visit to Smithfield makes it a legitimate expense I can charge to my pay-day investigation.'

'That'll go down well, if she knows we're working together again.'

Jack dismissed Alexi's concerns with a casual wave of one hand. 'She'll get over it.'

'We ought to be at the hotel ourselves tomorrow.'

'Yeah, we should. I dare say the studio will have put out an announcement, now that Juliette's father's been told of her death, so the press will be swarming all over the place like ants. So will the studio suits and, I dare say, your ex. I'd like to see how they play it, although I have a pretty good idea what the official line will be.'

'You still think they'll take the show-must-go-on route?'

He flexed a cynical brow. 'Don't you? Especially since the other four regional heats are on-going. They can hardly cancel the whole lot. They have too much invested in it.'

Alexi conceded the point with a shrug. 'I wouldn't bet against it. Vickery will be there, presumably.'

'Count on it.'

'I could try and have informal chats with everyone involved, as and when. See what they know, where they were last night, all that stuff.'

'That would help.' He stood up, reclaimed her hand and pulled her to her feet. 'Come on, it's getting late and you look done in.'

'Thanks. Just what a girl needs to hear.'

He kissed her cheek chastely. 'I'm going to take the spare room tonight. Not because I want to but because I want you to be sure about this.' He grasped her shoulders and fixed her with a smouldering look. 'Besides, when the time's right, I need your complete attention and right now I'm pretty sure I wouldn't get it.'

Alexi yawned, then nodded. 'This isn't all about you, Maddox,' she said, grinning. 'Get over yourself.'

6

Jack didn't sleep well, mainly because he couldn't get past the fact that he and the woman he was fixated on were separated by a single flimsy wall. So near yet so far. He recited the alphabet backwards, thought about dead cats (sorry, Cosmo), all the things men are supposed to concentrate on to keep their minds off sex.

It wasn't working.

He thumped his pillows, turned onto his back and stared at the patterns dancing across the ceiling. If he and Alexi did decide to get involved, he needed her to invest totally in the relationship and he still wasn't convinced she was over that jerk Vaughan. He didn't intend to screw up his chances by putting her under too much pressure. Especially now, with all the shit going down at the hotel.

Jack was up before it was light and made his way to the kitchen to get some coffee on. Cosmo appeared from somewhere and wound himself around his legs.

'Morning, mate.' Jack bent to scratch the cat's big head. 'No good looking to me for food. You'll need to wait for your mum.'

Wearing a thick, tightly belted robe, a dishevelled Alexi

wandered into the kitchen, yawning and rubbing sleep from her eyes.

'Morning,' Jack said. 'Couldn't sleep either?'

'Too much going through my head.'

Not the same things that were going through his, Jack was willing to bet. Cosmo transferred his affections to Alexi and was rewarded when she shook some dried cat food into his bowl.

'Go hit the shower and I'll make us some breakfast.'

Alexi shot him a disbelieving look. 'You cook?'

He grinned at her. 'I make a mean omelette.'

'Well, in that case...'

He called Cassie the moment Alexi left him.

'What's happening?' she asked.

Cassie didn't interrupt while Jack related the events of the previous day.

'Where are you now?'

'At Alexi's cottage.'

'Ah.'

Jack said nothing, waiting to see which way Cassie would jump.

'Okay, I get it.' She sounded disappointed but resigned. 'So, what do you need from me?'

'A deeper dig into Davis's background to start with. If you can get into his mobile phone records it would help to know who he's been calling. I can't see Hammond being involved with the pay day lending scam. If he's an investment banker and as loaded as his fancy address implies—'

'Houses can be mortgaged, you know.'

'Yeah, but not to the tune that his gaff's worth. Regardless, I don't think he'd bother with something on such a small scale, especially if he can't control it himself. From what I've heard, the man's both a snob and a control freak. I want to know if there's a connection between Davis and him, which his phone records might tell us. I'd also dearly like to know why Davis went to see him last night.'

'Bankers have taken a hit recently so he might not be as well situated as he wants the world to believe. In which case, perhaps he *is* involved with the pay-day thing.'

'Good point. And er, can you look into his daughter as well?'

'Jack. Leave the murder to the police. I'll do what I can to help close *our* case but—'

'They could be connected.'

'Come on! You're just looking for excuses to hang out with Alexi.'

And there it was. Jack should have known Cassie's resentment would show itself sooner rather than later. 'I don't believe in coincidences, Cass. Besides, if Alexi weren't involved you'd be suspicious about Hammond's name appearing in both cases as well.'

'Even so, you can't be—'

'Just do what you're comfortable with.'

'Okay, there's a few new leads on your other cases. You need to stop by the office at some stage and catch up on them. I've been fielding calls from your clients. Other than that, I'm relatively clear at the moment so I'll knuckle down to your research.' She sighed. 'I guess you want me to look into the backgrounds of the other contestants while I'm at it.'

'And the producer, the show's host and some of the crew.' Jack held the phone away from his ear while Cassie vented. 'I take it you're okay with that,' he said, chuckling. 'I'll email you their details and I'll stop by the office later.'

By the time Alexi emerged from the shower, dressed in tight-fitting jeans and a thick sweatshirt, Jack had turned the meagre contents of her fridge into a massive omelette and made toast and coffee to go with it.

'Wow!' Alexi said, eyeing the mound of food with appreciation. 'I could get used to this.'

'All part of my seduction routine.'

'Nice try, Maddox.' She sat opposite him and picked up her fork. 'Lovely,' she said, closing her eyes as she took a bite.

'Glad you approve.'

'Was that Cassie I heard you talking to?'

'Yeah, she's getting onto the digging we need.'

'Good.'

Alexi's attitude towards him was reserved. Because of the situation at Hopgood Hall or because he, Jack, had opened his big mouth about wanting to be with her, putting her on the spot when he knew the time wasn't right?

Way to go, Maddox!

Jack switched on the small television in the corner of the kitchen. A background noise to ease the tense atmosphere. Unsurprisingly, Juliette's death was all over the news. A sombre-faced reporter who looked too young to shave was staring straight into the camera, asking if reality television had overstepped the mark.

'We don't know yet what happened to this young woman, Dale,' he said in response to a question posed by the studio anchor. 'All we're being told is that she was found dead under suspicious circumstances. The police are due to make a formal statement later this morning. In the meantime, we are left with questions about the impact of these reality shows and the pressures placed on the contestants to excel, shock, titillate... call it what you will. In the meantime, a grieving father is left wondering what could have happened to cause this senseless and untimely death and he will doubtless be demanding answers. All the people I've spoken to agree that the industry needs to take responsibility, learn from this tragedy and ensure nothing like it ever happens again.'

Jack snarled at the screen and switched it off.

'We ought to be with Cheryl and Drew,' Alexi said, pushing away her half-eaten breakfast. 'I'll tidy up here if you need to shower.'

Jack did need to, but didn't take long and didn't shave, mainly because he didn't have anything to shave with. If he was going to hang around, he'd need to bring some clothes and stuff back with him after he'd visited the office. It wasn't just Alexi who was the attraction; it was this case. It had already got to him and he didn't want to see a miscarriage of justice simply because Marcel was too convenient a suspect for the police to look past him.

Vickery was under pressure. Too many crimes, not enough crime fighters. This case was high profile and the brass would be pressuring him to get an early result. Just so long as it was the right result, Jack had no problem with that. But he didn't want to see Cheryl and Drew's reputation as hoteliers suffer, to say nothing of protecting Alexi's investment in their venture.

Yeah, he thought, making a wry face in the bathroom mirror as he finger-brushed his teeth; that would be it.

Ten minutes later, he, Alexi and Cosmo were in her car. There were uniformed police directing traffic at the end of the road leading to Hopgood Hall. As expected, the press were everywhere. Vans with antennae filled every available space and cameramen snapped pictures of Alexi's car as it was permitted to drive past the police cordon. Cosmo pushed his head against the window and snarled at them all.

'That's Cosmo!' someone shouted. The cameras went into overdrive.

'See what I mean about him being a poser,' Alexi said indulgently.

Jack chuckled and scratched Cosmo's ears. 'He'll be on all the front pages tomorrow.'

The car park was filled with police vehicles and high-quality cars Jack assumed belonged to the studio bigwigs.

'Looks like the cavalry's arrived,' Alexi said.

They gave their names to the uniformed policeman at the door and went directly to the kitchen. Cheryl and Drew were there. So was Patrick Vaughan and a couple of other suits Jack didn't know.

'Hey, you okay?' Patrick asked, pulling Alexi into a hug.

She shook him off. 'Fine,' she snapped.

'Oh.' Patrick offered Jack his hand and a scowl simultaneously. Jack flashed a smug smile, hoping he'd read too much into him arriving with Alexi. Childish but satisfying. Cosmo growled at Patrick and stalked off to join Toby in his basket. 'Didn't know you were here.'

Jack shot him a look. 'I'm surprised Alexi didn't mention it.'

Alexi introduced Jack to Evan Southgate, the show's producer, and Grenville Scott, a guy in a Savile Row suit who was the production company's chief lawyer.

'From now on, no one speaks to the police without me being there,' Grenville said assertively.

Jack wondered why he'd bothered to say that. No one in that kitchen was a suspect, or likely to be interviewed formally. Just flexing his muscles, Jack assumed, deciding he didn't like the man. He was still a copper at heart and the police and slick defence lawyers did not comfortable bedfellows make.

'They suspect Marcel of involvement,' Alexi said anxiously. 'Have you spoken to him yet?'

Patrick shook his head. 'We only just arrived.'

'Well, he's admitted to having sex with Juliette in his apartment early last night,' Alexi told them.

Patrick dragged a hand down his face.

'And one of his knives was found buried in her chest,' Jack added.

'Great,' Evan said. 'This is *so* not looking good for us.'

'It doesn't look too good for Marcel either,' Jack pointed out. 'To say nothing of the victim.'

'Marcel insists that he didn't kill her,' Alexi told them.

'Why would he?' Cheryl added. 'This show was making his name.'

Before anything more could be said, Vickery and DC Hogan joined them. Introductions were made and Cheryl's offer of coffee was accepted.

'We came to tell you what we suspected when we found the body. But we weren't in a position to divulge it until we were sure,' Vickery said. 'And we are telling you this as a courtesy, which we trust you will respect.'

Every head nodded.

'Ms. Hammond didn't die in her room as a result of a stab wound to the chest.' Alexi glanced quizzically at Jack, who manfully resisted an *I-told-you-so* look. 'She died elsewhere as the result of a blow to the head. Whether accidental or because she was attacked, we have yet to establish.'

'Any idea where she did die?' Drew asked.

'We are conducting a thorough search of the area,' Vickery replied non-committedly.

And had been ever since her body was found, Jack knew.

'Not in Marcel's apartment?' Cheryl made her question sound like a statement.

'I cannot confirm or deny that,' Vickery replied.

That's a no then, Jack decided.

'The post mortem is scheduled for this afternoon and we'll know more after that. But, obviously, she didn't accidentally hit her head, get up, walk back to her room and stab herself with a kitchen knife, so foul play is a near certainty. We will not be releasing details of the knife which, incidentally, pierced a silicone breast implant. We will simply say that she died as the result of a head injury and that we are treating her death as suspicious.'

'We appreciate you telling us,' Grenville said, looking worried, as well he might. It seemed increasingly likely that someone connected with the production was responsible for Juliette's murder. With the press already blaming her death on the pressures of reality TV, it was hard for Jack to decide if Grenville would tenaciously defend any suspects hauled in for questioning or distance his clients from them with a speed that defied gravity. Jack's money was on the latter.

'We'll be formally interviewing everyone involved with the production who was here yesterday,' Vickery added. 'Those interviews will take place at Reading Police Station. We've already cleared Mr Gasquet's two chefs who were working yesterday's lunch service. They can both account for every second of their time since leaving here and their stories check out.' Jack nodded, knowing this meant they didn't have criminal records. Vickery would have made sure of that. 'We also have people examining all the available film footage to see if we can trace Ms Hammond's last movements.'

'I shall be present at all the interviews, inspector,' Grenville said.

'I rather thought that might be the case,' Vickery replied drolly.

'Do you need my wife and me to come to the station to be interviewed?' Drew asked.

'No, sir, that won't be necessary. Your statements have already been typed up. You just need to sign them. I need to speak with the other three contestants, your chef and the two members of the production team who were here. Oh, and I believe the show's host was around.'

Patrick and Evan shared a surprised look that didn't escape Vickery's notice. 'What gave you that idea?' Evan asked.

'One of the crew mentioned it, sir. We'll need to talk to him as well. It's a case of establishing where everyone was and what they saw or didn't see of Ms Hammond.'

'Right, well anything we can do to help,' Drew said.

'I'm returning to Reading now, ready for the press statement. DC Hogan will stay here and arrange for the interviewees to be brought to the station as and when we're ready for them.'

'Can we go into the annexe again?' Alexi asked. 'Have your people finished there?'

'They have and you can. Whether the contestants will feel comfortable sleeping there again so soon after this tragedy is another matter.'

No one spoke for several minutes after the police left the kitchen.

'Will the show go on?' Alexi asked, breaking the silence.

Jack wasn't surprised when the producer nodded. 'Probably. The station bosses are making a final decision this afternoon but, just so long as no one involved is charged with murder, they have too much time and money invested to cancel now. Especially given that there are four other regional contests being shot simultaneously.'

'And Marcel will stay on?' Alexi asked.

'We're not into trial by television,' Evan replied. 'If we dropped him, it would imply that we thought he had something to do with the death which, as far as I know, he didn't.'

'I know he didn't do it,' Cheryl said staunchly.

'Of course he didn't, love.' Drew slid an arm around Cheryl's shoulders and gave them a squeeze. 'Why would he?'

'A lot of the evidence does point to him, albeit circumstantial,' Alexi pointed out gloomily.

'Except for a motive,' Jack said. 'He had means and opportunity but other than possible blackmail because he slept with Juliette, no real motive. Hard to get a conviction without one. Besides, we don't know much about where everyone else was. And Juliette was supposedly overheard arguing with someone else after she left Marcel, remember?'

Alexi nodded. 'You mean with...'

Jack nudged her and she abruptly stopped talking. He didn't want the TV people to know about Juliette's supposed argument with Paul Dakin until they absolutely had to. They would support Marcel if they could but if the only alternative suspect was Dakin – one of their own – then the cynic in Jack didn't doubt that the production company would feed Marcel to the wolves in order to protect the show's host.

'I gather the others are all upstairs in the residents' lounge,' Alexi said. 'I might as well wander up there and see what they have to say for themselves. No one said we couldn't talk to them before they give their statements. Besides, I've got to know them quite well in the short time they've been here and they'll probably open up to me.'

'Alexi, have you got a moment?' Patrick grasped her elbow and drew her aside. 'This probably sounds indelicate,' he said in a lowered voice that Jack could still hear because he made a point of loitering close enough to eavesdrop, 'but you know how it works. If we don't print the truth then someone else will.'

'Ever the newsman, Patrick,' she replied, sounding weary yet resigned. 'Just let it be for now. When the dust settles, we'll see where we stand.'

'Can we have dinner together later?' he asked, casting a wary glance Jack's way.

'I don't think so.' She turned away from him. 'I'll call you,' she said in a tone that made it clear the subject wasn't up for debate.

'He doesn't give up,' Jack said as he followed Alexi, Cosmo and Toby up the stairs.

She sighed. 'He's right about one thing, though. If I wasn't so closely involved, I'd be busting my gut to get the inside scoop too.' She flashed a wry smile. 'I'm starting not to like the person I used to be.'

'That's not what I meant.'

She expelled a long breath. 'No, I know you didn't.'

'Okay with you if I sit in while you talk to the contestants? I don't know them so might see something you miss.'

'Sure. If they don't mind me asking questions or you being there while I do then it's fine with me.'

Only Greta was in the lounge, engrossed in something on her iPad.

'Hi, Greta,' Alexi said. 'All alone?'

'John and Anton appeared for breakfast but have been back in their rooms ever since.' Greta shrugged her wide shoulders as she shot a wary look in Cosmo's direction. Cosmo stalked across the room, looking for somewhere comfortable to snooze, and ignored Greta. 'We're all a bit on edge, which is hardly to be wondered at, I suppose.'

Jack hadn't seen Greta in the flesh before but recognised her from the programme. She was tall, slightly overweight, with a round face and a button mouth that looked too small for it. Her hair was arguably her best feature. Dark brown, thick and sleek, it bounced on her shoulders when she moved her head, not a split end in sight. She had a habit of twirling the ends around her fingers when she spoke, as though it was one aspect of her appearance she felt she didn't have to apologise for. She wore a trendy pair of glasses, no makeup and tent-like clothing that disguised the shape of her body.

She wasn't unattractive but didn't make the best of herself. Because she didn't care about appearances or because she was too serious about cooking to worry about how she looked? Then again, trying to compete in the looks department with Juliette would have been beyond most women's capabilities. She was probably intelligent enough to know she'd been selected for the programme partly because she and Juliette were chalk and cheese.

Jack had studied all the notes Alexi held from the studio, supplied to her by Patrick, regarding each competitor's background. He knew that Greta was twenty-six, had a high IQ and worked for an IT company. But, like all the competitors, her passion was cooking and she wanted to make it as a professional chef. Being selected for the programme was her best chance of achieving that ambition. Now it all hung in the balance.

'Mind if we join you?' Alexi asked, sitting down before Greta could respond. 'This is a friend of mine, Jack Maddox.'

'Pleased to meet you,' Jack said, extending his hand. 'Sorry it has to be under such circumstances.'

Greta shook Jack's hand and shrugged. 'Selfish bitch,' she muttered. 'Sorry if that sounds harsh,' she added, 'but I've never been one to shed crocodile tears. She and I didn't like one another; that's no secret. It came out on the screen and I've told the police that it's the truth. Even so, I wouldn't wish her dead. I'd have preferred to have put her firmly in her place by beating her fair and square in the contest. I told the police that too.'

'I take it you're referring to Juliette,' Alexi said. 'Probably better not to speak about her like that too often. The police might think you had a hand in her demise.'

'They probably already do. Like I say, all that antagonism between us on screen wasn't play-acting.' She lifted her wide shoulders in a belligerent gesture. 'Didn't see any reason not to be straight with them. We were all getting sick of the cameras following our every move twenty-four seven, but for once I'm glad they did. I was either in the residents' lounge in the annexe all evening or elsewhere under the eagle eye of a camera, and the footage will prove it.' She looked smug. 'So I'm in the clear, which means I get bragging rights and can say I'm not particularly sorry that she's dead.' Her head shot up. 'What? Don't look at me like that, Alexi. I have many faults but no one's ever accused me of being a hypocrite.'

Alexi managed a sardonic smile. 'Obviously not.'

'I really didn't like her but at the risk of repeating myself, I did want the show to go on so I could beat her fair and square. I would have done it, too. She might have waggled her dainty little backside at all the men who mattered, but I'm a better chef than she would ever have been.' Greta sighed. 'Still, I guess they'll cancel the series now as a sign of respect, or some such garbage, and it'll have all been for nothing.'

'Actually,' Alexi said, sharing a raised eyebrow look with Jack, 'I think they plan to carry on.'

'Really?' Greta brightened considerably. 'Cool.'

'Murder is good for ratings, apparently,' Jack said but his sarcasm was clearly lost on Greta.

'Why didn't the two of you get on?' Alexi asked. 'I get it that you resented her using her feminine wiles on the men. That would have annoyed me too, but I think you're bright enough to realise she was put on the show with that purpose in mind. That the suits encouraged it because they always have one eye on the ratings.'

Greta sighed in a considering way that Jack had seen many times before during interviews with suspects. She knew something and was trying to decide how much more to say to them.

'It's not common knowledge,' she said, 'but I expect it will come out now that she's dead so you might as well hear it from me. The thing is, we'd met before.'

'What!' Jack and Alexi said together.

'When?' Jack asked alone. 'Did the producers know?'

'At school. I left eight years ago when I was eighteen. And yes, they did know but I didn't tell the police. I'd been waiting for that sleaze ball Dakin to throw our acrimonious past up in the questions they set us in recreation,' Greta said. 'Bet they regret not getting that one in earlier. Anyway, Juliette and I both went to Eversham.'

'That posh, fee-paying place near Arborfield?' Jack asked.

'No need to look so shocked,' Greta replied huffily. 'Juliette went there because her old man stumped up the fees. I got offered a scholarship place. She was a year behind me but I remember that she was a right little madam even then. Her dad expected her to excel at everything, which was daft because nobody can. Anyway, she wasn't going to disappoint him so used anyone and everyone she could to do her work for her. You know, giving her all the right facts to put in essays, pointing out the most likely areas to swot for in exams by going through past papers, stuff like that.'

'You helped her?'

Greta nodded. 'She paid well and I needed the money.'

'Isn't a lot of that stuff available online nowadays?' Jack asked.

'Yeah, if you know where to look, or can be arsed to do the looking. But the teachers were on to that. They could spot stuff cribbed from the net at twenty paces with the wind in the wrong direction. They'd seen it all before so you needed to be inventive to get it past them, and Juliette simply wasn't that clever.'

'So why did you fall out?' Jack asked. 'You had a business arrangement. Doesn't mean you had to like one another. But it's obvious you despised Juliette.'

'It was over a boy,' Greta said after a significant pause. 'I was passably pretty in those days, with assets that got me noticed. And I had great hair.' Another twist of the hair in question. 'My appearance wasn't in Juliette's league, of course, but no one's was. Anyway, ours was an all-girls school but there was a kid of about twenty who came once a week and worked in the grounds with the gardeners.

He and I got along and... well, we did more than just tinker in the potting shed, if you get my drift.'

Alexi and Jack nodded.

'There's not much more to tell. Juliette found out about it and took him from me. Not because she wanted him but because she was a spiteful mare and because she could.'

'Ouch!' Alexi touched her hand. 'That must have hurt. I assume she could get any guy she wanted, even then, so why do that to you?'

'Because she was always doing outrageous things to impress her friends. But even she had never had sex on the school grounds.' Greta scowled. 'I'd eclipsed her, you see, and I realised only when it was too late to change things that it had seriously pissed her off.'

'How did she know? Did you go around telling people what you'd done?' Jack asked. 'Wasn't that taking a bit of a risk? Presumably you'd have been expelled if the headmistress found out.'

'Yeah well, I did boast to one or two people I thought I could trust. Stupid! Stupid! I should have known better. I never really fitted in with all those rich girls and I thought it might gain me some street cred if they knew what I'd done. Like I say, it was stupid but when you're that young and find your first love, you think the whole world will be glad for you and that it will last forever.' She shook her head. 'Ha, much I knew!'

'So how did you find out that your boyfriend had cheated on you with Juliette?' Alexi asked.

'She deliberately fixed it so I'd catch them together. I've never forgotten her smirk when I did, the vicious little cow! Anyway, she had to find someone else to do her homework after that. All the money in the world wouldn't have persuaded me to help her and I never spoke to her again until this programme started. And only then under sufferance.'

'How did you feel when you knew you'd be competing against her?' Jack asked.

'Pleased,' Greta said succinctly. 'The only time I'd ever lost to her was over that boy. The competition for the final places on this show was brutal. And I'll give Juliette her due; she'd always liked to cook, even back at school. But it's more than just that. There's planning involved, timings, allowances for nerves and, of course, having the balls to be innovative enough to stand out.' Greta screwed up her nose. 'Juliette was going about it a different way by trying to get Marcel, Paul and who the hell knows who else to favour her by... well, returning the favours she was willing to dish out. In other words, history was repeating itself.'

'You think she was sleeping with them both?'

Greta shrugged. 'Wouldn't put it past her but I don't see how that would help her with the other stuff.'

'What stuff?' Jack asked.

'Well, I know how to schedule my menus, how to make them ground-breaking, if you like, and how to ensure I have enough time to complete them.' Greta grinned. 'Juliette didn't and had no one to do it for her. Unless, of course, she cozied up with Marcel, although I'm not sure he would fall for that one. He's a dedicated chef and wouldn't countenance cheating.'

Before Jack could ask more questions, Anton and John came into the room.

'The police are just about to... oh, hi, Alexi,' Anton said.

Alexi introduced them both to Jack. 'What are the police about to do?' she asked after the men had shaken hands.

'Give a statement to the press,' John replied, switching on the television.

A high-ranking uniform stood in front of a bank of microphones, Vickery at his side, and said more or less what Vickery had told them to expect. There was a barrage of questions, all of which were fielded without giving anything away. Then it was over, having taken no more than three minutes. A number flashed up on the screen for people to ring with any information pertinent to the enquiry. Jack knew it would be flooded with time wasters but anything they said would still have to be followed up.

'So she wasn't killed in her room,' John said pensively.

'Course she wasn't,' Greta replied. 'I was in the lounge. I'd have heard something.'

'So, what happens now?' Anton asked in his soft, lilting, Caribbean accent. 'What are we supposed to do? Will the show go on?'

'Alexi seems to think so.'

'Good,' John and Anton said in unison.

The door opened and DC Hogan stood there. 'Time for the three of you to come down to the station,' she said. 'Shouldn't take long. We just need to go over what you told us about your where-abouts yesterday and get you to sign your statements.'

Alexi and Jack watched them gather up their coats and head off with the DC.

'What did you make of Greta?' Alexi asked.

'She didn't tell us the complete truth.'

'What, about her prior relationship with Juliette?'

Jack nodded.

'Doesn't matter, does it, if she can prove where she was when Juliette was murdered?'

'Precisely. So why lie?'

'I don't think she did. She just left a few things out. Things that probably didn't show her in a good light. People have selective memories, you know.'

'Hmm.' Jack's phone pinged. 'Good old Cass,' he said, checking the message. 'She's got some stuff for us already. Look, there's not much more I can do here until all the suspects have been formally interviewed. So, I'm going to head back to Newbury. I need to stop off at the office, clear up a few things, see what Cassie has for me and pick up some clothes. Then I'll be back.'

'Drive carefully. That bike's an accident waiting to happen on these frosty, narrow roads.'

Jack grinned at her and waved over his shoulder as he headed for the stairs, wondering if she'd noticed that he made no reference to finding accommodation when he got back.

7

Alexi watched Jack go, then collapsed onto a couch in the corner of the lounge, already exhausted and the day had hardly begun. Cosmo rubbed against her legs while Toby hopped onto the seat beside her, looking to have his ears scratched. She was glad Jack intended to hang around and was confident that he would get to the truth, even if the police bungled the investigation. It was like he had a point to prove after the way he'd been treated by the Force and she couldn't blame him for that. She felt the same way about journalism after being all but sacked from the *Sentinel*.

Her feelings about Jack wanting a relationship with her were harder to define. When it came to picking men, to seeing through their bullshit and getting a handle on their real motives, she was a total failure. She liked Jack. More than liked him. He turned female heads everywhere he went and was kind, funny and clever. He exuded virile power *and* he could cook. What was not to like? But she still wasn't sure if she was ready to commit.

'Cosmo,' she said, leaning down to stroke the big cat, 'I think you and I ought to stick together. Fewer complications that way. Yes, I know you like Jack, but what if he breaks my heart?'

But then again, what's life without a few risks? she asked herself as she pushed herself to her feet. Jack hadn't made it clear if he was thinking long or short term, long or short distance. Of more immediate concern, where did he think he'd be staying if he hung around Lambourn for a while? The production company still had the hotel booked solid and the press would have snapped up every other room within a ten-mile radius.

'He might have asked, instead of just assuming,' Alexi said, peeved. 'Come on, Cosmo. Let's see what's happening downstairs.'

Toby and Cosmo ran ahead. Alexi descended the stairs at a more leisurely pace and headed for Cheryl's kitchen, expecting to find her or Drew there. Neither of them were, but Paul Dakin was, flipping through the morning's paper but obviously not reading it. Probably looking for references to himself. Alexi had a low opinion of Paul. Cosmo didn't like him either and proved it by growling as he stalked past, erect tail vibrating with annoyance. Paul hastily got out of the cat's way, putting the barrier of the table between him and Cosmo.

Wuss!

'Oh hi, Alexi.' Paul put aside the paper and turned on the fake megawatt smile he used in front of the camera and which irritated the hell out of Alexi. 'I was hoping to catch you.'

Alexi poured herself some coffee from the pot that was kept permanently on the go on the kitchen worktop. She waved it in Paul's direction but he shook his head. Caffeine would probably stain his whiter-than-white dental implants, Alexi supposed, suppressing a grin at the thought.

'What brings you to the bowels of the house, Paul?'

Alexi seated herself across from him. He wasn't as impeccably turned out as usual, she noticed. There were dark shadows under his eyes, his clothes were rumpled and his usually perfect bouffant hair do was wilting.

'Terrible business with Juliette,' he said, shaking his head. 'Simply shocking. Who would do such a thing?'

'That's what the police hope to find out.'

Alexi knew he didn't just want to lament Juliette's passing and, stirring her coffee even though she hadn't added sugar to it, she waited him out.

'I hear the show's going to continue,' he said into a loaded silence broken only by the jingling of the tags on Toby's collar as he energetically scratched at a spot behind his left ear. 'Not sure if they're going to replace Juliette or just continue with three contestants.'

'I'm sure you'll be the first to know.'

He sighed. 'She wasn't a bad kid, you know.'

'You're in a minority there, Paul. Almost no one else I've spoken to other than Cheryl has a good word to say about her.'

'Because they didn't know her.'

Alexi flexed a brow. 'And you did? Tell me about her.'

'She was funny, self-deprecating when the cameras weren't on her. I think she had daddy issues, though. A love-hate relationship with him that was never far from the surface. She wanted to impress him but he disapproved of her being on the programme so she knew she never would. She was conflicted about that.'

'Someone else mentioned her fixation with her father,' Alexi replied, drumming her fingers restlessly on the table.

'I'm in trouble, Alexi,' Paul said after another long pause. 'I need a sounding board.'

'Then talk to Grenville Scott. That's what he gets paid his telephone number salary for,' Alexi said briskly. 'I don't know much about legal matters which, I assume, is what this is about. Besides, you're under contract to the production company. They won't thank me for giving you layman's advice but, if you're desperate then I guess you could try me.'

'I was hoping to talk to you in confidence,' he said, running his hand through the deflated bouffant. 'As a friend.'

A friend? They'd barely exchanged a dozen words in all the time the contest had been running.

'I take it you were sleeping with Juliette,' Alexi said, cutting to the chase.

Paul's head shot up. 'How did you know?'

'Lucky guess. Besides, you were seen here last night and heard arguing with her.'

'Oh God!' Paul dropped his face into his hands and groaned. 'Who heard me?'

'Come on, Paul. You know better than most that this place is a goldfish bowl.' Alexi wasn't prepared to name names. 'That's rather the idea of fly-on-the-wall television, isn't it? Nothing goes unnoticed.'

He sighed. 'I suppose.'

'You're thinking of your wife and kids if this gets out?'

Paul nodded. 'I stand to lose everything. My wife will bail if she knows I've been unfaithful and, worse, I have a morality clause in my contract. If Far Reach find out then I'm history.'

Alexi thought he had more immediate concerns, like what the police would make of his having slept with the victim, but refrained from saying so.

'If you have so much to lose, why did you do it? Sleep with her, I mean.' Alexi asked.

'What can I say?' Paul spread his hands. 'She came on to me. I was flattered.'

'You must have women hit on you a lot in your line of work.' Alexi didn't get it herself but figured that a certain type of person would do whatever it took to get themselves noticed by someone in Paul's position. Besides, she was pretty sure that he was the one who often did the trawling, promising his victims he could do things for their careers. The TV equivalent of the casting couch.

'Yeah, but Juliette was different. There was just something about her. Oh, she seemed over confident on the surface but underneath, she was vulnerable and needy.'

Alexi was reminded that Cheryl had said something similar about her, causing her to think that perhaps she'd been too quick to judge, just because Juliette had tried to kick Cosmo. 'It didn't occur to you that it might be an act to get you to use your influence? She was pretty determined to win the contest and doesn't seem to have cared too much about what she had to do to ensure that win.'

'What influence? I'm the host. I have no say in who wins.'

'But you could make her look good on film. You're the one who fired questions at the contestants. It was up to you how hard you were on them and, just for the record, I'm not the only one who noticed how easy you went on Juliette.'

'She wasn't as bad as the show made her look and deserved a break,' Paul said defensively. 'They didn't broadcast any footage of her being considerate.'

'How often did that happen?' Alexi asked. 'She didn't go out of her way to make herself popular with anyone who couldn't help her.'

Paul smiled. 'She knew how to come across all sweetness and light on camera but not much of that footage got shown. I think the producers decided that didn't make for good TV.'

'Because they knew it was an act?'

'Possibly. They don't confide in me.' Paul sighed. 'Look, she was ambitious, but that isn't why she came on to me. You think I don't have experience in these things?' he asked with a touch of his former arrogance.

Alexi shook her head. 'Don't be naïve, Paul.'

'What a bloody mess!'

'I take it you can't decide whether to tell Grenville for fear of invalidating your contract.'

Paul nodded.

'But if you don't tell the police then you're withholding information, especially since you were seen and heard arguing with Juliette yesterday.'

He looked to be on the verge of tears. 'She'd asked me if I could get down here and I said I'd try but couldn't promise. Something came up so I called her mobile and told her I couldn't make it. Then my commitment got cancelled so I thought I'd come down and surprise her. I mean, she couldn't leave the grounds so I figured she'd be bored, at a loose end, pleased to see me. She didn't get on with the other contestants so was often lonely on her down time.' He scrubbed a hand down his face. 'I came in the back way and caught her sneaking out of Marcel's apartment.'

'Ah, she replaced you with someone who *could* help her.'

'That's what we argued about. Her going with Marcel. She said I didn't own her and if I couldn't be there for her, she'd find someone who could be.'

'The police will see that as sufficient reason to kill her,' Alexi said briskly, seeing no point in sugar-coating it. 'You risked your marriage and your career for her sake but she cheated on you the first chance she got. A real ego deflator and a solid motive. The only motive they have. Sorry, Paul, but I'm not telling you something that hasn't already occurred to you, am I?'

'But I didn't kill her!' His eyes filled. 'I swear to God I didn't. We argued, I left and drove home to London. I stopped for petrol on the motorway so I have an alibi.'

Alexi lifted one hand and tilted it from side to side. 'Depends on how soon after you left that she was killed.'

The air left his lungs in an extravagant whoosh as he buried his face in his hands and sobbed. Alexi would have felt sorry for him, but for the fact that he was only broken up about his own situation and didn't seem to care that Juliette had been brutally murdered.

'Look, Paul, you came to me for advice and, far as I can see, you have graver concerns than your marriage or your career. Talk to Grenville, tell him what you told me, and I'm betting he'll insist that you tell the police exactly what happened.'

'Yes, but—'

'If you lie, the chances are you'll get caught out, which will only make matters worse.'

'What about Marcel? He was sleeping with her too. Perhaps she used sex to try and influence the outcome of the competition—'

'I'm sure she did, but Marcel wasn't a contestant, isn't married and doesn't have a morality clause. All he can be accused of is bad taste in sleeping with a contestant, which would probably enhance his reputation in some quarters. He had no reason to kill her.'

'But I do.' Paul hung his head. 'Shit, why did I let myself be drawn in by—'

DC Hogan poked her head round the door. 'Oh, there you are, Mr Dakin. We're ready to take your statement at the station now. Mr Scott said he would meet you there.'

Paul stood up, looking like he was about to face a firing squad. Alexi said goodbye and watched him as he left, trying to decide if he was guilty of anything more sinister than arrogance and loose morals. Either way, at least it would take some of the pressure off Marcel now that the police had an alternative suspect who *did* have a motive to kill. And, more significantly, one who had seen Juliette leave Marcel's apartment alive and well.

What to do with herself now? Alexi stood up and stretched her arms above her head, hearing the vertebrae in her spine pop. Presumably, the contestants were back from making their statements. Alexi would like to talk to Anton and John but decided to wait until Jack returned. He'd probably want to hear what they had to say first hand.

Alexi, Cosmo and Toby wandered outside. She looked towards the annexe and saw Drew tearing down the crime scene tape from the perimeter. She went to join him.

'Where's Cheryl?' she asked.

'With the baby. I wanted to put this place back together without her seeing it the way it looks now. It's a mess inside. Fingerprint powder everywhere. Those police are not good housekeepers.'

'I'll help you put it straight.'

'You don't need to do that.'

'Hey, what are partners for? Besides, I'm under-occupied right now, waiting for Jack to get back from Newbury so we can continue with our sleuthing.'

Drew sent her a mischievous grin. 'Is that what they're calling it this week?'

Alexi thumped his arm. 'It's not like that with us, Drew.'

'Well, it ought to be. You could do a lot worse and I can tell he's got the hots for you, sensible man that he is.'

'Told you that, did he?'

Drew grinned. 'He doesn't need to. You women aren't the only ones who speak fluent body language.'

Alexi laughed but really didn't want to go there, not until she had a surer idea of her own feelings. 'Come on,' she said instead. 'Let's take a look inside.'

'Okay, I get it. I shall mind my own business.' Drew threw an arm around Alexi's shoulders. 'But has it occurred to you that we care about you and want to see you happy? I have it on good authority from my wife that Jack is the sort of guy who would amply satisfy any woman's needs.'

Alexi shook her head, laughing in spite of herself. 'There's obviously nothing wrong with my friend's eyesight.'

Drew pulled an affronted expression.

'Oh my goodness!' Alexi clapped a hand over her mouth when they entered the annexe's reception room and she saw the state the police had left it in.

It looked as though it had been ransacked. Every book, DVD, file of papers... absolutely everything had been moved and examined but not put back in its proper place. Every drawer was pulled open, every cushion removed from the seating and not replaced properly. Rugs had been rolled up to expose bare floorboards. The pictures hanging on the walls were crooked.

The annexe had been Alexi's pet project. She'd been passionate about it but it now felt as though her lovely new, carefully decorated reception room had been violated.

'Did they expect to find a written confession somewhere?' she asked, shaking her head.

'Wait until you see Juliette's room. If you *want* to see it.'

'Yeah, I do actually.' Alexi glanced around suspiciously. 'Are the cameras still rolling?'

'No, they're off for now.'

'Come on then. Let's take a look.'

Alexi felt a chill as she entered Juliette's room, even though she told herself Juliette hadn't actually been killed there. The fingerprint powder Drew had told her to expect coated every surface like a grey shroud. The bed was stripped, the brand-new mattress stained with blood and traces of other fluids. Alexi preferred not to guess at their origin. Juliette's extensive collection of clothing had obviously been checked over and now dangled at drunken angles from hangers. There was no sign of her iPad or personal papers. Presumably the police had taken them.

Drew opened the door that led directly outside, in spite of the fact that the temperature was barely above freezing. It helped to dispel the gloom of a life needlessly taken.

'That mattress will have to go,' he said, as though speaking to himself.

Alexi prowled around the room, touching Juliette's things. She had no clear idea what she was looking for but looked anyway.

'Where were the cameras in this room?' she asked.

'There was one there, above the door, pointed directly at the bed,' Drew replied. 'And the other was above that wall light fitting, getting a different angle of the room.'

'Leaving no privacy,' Alexi muttered to herself. 'Those cameras not working bother me, Drew. It's too much of a coincidence to imagine they just happened to go on the blink at the time when someone wanted to dump a body in here and symbolically stab it through an implant.'

'Symbolic?'

'That's what Jack reckons but he can't say why. It does seem a bit futile, if Juliette was already dead, so I suppose it *could* be symbolic.' She subsided into thought. 'How do you decommission a spy camera?'

'Far as I can make out, they're wireless, activated by movement. In other words, the camera only transmits when there's something to transmit. The signal goes to a receiver that's connected to the recording device and whoever's on duty can watch the monitors in the different rooms to see what's what. They work through that thingy over there,' Drew added, pointing to a small device that looked like a satellite box. 'Someone only needed to disconnect them and they'd go down.'

'I thought you said the cameras operated wirelessly.'

'The cameras do but a live feed goes into that box, which is what picks up movement and wakes the cameras up.'

'Why wasn't that person captured doing the deed then?'

'Probably crawled on hands and knees. He or she could have

come in through the side door. Neither camera captures that door actually opening.'

'I wonder why Gerry didn't notice that both of Juliette's cameras had gone down,' Alexi said, almost to herself. 'It was Gerry Salter on duty last night, wasn't it?'

'Yeah, but if there was no one in the room, he wouldn't expect to see any movement.'

'Wouldn't he get a warning light to say they'd gone off line?'

'No idea. We'll have to ask him. No doubt the police already have.'

'Come on, Drew,' she said, indicating the mattress. 'Let's get this out and have a new one sent over from the hotel's supply. We can clean up while we're waiting for it to arrive.'

'Earning your keep,' Drew said, grinning. 'I like that.'

They both returned to the reception room where Drew had deposited cleaning supplies, donned rubber gloves and set to work. Two hours later, when Cheryl came in search of them, the place was almost as good as new. But Alexi knew it would take a lot longer for the stigma of death to leave the place.

* * *

'You work fast.' Jack nodded his approval as he read through the stuff Cassie had found for him, having printed it out. 'I'm impressed.'

'Don't be,' she replied, her fingers flying over her keyboard. 'I'm just getting started.'

Jack flipped through Dean Davis's mobile phone records. 'Do we know who all these numbers refer to that Davis called so regularly?'

'The most frequent one is his mother. Well, his home number

but he lives with his mother so I guess that's who he called so frequently.'

Jack frowned. 'No father on the scene? Siblings?'

'Give me a chance.'

'Sorry.'

Jack's phone rang. He spoke to a client about one of his on-going cases, got side tracked and decided he might as well deal with the work that had come in regarding all of his assignments. He didn't want to give Cassie any reason to complain about him not pulling his weight. It was an hour before he could return to Dean's phone records. He wondered how Cassie managed to get her hands on them so quickly but probably wouldn't understand, even if she tried to explain it to him. His online skills didn't extend far beyond picking up his email and he was perfectly content for it to remain that way.

'Dean Davis is nineteen and has a steady job,' he said, thinking aloud. 'Why would he want to still live with his mother—'

'A lot of kids do nowadays. They get free board and accommodation, their washing done and can come and go as they please. No house rules about overnight guests and the sleeping arrangements as far as I can tell from speaking with friends with kids in their teens and twenties.'

'Okay, but why call her several times a day? That's definitely not natural.'

'Let me do some more digging.'

'Any more kids in that household?'

'Don't think so. According to the Council Tax records, it's just the two of them.'

'So Dean looks after her maybe, not the other way around.'

'It looks that way.'

'Does she work?'

'She has a chequered work history. Never stayed anywhere for long. Last job was for more than two years, her longest until... holy shit!' Cassie turned to look at Jack, her jaw dropping. 'She had a job as a receptionist at Cash Out until a few months ago when she was fired.'

'You're kidding me?'

'See for yourself.'

'Hell, perhaps I've been coming at this job the wrong way.' Jack slapped his thigh. 'Dean Davis is protective of his mum, judging by the number of times he calls her every day. She loses her job and so, and I'm surmising here, he decides to teach her ex-employers a lesson. I thought Davis was just a worker bee but what if he's the brains behind the scam.' Jack blew air through his lips.

'You need to tell the client.'

'No, what I need to do is talk to Davis first.'

'Jack, we're being paid by Cash Out.'

'And they're getting their pound of flesh. But they also want confidentiality so I need to discover first if there's any connection between Juliette's murder, Dean and Hammond, or whether that's purely coincidence.'

'You know Dean didn't murder her because you followed him last night. Anyway, why would he...' Cassie gasped. 'Oh God!'

'What is it?' Jack jumped up and read her screen over her shoulder.

'I hate to say this, Jack, but you were right. There is a connection between your case and Juliette's murder.'

'How so?'

She pointed to an entry on her screen from the marriage register. 'Look. Dean's mum used to be married to Hammond.' She sent Jack a wide-eyed look. 'She could be Juliette's mother.'

8

Jack stopped at his flat to pack a bag and then drove back to Lambourn, using the short drive to try and make sense of what he'd just learned about Davis's family connections. All the employees in the jewellery shop could talk about was *What's For Dinner?* Since it was being filmed locally, they felt that their views counted for something. They all had opinions about who would win, if the contestants would come to blows, if anyone would walk out and, the most contentious point of all, if Marcel would blow a fuse.

Every word, nuance and disagreement had been debated in depth after the first two episodes aired. Jack had been so astonished by the degree of their interest that it hadn't occurred to him until now that Dean hadn't joined in the speculation. Nor had he mentioned that Juliette and he were related.

'Not natural,' Jack muttered to himself as he reached the outskirts of Lambourn mid-afternoon and slowed down as he got caught behind a string of racehorses.

The press were still camped outside Hopgood Hall when he finally got there. He was waved through the police cordon but almost blinded by multiple camera flashes as he negotiated his way through to the visitors' car park.

'Hey,' he said, entering the kitchen and finding Drew, Cheryl and Alexi sitting around the table with a very glum-looking Marcel. 'That bad was it, mate?' he asked Marcel, pausing to touch Alexi's shoulder and bending to stroke Cosmo when he stalked over and demanded attention.

'You probably missed the grand announcement,' Alexi replied, 'but don't worry, Drew recorded it for you.'

Drew pressed a button on the VCR and Paul Dakin appeared on screen, all bouffanted up, wearing a dark suit and tie and looking sombre. He made a sickening announcement about the show having to go on, that everyone involved with it was cooperating with the police and were confident they would bring Juliette's killer to justice.

'Clever,' Jack muttered. 'By publicly offering their cooperation the implication is that if anyone involved proves to be the killer, they will be hung out to dry and Far Reach Production's reputation will remain intact.'

Alexi nodded. 'Covering their own backs, in other words. Why am I not surprised?'

They returned their attention to the screen. Paul went on to say the rest of the series would be dedicated to Juliette, who would be greatly missed and whom everyone had loved.

'He certainly did,' Alexi mumbled.

Paul then introduced Juliette's replacement, a lady who was first reserve after the elimination rounds. Jack wasn't a bit surprised to see she was of a similar age to Juliette, albeit a brunette, but equally stunning.

'And people fall for this shit,' Jack said, shaking his head.

'Do you think they had replicas for each contestant waiting in the wings, just in case?' Drew asked with a sardonic grin.

'The station has been inundated with calls of support,' Marcel replied, sneering at Dakin's image, now frozen on the screen.

'How did you get on?' Jack asked him. 'Did they get the thumbscrews out?'

'Don't joke about such things, mate.' Marcel shuddered. 'Granville protected me but I'm not sure how much longer he'll carry on having my back.'

'He'll have to if the show's continuing,' Jack replied. 'This is a great opportunity for them to top the ratings and you're pivotal to their success.'

'If I don't get arrested for murder.'

Alexi told him about her remarkable conversation with Dakin. 'I'm assuming,' she said, 'that if the studio has to pick a side, they'll take Dakin's.'

'If he has a morality clause, they should kick him off the show,' Cheryl said indignantly. 'What's the point of having one otherwise?'

'Alexi's right. I suspect they'll want to keep what happens on the set,' Jack replied. 'The viewers love Dakin's clean-cut image and it won't reflect well on the production company if the truth about his philandering comes out. Especially since they've just publicly backed him to the hilt by having him announce the show's to continue with him hosting it.'

Marcel shot Jack a baleful look. 'But I could be collateral damage?'

'Afraid so,' Jack replied. 'The station wants you and probably fought to keep you. You're a great chef: moody, pedantic and charismatic on camera. Every woman who watches probably loves your bad-boy image and thinks she could reform you. Half the men want to be like you. But you aren't a direct employee of Far Reach Productions. Therein lies the difference between you and Dakin. The suits at the studio have to answer to their sponsors, remember.'

'Like I could forget.'

'If Marcel's activities become common knowledge, if someone knows you slept with Juliette and leaks that information, the studio will most likely deny all prior knowledge, pretend to be shocked and kick you off the show.' Alexi flashed an apologetic smile at the downbeat chef. 'Sorry, Marcel, but the cable company is owned by my old boss at the *Sentinel* and I know from personal experience just how lethal he can be, even with long-time loyal employees.'

'It's okay.' Marcel shook the hair out of his eyes. 'I think Grenville threatened the police with a lawsuit if details of Dakin's activities leaked into the public domain. He didn't make similar threats about mine, which told me all I needed to know about their loyalties.'

'They still have to prove you actually killed her, or at least had a solid motive, if they want to make a case against you, Marcel,' Drew reminded him.

'Yeah well...'

'Dakin told the police about his affair with Juliette and also produced his petrol receipt for his return journey,' Alexi explained. 'Presumably they'll check that against the time of death, which he seems to think will clear him.'

'Time of death isn't usually an exact science,' Jack pointed out, 'but with all these cameras around it's possible that in this case they'll be able to pin it down more accurately.'

'I thought Dakin having seen Juliette alive and well after she left me would put me in the clear,' Marcel said gloomily. 'But Inspector Vickery suggested that I saw them together, realised why Dakin was sniffing around her and lost my rag. As he took pleasure in reminding me, I have a very short fuse on the small screen and, according to him, jealousy is one of the main motivations for murder.'

'Look on the bright side. You're not under lock and key,' Jack said.

'Yeah, but for how much longer?' Marcel pushed himself to his feet. 'I need to be in the kitchen to oversee prep. We have two full sittings tonight, and as many more on the waiting list.' He flashed a rueful smile. 'Murder is definitely good for business, Drew.'

'Not my preferred method of pulling in the punters,' Drew replied with a wry smile, 'but I'll take the trade any which way I can get it.'

'Don't tell Vickery that or your name will be added to the list of suspects.' Marcel waved over his shoulder. 'Later, guys.'

'What now?' Drew asked Jack. 'Any suggestions? Aw, damn.' An indignant squall echoed through the baby monitor.

'I'll see to her,' Cheryl said, getting to her feet. 'You're needed to cover in the bar, Drew.'

'I'm on my way but only after I've come with you and kissed my daughter.'

'He never says things like that to me,' Cheryl complained. 'Who knew I'd have to compete with my own daughter for my husband's affections?'

Drew placed a big, smacking kiss on Cheryl's cheek, making Jack and Alexi laugh. 'Oh, I think I can make time for you in my busy schedule, Mrs H,' Drew said as he opened the door for his wife.

'Right,' Alexi said, her smile fading as she turned to face Jack. 'You have news. I can see you're bursting with it. Come on, don't keep me in suspense.'

Jack got up and poured coffee for them both, then resumed his seat and told her about the connection between her case and his.

'I knew it! Do you think Hammond arranged to have his daughter killed?'

'Don't get carried away.' Jack held his hands out to her, palms foremost. 'I only said there's a connection, a tenuous one. I have absolutely no idea what it means. That's why I thought we could pay a call on Davis when he gets home from work tonight. I assume you'd like to come.'

'Count on it. But shouldn't we tell Vickery?'

'After we've spoken to Davis, if I think there's anything he needs to know.'

'Shouldn't you be hard at work at the jewellery store?' she asked.

Jack grinned. 'I called in sick.'

'That'll make you popular.'

Jack's smiled widened. 'Something tells me I shall be quitting altogether within a day or two.'

'I know you have to put your client's interests first,' Alexi said, her expression sombre. 'I respect that, but all the time we wait, the greater the risk becomes that Marcel will be arrested. If nothing else, this will give Vickery a different direction to look in.'

'He'll find Juliette's mother without our help, I expect. I don't see that Davis ripping off Cash Out has anything to do with Juliette's murder but if I find any link at all, Vickery will be the first to know.'

'How can you be so sure he didn't do it? Davis has already surprised you.'

'True, but I've been doing this for a long time. You get a feel for these things. Besides, Davis only seems to care about his mum's welfare. I don't want to pre-empt whatever he'll have to tell me, but on the surface, it looks as though he only stole from his employers to get revenge for his mother's dismissal. Killing Juliette, even if he could have somehow got into the private part of the hotel and knew where all the cameras were, wouldn't benefit him at all. And even if he *had* decided to take her out, why go to the trouble of framing Marcel? He's already surprised me with his intelligence and anyone with half a brain must have known that staging Juliette's death that way greatly increased his chances of being caught.' Jack fixed Alexi with a determined look. 'Anyway, are you okay with my not telling Vickery about the Cash Out angle?'

'I guess I'll have to be.'

'I know you have a soft spot for Marcel, but—'

'We get along okay because I won't put up with any of his prima donna crap and he knows it.' She grinned. 'He's also easy on the eye.'

Jack scowled. 'I've just decided he's as guilty as hell.'

'I hate to see Marcel treated like the prime suspect when his only crime, far as I can tell, is letting his libido overcome common sense.' She sent Jack a mischievous smile. 'If every man who got himself into that sort of trouble was accused of murder, our prisons wouldn't be able to cope.'

'Yeah, point taken, but don't worry about Marcel being arrested. If Vickery had enough evidence, he'd have taken him in by now. He was interviewed under caution, which isn't good, but wasn't held, which is.'

'Why do you think that is?'

'The interview under caution?'

She nodded.

'Because they need to find out where Juliette was killed and figure out why she was moved. That's vital. Unless they find blood, or a convenient blunt object with her blood and hair on it, they'll have their work cut out. Assuming she was killed out of doors, it was a freezing night and the ground's rock hard.'

'Do you think she was killed outside?'

'Yeah, given all the cameras everywhere else and the fact that she couldn't leave the grounds. They must have ruled out Marcel's apartment as a killing field and we know it wasn't done in her room. It's also good from Marcel's perspective that Dakin has admitted being here, which means they'll be searching the area where they argued. Vickery knows that any decent defence lawyer will use that

angle to cast doubt on Marcel's guilt if they don't. That's why
they've released the annexe but still have the courtyard between
Marcel's apartment and the direct route back to the annexe
cordoned off.'

Alexi nodded. 'And why police have been conducting a meticu-
lous search of the area today?'

'Right. Just so long as they found nothing they can connect to
Marcel in Juliette's room, I don't think there's any immediate cause
for concern.'

'Since he's adamant that he never set foot in it, we have to
assume that they won't.'

'Right.' Jack didn't bother to tell her that he'd heard such
genuine-sounding protestations of innocence too many times to
recall. 'Have you been into the annexe?'

'Yes, Drew and I cleaned it up. It was a right old mess. The new
contestant, Becky Faraday her name is, is now settling in. The
others are over there getting to know her and the cameras are
recording the whole thing.'

Jack pulled a disgruntled face. 'The show really does go on. I
take it Becky isn't in Juliette's old room.'

'No, she took one of the others.'

'Did you see anything interesting in the annexe before you
cleaned it up?'

'Other than that the police turned the place upside down and
didn't tidy up after themselves? No wonder they're called pigs. No
offence.'

Jack bit back a smile. 'None taken.'

'Anyway, to answer your question, no, not really, but then I
didn't imagine that I would. I am intrigued though about both
cameras in Juliette's room being out and no one noticing.' Alexi
wrinkled her brow. 'It makes the whole thing of putting Juliette
back in her room seem pre-meditated to me. I mean, they could

hardly have put her back with the cameras running, so someone had to have gone in there beforehand and disabled them, don't you think? That means the crime was planned, not spur of the moment.'

'You're thinking someone really had to hate her to go to all that trouble.'

'Exactly. I know she wasn't popular, but being disliked is very different to being despised enough to drive a person to murder.' Alexi lifted both shoulders and spread her hands. 'I mean, if you want to kill someone, why do it when they're starring in a TV show and the spotlight's on them relentlessly?'

'Unless you want to boost the show's ratings.'

Alexi gaped at him. 'You don't believe that, surely?'

'I don't discount it any more than I discount the possibility that one of the other contestants might have done it. He or she – we'll refer to the killer as *he* for the sake of argument – wants to win so badly that it's become a contest worth killing for. We still have to talk to the two guys. It will be interesting to see if they have any theories.'

'I just don't see any of the contestants taking the chance.' Alexi accompanied her words with a firm shake of her head. 'Besides, as you already pointed out, killing her so publicly greatly increases the chances of being caught.'

'I also pointed out that it's symbolic. Her body wasn't just dumped on that bed; her limbs were carefully arranged for some reason. The killer has a point to make and thinks he's clever enough not to get caught.'

'Well, so far he's right about that. But why make a point when no one else understands it?'

'It means something to the killer and that's what this is all about. Trust me on this. Serial killers make obscure points all the time. Not that I think we have a serial on our hands, but the same principle applies. But, for what it's worth, I agree with you about the cameras.' Jack took her hand and ran his forefinger down the length of hers. 'And I doubt whether that fact has escaped Vickery's notice, which is another reason for him to have doubts about Marcel's guilt. Marcel doesn't know enough about how the cameras are monitored to be sure he wouldn't be caught tampering with them.'

'You should have mentioned that to Marcel. Put his mind at rest.'

'Better not to. If Vickery does raise the subject with him, I want his reaction, his denial that he knows anything about their workings, to seem genuine.'

'Okay, that's good, but we need to talk to Gerry Salter. Why didn't he notice they were down and do something about it? Drew says if there wasn't any movement in Juliette's room then he would have no way of knowing that someone had disconnected the cameras from the control box. I don't buy that. There must be warning lights, or something, if they're tampered with. Otherwise... well, the contestants could unplug them whenever they felt like it and get up to whatever the hell they wanted to.' She scowled. 'Like murdering one another.'

'Right, we will talk to Gerry but I gather he and the PR woman... Hayley, is it?'

'Yes, Hayley Wood. She works for the studio and is here all the time, troubleshooting.' Alexi pulled a face. 'She was kept on her toes with Juliette around.'

'She and Gerry are down at the station right now, giving their statements. We can't talk to Davis until he gets home around six, so we've got a couple of hours to kill. Might as well try and speak with the other contestants.'

'Okay.'

Jack and Alexi, cat and dog in tow, took the long route round to the annexe, avoiding the cordoned-off courtyard which was still being searched by officers in protective clothing. The three original contestants were seated around the fireplace in the recreation room. With the exception of Anton, they all looked tense but Anton never seemed to let anything get to him. The newcomer sat perched on the edge of her seat, clearly terrified of the cameras.

'Hey, Alexi,' Anton said, waving a languid hand. 'How's it going? Hey, big guy.' He dropped a hand to try and scratch Cosmo's ears. Cosmo snarled, gave him an aloof look and stalked off, tail aloft. Anton chuckled. 'I'm damned if that cat'll keep ignoring me. I'm one of the good guys, mon, and you're just a moggy with attitude,' he called to Cosmo's retreating back.

'Don't take it personally, Anton,' Alexi said. 'He doesn't like anyone much.'

'He appears to like Jack.' Anton turned his head and shook a finger at Cosmo, setting his dreadlocks dancing across his shoulders. 'That's insulting, Cosmo my mon. In fact, my grandma would say it's downright rude, and no one dares to disagree with my grandma. So, Cosmo, unless you wanna make friends, I shall just have to send my grandma over from Trinidad to sort you out.'

Cosmo's tail twitched but he didn't turn around.

'I think you've got him worried,' Alexi said, laughing.

'He'd better be. My grandma is five foot nothing but she scares the crap out of me. When we were kids, once she reached for her wooden spoon we knew to scatter. Fast.' He chuckled. 'She sure wasn't gonna use it to stir the dinner.'

'You must be Becky,' Alexi said, offering the new girl her hand. 'I'm Alexi Ellis, part-owner of the hotel. Sorry we have to meet under such circumstances. This is Jack Maddox, a friend of mine.'

'And a PI,' John, the quietest of the original contestants, added, 'so don't tell him anything you might later regret.'

Becky blushed as she shook Jack's hand and he turned on the

charm. At the same time, Jack wondered how John knew what he did for a living. He hadn't mentioned it but, then again, his name had been all over the papers when the Parker case broke. Still, it was odd that he'd made a point of mentioning his occupation. Jack also happened to know that the quiet ones, the loners, who were easily overlooked, were often not what they appeared to be. Jack wouldn't forget about John and needed to know a lot more about his background. Vickery would be digging, of course, but John would not be a priority for him. He now had Marcel and Paul as prime suspects, and would be concentrating most of his resources upon tearing their lives apart.

'Being here must seem a little surreal,' Jack said to Becky.

'Just a bit. I thought I'd missed my chance to be on the show. But to get that opportunity because someone died... well, it doesn't seem right.'

Greta looked as though she wanted to disagree, then obviously remembered the cameras and kept her mouth shut.

'Juliette came across as a real nice person,' Becky added.

Greta spluttered. John and Anton remained tactfully silent.

'Got a minute, Anton?' Alexi asked.

'For you, any time.'

It occurred to Jack that they couldn't talk in the annexe, not with the cameras recording every word that was spoken. If Anton knew or suspected anything, he was unlikely to admit it under such circumstances. The same idea must have occurred to Alexi since she suggested returning to the hotel's kitchen for coffee.

'Why do I feel I'm about to undergo an inquisition?' Anton asked in his lazily hypnotic drawl. 'Send out a search party if I don't return soon, guys.'

'You're such a drama queen, Anton,' Alexi chided. 'Almost as bad as Marcel.'

Anton's deep chuckle vibrated through the cool afternoon air as they returned to the house. 'Mon, I copy everything he does. He's my idol.'

'Why's that?' Jack asked as they sat themselves around the kitchen table and Alexi poured coffee for them all.

'I like his style. He's a brilliant chef, doesn't take crap from anyone and works and plays hard.' Anton leaned his rangy body back in his chair, managing, as he always appeared to do on screen, to look totally relaxed. 'I admire him.'

'This hero worship wouldn't be a way to get ahead in the contest?' Jack asked.

'Jack!' Alexi protested.

Anton waved a hand to silence her protest. 'That's what Inspector Vickery asked me and I'll tell you what I told him. Marcel won't let flattery influence him, which is why it didn't bother me that Juliette was trying to get ahead by jumping his bones. He'd take what was on offer, like any red-blooded male would, and then follow his conscience when it came to the day job.'

'You knew what Juliette was doing?' Alexi asked, permitting her surprise to show. 'And didn't call her on it?'

'I saw the way she flirted with him every chance she got.' He shrugged, still casually draped over his chair. 'It didn't take a genius to figure out what she intended. Same with Paul.'

'What did you make of her?' Jack asked.

'Couldn't stand her.'

'Well,' Jack replied, blinking, 'thanks for your honesty. Is that what you told Vickery?'

'Sure, mon. Why not? The four of us were in competition but we are, or were, also committed to living in close quarters for six long weeks. No reason why we shouldn't get along when we weren't cooking against one another, but Juliette loved stirring up trouble, trying to set us at odds all the time. It was like she found it amusing.'

'How do you mean?' Jack asked.

'I'll give you an example. Just before we were due to go on set for the first episode, she joined John in the courtyard and was all over him like a rash. Now John's kinda awkward around women, especially women who look like Juliette did. But she flattered him. Said he was a brilliant chef and could he give her some tips? Of course, John fell for it. He asked her which areas she needed help in. All the while, Juliette was... well, touching his arm, his hand, any part of him that was within range, and standing far too close. I know because I watched her performance through the window and could hear what she was saying to him.' Anton shook his head. 'Poor John. His glasses must have steamed up. Of course, Juliette timed her attack so he was too turned on to think straight moments before we were due in the kitchen. John's performance was woeful in a situation where he ought to have excelled. We were baking and that's his specialty.'

'I didn't know she did that,' Alexi said. 'That was mean of her!'

'You have no idea how mean that little madam could be, darlin'.' Anton sighed. 'I took Marcel aside afterwards and told him why John had performed so badly. I also told Juliette what I thought of her for foolin' with him. She was a good chef. She didn't need to resort to cheating, but Juliette thought it was funny.'

'I know she and Greta didn't get along,' Jack said. 'What else did she do, apart from fooling around with John, to piss you off?'

'How long have you got?' Anton sipped his cooling coffee but, for the first time, failed to meet Jack's gaze. In fact, his gaze drifted off to the left, a sure sign that he was lying, if only by omission. 'After the incident with John, she knew I was on her case. She hated that I could see through her and wouldn't let her manipulate me. She seemed to think that every man on the planet should fall for her charm. Anyway, all I can say is that I'm not sorry she's dead and, in case you're wondering, I told Vickery that, too.' Anton stood up.

'Thanks for the coffee. I'd better get back. Paul is joining us to do a gentle meet and greet with the new girl. Wouldn't want to miss the fun.'

With a casual wave, he left them and ambled back to the annexe.

'We'll have to leave John until later, then,' Alexi said. 'Can't interrupt the filming.'

'John will keep but we mustn't overlook him.'

'Are we any further forward?' Alexi asked, looking discouraged.

Jack shook his head. 'Vickery's problem isn't a lack of suspects; he's got too darned many of them.'

'Hmm, all three contestants disliked her. Greta holds an old grudge against her and she humiliated John. But I can't see John dreaming up such an elaborate murder.'

'She insulted his manhood. That would be enough motivation for a lot of men, especially the mild-mannered ones. You'd be surprised.'

'Well, at least Anton doesn't have a motive. He seems like a decent guy and tried to set Juliette straight over her treatment of John. He wouldn't get personally involved with her and she had no way of controlling him, so he wouldn't have a reason to kill her.'

'As far as we know.' Jack propped his feet on a vacant chair. 'He was holding something back, though.'

'How do you know that?' Alexi asked irritably. 'He seemed forthcoming enough to me.'

'Too forthcoming. What he told us about John has to be true. He knows we'll confirm it with John. But he told us too quickly. Almost as though he wanted to stop us from asking him anything more personal.'

'Then why didn't you, if you thought there was something there?'

'Because he wouldn't have told me, and I doubt if he told the police, either.'

'You suspect him?'

Jack grinned. 'I suspect everyone. I can't seem to help myself.'

'But if there's something that Juliette was using against Anton, how did she find it?'

'The same way as I hope Cassie will. The moment Juliette knew the names of her opponents, she will have surfed the web, looking for anything that she could use to get an edge. And don't forget, Daddy's a powerful man. I doubt that Juliette could hack into sensitive areas like Cassie can, but you can bet your bank balance that Daddy knows a man who can.'

'But her father didn't want her competing,' Alexi pointed out. 'Why would he make it easy for her?'

'She stood her ground so I'm guessing he decided to make the best of it and gave her a helping hand. Whether she asked him to or not is another matter but we know from what Greta told us that he doesn't expect anything other than excellence from his daughter.' Jack yawned. 'Anyway, if there are skeletons in Anton's cupboard, Cassie will find them.'

'Well, I still don't think any of the contestants did it. Greta's grudge goes back years. She must be over that by now. And as for John and Anton... well—'

'Perhaps they're all in it and covering for one another.'

'Now you're just being silly,' Alexi said.

'Yeah well, we still need to talk to Gerry. We'll try and catch him later. After we've—'

'Oh shit!'

'What is it?' Jack asked, jumping up and staring out the window in the same direction as Alexi. 'Oh dear,' he said, laughing when he saw Cosmo, encouraged by Toby's barks, backing the terrified crime scene techs into a corner of the courtyard. 'You'd best go and rescue them before it's their blood that's split.'

'I really am going to have to start leaving Cosmo at home,' she said, shaking her head as she dashed through the back door.

Jack watched from the window as Alexi called Cosmo off and apologised profusely to the embarrassed techs. But when she returned to the kitchen, chastised dog and cat in her wake, she looked pale and visibly shaken.

'What is it?' Jack asked.

'I couldn't help seeing what they found,' she said, falling into the nearest chair. 'They were just photographing an area of gravel that had dark stains on it and, I'm pretty sure, some long, blonde hairs. They bagged a couple of the decorative rocks Fay used to create that water feature close to the door to Marcel's apartment.' Her eyes widened with apprehension. 'I think they've found the place where Juliette died.'

9

'No use trying to make it up to me,' Alexi told Cosmo, wagging a finger at him and trying not to laugh. Her recalcitrant cat sat on her lap in Jack's car, all sweetness and light, sending her innocent looks through piercing hazel eyes. 'Any more of that malarkey and it's straight back to Waterloo arches for you.'

'Meow!'

Jack laughed. 'I swear to God he understands every word you say.'

'I'm absolutely sure that he does. He knows he was out of line back there, which is why we're getting the *sweet kitty* act. Just because he was bored, that's no reason to terrorise people.'

'He was only having a little fun,' Jack said, reaching across to scratch Cosmo's ears.

'Fun! The poor woman was traumatised. She started talking about the Wild Animal Act, whatever that is.'

'I don't think it exists.'

'Whatever, it was a hell of a job to talk her down.' Alexi stroked Cosmo's gleaming flank. 'Still, at least I was able to find out what they'd discovered.'

'Cosmo knew that. That's why he created a diversion.'

Alexi rolled her eyes. 'Don't encourage him.'

'Here we go. The place we need is just down here.'

Jack returned to the terrace of run-down houses where Dean Davis lived with his mother. They looked as though they'd been built before indoor plumbing had been invented.

'Hammond can't have given his wife a very generous divorce settlement if she's reduced to living like this.'

Alexi screwed up her nose at graffiti-covered walls. Rubbish spilled from bins that had been overturned, not necessarily by wildlife, and a general air of depression clung to an area that progress seemed to have bypassed. A gang of youths wearing hoodies loitered, staring belligerently at Jack's car as he crawled along the street looking for somewhere to park. Alexi saw more than one car up on blocks in scrappy front yards; more than one broken window boarded up with plywood that would pose few problems for a determined burglar. Presumably the residents had run out of things worth stealing.

'I should have asked Cassie to check on the terms of the Hammonds' divorce. Oh well.' He found a vacant spot a short distance away from the Davis residence and reversed his car into it. 'Perhaps Davis will enlighten us.'

They left Cosmo in charge of the car. He curled up on the passenger seat and watched them through one eye as they walked towards Davis's house. Jack's expensive car would be safe from the loitering kids with Cosmo on guard duty. They reached the house, which looked slightly better maintained than those on either side. There was fresh paint on the sills and the front garden looked as though someone had made an effort to maintain it. It was hard to be sure in the dead of winter.

Jack pressed the bell. They heard it echoing inside the house but no one responded. Jack repeated the process, keeping his thumb depressed this time. Still no response. They shared a look and were on the point of giving up when the door was opened a few inches, the chain left on. A sensible precaution, given the state of the neighbourhood, Alexi thought. A young man peered through the opening.

'Yeah,' he said. 'What do you... bloody hell! What are you doing here? I thought you were off sick.'

'I got better. Can we come in, Dean?'

'Why?' Dean asked suspiciously. 'How did you know where I lived?'

'We need to talk, but inside.' He looked over his shoulder at the group of kids who had ambled down the road, pretending not to listen.

Dean reluctantly released the chain, opened the door wide enough to admit them both and then double locked it behind him. What a way to live, Alexi thought, feeling sorry for Dean.

'This is Alexi,' Jack said. 'Alexi, Dean.'

'Nice to meet you,' Alexi said, thrusting out her hand. Dean ignored it.

He leaned against the wall in the narrow hallway, glaring at Jack with dawning awareness. 'You know, don't you?'

'Let's sit down somewhere and talk about it,' Jack said.

Dean led them into a small sitting room. There were lots of feminine touches – candles, ornaments, flourishing plants, hand-made cushion covers – and it was spotlessly clean. There was no sign of the woman, his mother presumably, who took such pride in her home. Dean fell into the only armchair, which was situated in front of a large, flat-screen TV, and indicated that they should take the couch opposite.

'Will I go to prison?' he asked, dropping his head into his splayed hands. 'I can't go to prison. Who'll take care of Mum if they lock me up?'

'Tell me what made you do it?' Jack asked.

'You were sent there to catch me?'

Jack nodded.

'I thought you might have been. You seemed too good for that job. I'd decided to stop anyway. I'd made my point.'

'What point—'

'Dean, have we got visitors? Is it William?'

A woman drifted into the room, light-brown hair threaded with grey falling around her shoulders. Alexi was transfixed by her astounding beauty: her delicate features, high, Slavic cheekbones and huge, haunted, brown eyes. She had to be in her mid-forties but her complexion was still creamy, her face almost totally unlined. There was something about the sensuality in her elegant movements that held Alexi's attention. And Jack's too, she could see. The tough PI was staring at her in awe.

The lady had to be Juliette's mother. The resemblance was too marked for there to be any doubt about it. And yet Alexi hadn't found Juliette nearly so captivating. There had been a tough determination about Juliette that wouldn't stir a man's protective instincts in the manner that Melody Davis's ethereal qualities had clearly stirred Jack's. Her serenity, her detached air of non-availability, would make her irresistible to a man like Hammond. He may not have been wealthy when they'd met twenty-five years ago but, Alexi suspected, he would already have developed a determination to get whatever he wanted.

'Where's William?' Melody was starting to get agitated. 'You said he was here, Dean. He'll want to see me. I have to get ready.'

'He's not here yet, Mum,' Dean said gently. 'These are friends of mine, come to visit.'

'Oh, friends.' She waved a hand, quickly losing interest in them. 'Where is William? Why is he always late?'

Dean took her by the shoulders and turned her towards the

chair he'd just vacated. 'Come on, Mum. You sit down and I'll put your programme on. It's about to start.'

Jack and Alexi exchanged a glance as Dean switched on the TV and then knelt beside his mother, holding her hand and talking quietly to her until she became less agitated. It was the most touching scene Alexi had witnessed for years. The child had become the parent, sacrificing his youth in order to take care of the mother he clearly adored. She felt tears spring to her eyes when Jack squeezed her hand. The two of them went to stand in the hallway, giving Dean the space he needed.

'The poor guy,' Alexi whispered. 'You have to help him. Anyone who loves his mother as much as he obviously does can't be all that bad.'

'I'll do what I can for him. Let's hear what he has to say for himself first.'

Dean joined them a short time later. 'Come on, we can finish our chat in here.'

He led them into a small kitchen that had been refurbished with modern cabinets and appliances. It was as homely and as clean as the rest of the house. There was a table jammed against one wall. Dean indicated that they should sit there, which they did.

'Does that answer your question?' Dean asked, sighing. 'About why I did it, I mean.'

'What's wrong with her?' Alexi asked gently.

'She's bipolar.' Dean stared at the shopping list anchored with a magnet to the fridge door as he spoke. Clearly, he didn't like discussing his mother's problems and Alexi didn't blame him for that. There was a stigma attached to mental incapacity and most people wouldn't understand. 'She's okay when she's on her medication but she doesn't always take it. Says it makes her muddled and she misses her highs.'

Alexi nodded, feeling great sympathy for all the responsibility that rested on this young man's shoulders. She really hoped that Jack *would* go easy on him. He didn't strike her as a natural thief and had probably done what he did for a very good reason.

'I've heard that said before about people who suffer from bipolar disorder,' Jack said. 'It can't be easy for you.'

'I'm not asking for your sympathy.' He rubbed his face with his hands. 'Mum's been through a lot but we finally got her stabilised on medication that we thought suited her. She was doing okay. Well enough to get a job as a receptionist, in fact. She's very good with people, very caring, when she takes her meds.'

'Let me guess,' Jack said. 'She worked at Cash Out.'

Dean's face hardened. 'For nearly two years. I heard about the vacancy just after I got my job and was chatting with someone at Cash Out. We talk to them a lot... well, you'd know that,' he said, nodding at Jack. 'There's often stuff we need to pick up the phone about with new clients, delays and stuff. They always seemed to be short-staffed and mentioned the vacancy to me. I thought it might suit Mum but made sure they knew what was wrong with her before she went for the interview. Mum thrived there and I was delighted. It took the pressure off me and I was in danger of getting a life of my own for a while.'

'Are you her sole carer?' Alexi asked.

He shrugged. 'Might as well be. Social Services are worse than useless.'

'What happened at Cash Out?' Jack asked.

'I thought Mum finally understood about the need to take her pills. There had been incidents before when... but, anyway, I put them out for her every day and watch her take them. Problem is, periodically she decides she doesn't need them and she can be very evasive. She holds them under her tongue, then spits them out when I'm not looking.' He shrugged. 'What am I supposed to do? Stand over her until she swallows? Anyway, something happened one day at work, presumably when she'd avoided taking her meds. There was an incident in reception when she got aggressive with a client and was sacked on the spot for gross misconduct.' He thumped the arm of his chair. 'It was so unfair. I explained what had happened and promised I'd make sure it didn't happen again, but I think they used it as an excuse to get rid of her. They had no right to do that. They didn't even go through the proper disciplinary channels that they'd have to with anyone else.'

'I'm sorry,' Alexi said softly. 'Could you not have taken it up with them?'

He shook his head. 'Mum was going through a prolonged bout of depression. If she attended a hearing in that state, it would have reinforced their opinion that she was unstable.'

'And so you decided to get your revenge another way.'

'Yeah, stupid perhaps, but I was so damned mad, and feeling a bit sorry for us both, I guess. People can be so judgemental.' He ran a hand through his hair. 'Anyway, I only did it until I'd got back the money Mum ought to have been paid for two years loyal service, minus what I had to pay to the two people who helped me with the scam, obviously. I didn't think I'd be caught.'

'And I didn't think you were the brains behind it,' Jack replied. 'I underestimated you. I thought whoever masterminded it was using you.'

'Just because I work in a shop doesn't mean I'm stupid.'

Jack leaned back in his seat, crossed one foot over his opposite thigh and sent Dean an assessing look. 'I'd say you were just the opposite. You are, or have the ability to be, a high achiever.' He paused. 'Just like your father.'

Dean scowled. 'My father took off years ago, when I was still just a kid, and took most of my mum's money with him.' He kicked at the leg of the coffee table. 'Bastard!'

'I meant your biological father.'

Dean's head jerked up. 'You know about him?'

'I should have explained that Alexi is an investor in the hotel where your sister was murdered.' Jack sent him a look of sympathy. 'I'm sorry about that.'

'Yeah well, I barely knew her.'

'Have you told your mum yet?' Alexi asked.

Dean sucked his teeth. 'No. I'm waiting for the right time. She doesn't talk much about Juliette but she does remember who she is. Him, on the other hand, she talks about all the time. You just saw that for yourself. She's convinced he'll be back for her any day now. It's heart-breaking.' Dean exhaled slowly. 'Anyway, I'll know when she's feeling strong enough to take the news about Juliette.'

'Why don't you start at the beginning and explain your relationship with the Hammonds,' Jack invited.

'If it means the police won't come round harassing Mum, then I suppose there's no harm in it. She's not good with officialdom and if she's on a downer, it'll either make her more depressed or aggressive.'

'I understand,' Alexi said. She'd done a feature on bipolar sufferers when she'd worked for the *Sentinel*, exploring the prejudices and misunderstandings they endured.

Dean threw back his head and sighed. 'Mum married Hammond when she was just eighteen. I've seen pictures. She was a vision and, apparently the life and soul, on a perpetual high with a natural ability to light up any room she walked into. She was a secretary in his office; Hammond was a trainee banker with all the right connections to make it with the big boys. She tells me he was charming and swept her off her feet. They had a whirlwind romance and married within three months of meeting. Hammond came from a moneyed back-ground and there was no question of Mum working once they tied the knot. Hammond was very possessive and wanted her all to himself.'

Alexi nodded. From what she knew of Hammond, she wasn't surprised to hear it.

'Juliette was born within a year of their marriage. It was a diffi-cult birth and I think that's when Mum's illness started to be appar-ent. Anyway, nothing in Hammond's life was allowed to be defective. The marriage fell apart, Hammond accused Mum of having an affair, which she did not, and when she told him she was pregnant again—'

'With you?' Jack asked.

'With me. He refused to believe the child was his and threw her out. She got a fraction of what was due to her because she couldn't afford a good solicitor to fight her corner. Anyway, Davis came along, married her, exploited her and ran off with the rest of her money. Hence we've been reduced to living like this,' he said, spreading his arms to encompass the small room. 'Mum has been getting steadily worse and, like I already said, Social Services are sod-all help. So I left school as soon as I could, and have been taking care of her ever since.'

'What had you planned to do?' Alexi asked.

'I wanted to be an architect. I'm told I have a flair for design.' He scowled. 'Fat chance of finding out if that's true now.'

'I think you could do anything you set your mind to,' Alexi replied. 'It's never too late.'

'Yeah well, I took A levels at night school, just so my brain didn't wither. I got four A stars but there's no way I can take a degree online; not work and look out for Mum, so that's that. My life revolves around working in a shop and looking after Mum.'

'Then I can understand why you feel such bitterness towards Hammond,' Alexi said.

'You look a lot like the pictures I've seen of him,' Jack added. 'If you've met in the flesh then he must be able to see it too.'

'I got his looks and brains; Juliette got Mum's looks and wasn't quite so smart, although I hear she was sly.'

'Does Hammond now accept that you're his son?' Alexi asked.

'Look, I love my mum and don't mind looking after her, but I did resent having to give up my education because that bastard refused to accept his responsibilities.'

Alexi nodded. 'I'd feel that way too in your position.'

'I tried to contact him several times but he refused to take my calls or answer my letters. I even tried knocking at his door but got turned away. Accosting him at his workplace didn't get me anywhere either. All I wanted was enough money to get Mum the professional help she needs.' Dean shook his head. 'He owes us that much.'

'But you have met him now,' Jack said.

Dean shot Jack a look. 'How the hell do you know that?'

'Humour me.'

'Yeah, okay, why not? We met for the first time the other night. Juliette tracked me down at the shop, out of the blue. I knew who she was the moment she walked through the door. We went to lunch. She told me she overheard her father giving instructions that I wasn't to be allowed anywhere near his precious property. She also heard her name mentioned in connection with me and got curious. So, she checked his desk, found my name and number scribbled on the corner of his blotter and did some digging. She said the moment she looked at me she knew we had to be related. Like you say, I resemble *him*. She was also astounded when I told her our mother was alive and well. He'd told her she died years ago, you see. Anyway, she wanted to meet Mum and I saw no harm in that.'

'She came here?'

'Yes, and lit the place up, just like Mum would have done at her age, I would imagine. She was delighted to have a brother. She said it would take some of the pressure off her. Ha, I wasn't about to tell her that I'd stick pins in my eyes before I let Hammond be a father to me at this point.'

'When was all this?' Jack asked.

'Just before she moved to your hotel for the TV programme. She was excited about bringing Hammond and me together. So she went to him and said if he didn't agree to meet me and allow me to take a DNA sample for comparison, then she'd get a sample without his help. She didn't stand up to him often so I guess the threat worked. I went round there the other night, we talked for ten minutes, he gave me a few strands of his hair and I left.'

'Nothing more than that?' Jack asked suspiciously.

'I explained I only wanted support for Mum and he said that if I was his son, if he'd got it wrong and Mum hadn't cheated on him, then he would pay for her care.' Dean snorted. 'Very big of him. It's thanks to his treatment of her that she's gone so far downhill. She adores him, even now, which is infuriating. Every time a visitor calls she asks if it's William, like she did just now. He has absolutely no idea what he did to her.'

Alexi wasn't surprised to hear it. Ruthless men like Hammond, control freaks who wanted everything on their terms, seldom made allowance for any weaknesses, especially mental ones.

'You didn't answer my question about Cash Out,' Dean said, turning to Jack. 'Will I go to prison?'

'Not if I can help it,' Jack replied. 'I'll explain the circumstances to Mick Bailey and hopefully he'll let it go, if you agree to repay the money stolen.'

'How the hell I am supposed to do that?' Dean threw up his hands. 'You might as well lock me up now. I don't have it any more.

There were debts I had to clear, and I paid the people who helped me.'

'Perhaps it won't come to that,' Alexi said. 'Hammond only has one child now and I doubt if he'd see you locked up for trying to help your mother, especially if your relationship happened to leak to the press.' Alexi grinned. 'I used to work on the *Sentinel*.'

Dean brightened. 'I thought I knew your face.'

'The police will get around to your mother,' Jack warned. 'And you, too. I can't keep it from them.'

'I thought they would the moment I heard Juliette was dead. But I didn't kill her. I've never set foot in that fancy hotel. Couldn't afford their prices. Besides, I wanted her alive. It was only thanks to her that I stood any chance of getting Hammond to face up to his responsibilities.'

'I know you didn't kill her,' Jack said. 'I was watching this house on the night she was killed and followed you to your father's house.'

'Don't call him that. Still, I'm grateful that you did follow.' Dean smiled and the tension left his eyes. 'That gives me a rock-solid alibi at least.'

'How do you feel about helping us clear this business up?' Jack asked.

'How can I?' Dean spread his hands. 'You have connections with all the main suspects, not me.'

'I'd like to speak with your father... sorry, with Hammond, about Juliette, but I doubt whether he's receiving callers right now. But if you asked him—'

'Jack's a PI and, as I say, I'm a journalist and an investor in Hopgood Hall. We solved the Natalie Parker case recently.'

'Ah, I remember reading all about that. Well, it was impossible to miss it in this part of the world.' He fell silent for a moment, obviously considering his options. 'Okay,' he eventually said. 'Give me a moment.'

Dean left the room and they could hear him talking quietly on the phone in the hall. He returned a short time later, smiling.

'I told him who you both are. He'll see you as soon as you can get there,' he said.

10

Jack's car still had a wheel in each corner and a full complement of hub caps when they returned to it.

'Gangs nowadays,' he said, chuckling. 'No bottle. Afraid of a cute little pussy cat.'

The gang in question, having failed to relieve the car of its vital components, loitered a safe distance away from the BMW, muttering amongst themselves in teen-speak.

'Evening, lads,' Jack said cheerfully. 'Thanks for watching the motor for me.'

'What's that beast, then?' one of them asked, nodding dubiously in Cosmo's direction. Cosmo poked his nose through the gap in the window and dutifully growled.

'What's the matter, guys?' Alexi opened the door and let Cosmo out. There was a hasty shuffling of booted feet as the cat leapt agilely through the air and landed on all four feet, mere inches in front of the rapidly retreating group. He arched his back, hissed like he meant business and extended vicious-looking claws. Jack almost felt sorry for the little thugs. He would most likely have bottled it as well if confronted by Cosmo when he took a walk on the wild side. 'Never seen a cat before?'

Laughing as the gang lost all attempts at dignity and scattered, Alexi called Cosmo back to the car and patted his head.

'Good boy!'

'See,' Jack said, 'he only wants to protect you.'

'I feel so sorry for Dean Davis,' Alexi said, as she settled into her seat and Jack drove away. 'How can we help him?'

'I doubt whether my client at Cash Out will be anxious to pursue restitution, provided he knows the scam has been stopped. Especially when he learns that his company dismissed an employee with mental health issues without going through the proper channels.'

'Not forgetting that I might write about their dismissal procedures, or lack thereof, in connection with an employee with mental health issues,' Alexi added with a sweet smile.

Jack chuckled. 'The poor guy doesn't stand an earthly.'

'If that's how he treats his employees then he doesn't deserve to.'

'Doubt if he knows about the dismissal personally.'

'Perhaps not, but the buck still stops with him.'

Jack's mobile rang. He glanced at the display and shot a look at Alexi. 'It's Vickery,' he said, using the hands-free feature in his car to take the call. 'How did the post mortem go?' he asked, not bothering with any preamble.

'No signs of a struggle,' Vickery replied. 'She died from blunt force trauma.'

'A bash on the head.'

'Right. I gather you already know we've found the likely place where she died?'

'Cosmo did.'

'Hmm, our female techie needs counselling after meeting that damned feline.'

'Sorry about that,' Alexi said from the passenger seat, trying not to laugh.

'Yes well, anyway. I thought you'd like to know.'

'Any forensics?' Jack asked.

'Nothing obvious. Nothing under her nails, no convenient hairs on her clothing or torn off buttons from the assailant. That would be too easy. Nothing so far from her room either but we haven't got all the results back yet.' The fact that they had already got some meant that they must be giving the case the VIP treatment. 'She'd recently had sex but, of course, we already knew that.' He paused. 'What we didn't know was that she was pregnant.'

Jack and Alexi exchanged a look. 'How far gone?' Alexi asked.

'Just a few weeks. She might not have known herself for sure.'

'Or she might have done, which is why she didn't bother to have Marcel use a condom,' Jack speculated, 'and if push came to shove, was hoping to pin the blame on him.'

'What do you mean by that?' Vickery asked.

'Well, if her powers of manipulation didn't ensure she won the contest outright, the next best thing would be a place in Marcel's kitchen, working with him. That would give the seal of approval to her career. I'm just speculating here, but if she convinced him he was about to be a daddy and he wasn't too keen on the idea, there would still be time for her to have an abortion after the contest, provided she got her job.'

'You really think she could be that conniving?' Vickery asked dubiously.

'Just playing devil's advocate.' Jack exhaled. 'Anyway, the pregnancy pre-dates the contest so Marcel can't be the daddy because he wasn't involved at that stage. But he wouldn't know that if she lied about her dates.'

'The pregnancy doesn't pre-date qualifying rounds,' Alexi added. 'It's worth looking to see if anyone involved there is also involved with the filming at Hopgood Hall. If Juliette did know she'd conceived, confronted the father and refused his suggestion of an abortion, who knows what lengths a reluctant father-to-be might go to. Especially if he was already happily married and had his reputation as a family man to protect.'

'We're already onto that,' Vickery said.

'Of course you are. Sorry, Inspector. I was just thinking aloud.'

'Right.' Jack paused, wondering why Vickery was being so forthcoming. Presumably because he thought Jack and Alexi between them could get answers he couldn't. Or because he knew they'd dig anyway so might as well give them a little encouragement. Vickery was in the spotlight and obviously wasn't too proud to ask for help, albeit indirectly. 'There's something else you need to know,' he said. 'Hammond has a son, and an ex-wife. You'll find the son's mobile number in Juliette's phone records. His name's Dean Davis.' Jack reeled off his address.

'Blimey,' Vickery replied. 'Talk about opposite ends of the social scale.'

'Right. I was working on another case connected with Davis when Juliette's murder happened.'

'What case?'

'It's solved now and has absolutely nothing to do with Juliette Hammond. Trust me on this. And I know you'll check anyway, but Davis has no record. Suffice it to say that Dean Davis went to meet Hammond, thanks to Juliette's intervention, last night. I followed him there, so I'm pretty sure he had nothing to do with his sister's death.'

'We'll still need to talk to him.'

'He knows that. But, as for the ex-wife, she suffers from bipolar and is very fragile. Davis looks after her and is very protective of his mother. Treat her gently. She isn't involved.'

'I hear you. Okay, Jack, keep me posted if there's anything else I need to know.'

'Just so long as you return the favour. And in the spirit of co-operation, we're on our way to see Hammond. Dean phoned him and he agreed to see us immediately. We obviously need to see him about Dean's other problem but I have a feeling Hammond wants to talk to us about his daughter.'

'He was all over us, demanding answers we weren't in a position to give. Mind what you say to him, Jack, and let me know what he wants with you.'

'Will do.'

Jack cut the connection.

'It's funny,' Alexi said. 'We've heard nothing but bad things about Juliette from everyone we've spoken to. She was a spoiled princess, used to getting her way, and didn't care whose toes she trampled on in order to get it. You'd think she would hate to find she had a sibling to share all that paternal wealth and attention with. And yet, if Dean is to be believed, she welcomed him with open arms.'

'Everyone has some redeeming qualities and Juliette was obviously no exception. Her father smothered her spirit, is my guess. She couldn't alienate him completely or he'd withdraw financial support. She actually told Dean that he was similar to their father in looks and intelligence, so probably hoped that the majority of parental control would be transferred to the prodigal son.' Jack shrugged. 'She was still being selfish, just in a different way.'

'Are you surprised that Hammond agreed to see us?' Alexi asked after a short pause.

'Yes and no.' Jack halted at a junction and then made a left turn. 'Chances are he recognised our names from the Parker case. He will definitely know about your involvement at the hotel, and I expect Dean told him I'm a PI. If he thinks we're delving into the death of his daughter, he will want to know what we find out because Vickery won't tell him diddly squat. He can't because, unlikely though it seems, Hammond is a suspect.'

'Because he's a self-confessed control freak and argued about Juliette competing on the show?' Alexi nodded in answer to her own question. 'I get that, but I can't see him murdering her, or having someone do it for him. Besides, you can give him an alibi. You followed Dean here last night.'

'But we only have Dean's word for it that Hammond was actually home. Not that I doubt it, but I'm still a copper at heart and have a duty to view everything with suspicion.'

He turned between the gateposts he'd parked outside just the night before, triggering automatic lights as he drove down the gravel drive.

'Ready?' he asked, pulling up in front of the house and cutting the engine.

'Yeah. I'm interested to see what he's like.'

Once again, Cosmo was left in the car. Alexi and Jack approached a marble entrance portico flanked by Grecian pillars that led to a solid oak front door with polished brass furniture. A few miles away from the Davis residence, it might as well be a thousand for all the similarities there were. The door opened before Jack could ring the bell. A tall man with thick, curly, silver hair and an upright bearing assessed them through intelligent, grey eyes. Eyes that appeared strained, ringed by dark circles and situated in a face that was lined and drawn. Jack recognised the signs of deep grief in Hammond but sensed the last thing he'd welcome would be expressions of sympathy. Hammond was the sort of man who only dealt in answers.

And retribution.

'Mr Maddox,' he said, extending his hand. 'Ms Ellis. Please come in.'

'Thank you for seeing us,' Jack replied, following their host into a sumptuous lounge with a roaring log fire, in front of which an elderly Labrador slumbered, not bothering to stir when they entered the room. 'We're sorry for your loss.'

Hammond swallowed. 'Thank you.' He indicated a white leather settee. 'Please have a seat. Can I get you anything to drink?'

They both declined.

'I admire your work, Ms Ellis, and I followed the Parker case closely. I believe you were instrumental in closing it, Mr Maddox.'

'It was a joint effort,' Jack replied.

'The police haven't told me much about the cause of my daughter's death,' he said, a catch in his voice. 'I agreed to see you because I thought you might know something they don't. You have an investment in the hotel, I believe, Ms Ellis?'

'Yes. The Hopgoods are friends of mine.'

'I don't know them personally but I have had a drink on occasion in the bar and eaten once in the restaurant.'

'I understand you were against your daughter taking part in the contest,' Jack said, seeing no reason to prevaricate. Hammond was the type to take control of any situation and Jack wasn't about to give him the opportunity.

'She was better than that.' He turned up his nose. 'Any fool can cook.'

'I can't,' Alexi said.

'But you could if you took an interest, that's my point. It's not exactly on a par with finding a cure for cancer.'

'You didn't think making a career as a chef was good enough for your daughter?' Jack asked. 'Even though it was what she wanted to do and it made her happy?'

'Seems I was right to have my doubts, given the way matters turned out.'

Jack conceded the point with a nod. 'True, but...'

'Look, if she'd wanted to run a restaurant, I would have invested in one for her. She didn't need to make a fool of herself on national television. People like us don't get involved in all that sensationalist nonsense.' He scowled. 'It's tacky and degrading.'

'You argued about it?'

'I wanted to protect her. I knew that being under continuous scrutiny would be a strain and that anything she said or did would probably be taken out of context. It's what those shows do.' He curled his upper lip and took a healthy slug of what looked to be neat Scotch. 'It's how they stay up there in the ratings and they don't give a damn about the people who get hurt along the way.'

'Juliette defied you over taking part,' Alexi said. 'I don't think she went against your wishes very often, which probably told you how much she actually wanted to do it.'

Hammond shrugged. 'What is it that you want from me?'

Why did you agree to see us so readily? 'We actually came to talk to you about Dean Davis.' Jack paused. 'Your son.'

A brief blink was the only sign of surprise that Hammond permitted to show. 'I didn't know he was my son until I saw him yesterday. I still can't be absolutely certain but, having met him, I'm almost sure that he is.'

Jack was tempted to confront him regarding his treatment of his wife, but restrained himself. It wasn't his concern. Alexi opened her mouth, almost certainly to do the same thing, but Jack gave her a nudge and she shut it again. Succinctly, he told Hammond how he had come to know Dean.

'The fact is, he did what he did for his mother's sake. I shall explain that to my client and hopefully he won't press charges, but I dare say he'll want his money back.'

'I'll write you a cheque.'

Just like that. 'I'll be in touch once I've spoken to Bailey.'

'Then let me know.'

'The police will want to talk to Dean and his mother,' Alexi said. 'Dean's worried about exposing her to their questions. She's very fragile and hasn't yet been told that Juliette's dead.'

'Melody had nothing to do with our daughter's death. It won't take them five minutes to figure that out and then they'll have to leave her alone.'

'If you haven't seen your former wife for twenty years, how can you be so sure about that?' Jack asked.

'To the best of my knowledge, no one could get into the part of the hotel where she was killed. Is that right? I managed to get that much out of that tight-lipped detective,' he added in response to Jack's surprise.

Alexi nodded. 'Yes, it was well guarded and there were so many cameras around that an outsider would have been foolish to try it. But, at the same time, if an outsider did manage it undetected, suspicion would be very unlikely to fall on him or her simply because no one would know the perpetrator had been there. Daring but risky.'

'Well, from what you tell me about Melody's condition, she's too fragile to devise such a risky scheme, much less carry it out.'

'Perhaps not. Dean's mobile number will be on Juliette's phone records but there's nothing sinister about that,' Jack said. 'She made contact with him and Dean had no reason to want her dead. He's in the clear, but I thought you should be prepared for the fallout. It will come out that your ex-wife has been living in near poverty for the past twenty years, not ten miles away from here. Your son was forced to leave school early and give up the chance of making something of himself in favour of taking care of her. It won't look good for you and, no offence, but I suspect image is important to you. So on the face of it, the police might think your aggrieved son was out for revenge, but I can vouch for his whereabout on the night in question, as can you.'

'No offence taken.' Hammond sighed. 'I'll find them somewhere better to live and support them. Once it's been confirmed that Dean is my son, he can return to education if he so wishes. I gather he's intelligent. I'll get live-in help for Melody.'

Hammond had obviously done his homework, even before meeting Dean. That didn't surprise Jack but he did wonder if Dean would be willing to accept his help. He'd be a fool if he didn't but he hated Hammond for what he'd put his mother through and was young enough to stand on principle, to allow pride to get in his way. Whichever way Dean jumped, it would be done with his mother's welfare in mind. But if Hammond thought he had a son waiting in the wings to step into his shoes, Jack suspected that he'd be in for a disappointment.

'You didn't answer my earlier question, Mr Maddox. Are there any suspects in my daughter's killing?'

'To be frank, she was disliked by almost everyone on the show, with a few notable exceptions.'

'Such as?'

'Well, the show's host for one.'

'That frivolous moron.' Hammond's clipped phrases and lengthened vowels made the insult sound extra derisory. 'Juliette was attractive, very attractive. She got noticed by men but I doubt if she encouraged Dakin.'

'Candidly, I think your daughter would have done anything it took to get ahead,' Alexi said. 'I'm sorry if that sounds harsh, but you did ask. I also believe it's one of the reasons why she was unpopular with the other contestants. She made her looks work for her and was prepared to use her femininity to steal a march on the others. The male contestants couldn't fight back against such a weapon and, frankly, neither could the other female competitor.'

'The stupid, stupid girl.' Hammond slumped in his chair, suddenly looking a decade older, closer to the edge. 'I'm biased, I suppose, but she was passionate enough about food to have won on talent alone.'

'Possibly,' Alexi conceded, 'but by no means certainly.'

'Look, I asked you to come here because I need your help.' He sat forward, elbows resting on his thighs. 'I don't trust the police to get to the bottom of this without blackening my daughter's reputation. I imagine you are similarly concerned about the reputation of the hotel, Ms Ellis?'

'Well, yes but—'

'Then I would like to employ you in your professional capacity, Mr Maddox,' he said, straightening up again and suddenly looking every inch the autocratic banker. 'I want you to find out who killed my girl without assassinating her character.'

In other words, he wanted to protect his name, Jack thought. He doubted whether he would have considered taking such good care of his ex-wife and son otherwise. Jack didn't like the man but, then again, he wasn't leaving Lambourn until the case was solved, so he might as well get paid for looking into it. Besides, it would keep Cassie off his back if he had a legitimate excuse to hang around.

'Of course, Ms Ellis, it goes without saying that you can't write anything about my daughter without clearing it with me first.'

Alexi sat a little straighter and this time Jack didn't try to stop her from speaking her mind. 'You are not employing my services, Mr Hammond. But, just so that you know, I never write anything without first triple-checking my facts. If those facts are in the public domain and aren't palatable, then I'm not to blame. But I also don't make a point out of being needlessly cruel.'

'Forgive me, I didn't mean to imply—'

'Yes, you did.' Hammond blinked at her outspokenness. 'However, Jack and I work together, so in one respect you will be employing me as well. I know everything he does about this case, and a great deal that other journalists don't. But none of it has appeared in print, and never will.' She set her chin in a stubborn line. 'I hope that satisfies you with regard to my integrity.'

'Perfectly so, and I apologise for insulting you.'

Some of the stiffness left her posture. 'Apology accepted.'

'So,' Hammond said, relaxing also. 'What do you both know that isn't in the public domain?'

Jack held up a hand. 'It doesn't work that way. I'm not prepared to speculate. I only deal in hard facts. I know that isn't what you want to hear but, trust me, it's the only way to get this done.'

'Do you know...' He cleared his throat, eyes suspiciously moist. 'Had Juliette had sex? Was she raped?'

'She'd had consensual sex not long before she died,' Jack confirmed.

'With whom?'

Jack simply shook his head.

'Damn it, man, you work for me now!'

'I won't tell you anything that might encourage you to jump to conclusions, to conduct a witch hunt or hamper the official investigation.' Jack fixed him with a determined look. 'It's my way or not at all.'

Hammond looked away first. 'Very well. But how do you know it was consensual? You only have the man's word for that.'

'Forensics might throw up some clues.' Jack softened his voice. 'Suffice it to say, your daughter's body showed no signs of a struggle having taken place and she had no defensive wounds.'

'Good enough.'

'What we can tell you,' Jack said, not without sympathy, 'is that she was a few weeks pregnant.'

Hammond sat bolt upright. 'The father?'

'Sorry, no idea. The pregnancy showed up during the post mortem. We don't know if Juliette was aware. She didn't tell anyone if she was, as far as we know. Anyway, the police have her computer.

If she did say anything to her friends online, or had contact with the father, they'll find reference to it.'

'Right, I suppose they will.' He sighed. 'How can I help?'

'Can we see your daughter's room?'

Hammond looked surprised. 'If you like. The police have already been over it. They didn't find anything of interest, as far as I know.'

'Even so.'

'Very well.' He put his glass aside. The snoring dog opened one eye, closed it again and didn't move. 'Come this way.'

Hammond led them up a wide, sweeping staircase and headed for double doors at one end of the first-floor corridor.

'Through there,' he said. 'You won't mind if I don't... I'll wait for you downstairs.'

Jack let out a soft whistle as they entered an enormous sitting room with full length windows that probably looked over the back garden and the downs beyond. An area of outstanding beauty. Of course it was! Hammond clearly didn't do *ugly*. The sitting room led through to an equally sumptuous bedroom, with a four-poster double bed, feminine furnishings and draperies and a walk-in dressing room. There was an en-suite bathroom that would have taken up most of the floor space in Jack's flat.

'Be it ever so humble,' Alexi muttered.

'And soulless,' Jack added. 'She hasn't exactly stamped her personality on it.'

Alexi wandered into Juliette's dressing room, pushing her way through the racks of expensive clothes, eyes watering at some of the names on the labels. She gulped and was slightly envious when her gaze fell upon her racks of expensive shoes: nothing cheaper than Manolos. Jack was methodically looking through the sitting room. There was a desk where, presumably, her computer had sat. The only books, apart from a few romantic novels, were dedicated to cookery.

After twenty minutes, they had found absolutely nothing that offered them additional clues as to Juliette's personality: no diaries, letters, address books. Of course, nowadays people wrote blogs that they made public rather than committing their innermost thoughts to handwritten diaries. Letters had been replaced by emails and addresses were stored electronically. Jack would have to get Cassie to have a little look at Juliette's online activities.

'It's a gilded cage,' Alexi said, shaking her head. 'I never liked Juliette but now I find myself feeling sorry for her. What sort of man gives his daughter her own apartment within the family home?'

'The sort who wants to keep control over her. She was twenty-five. You'd think she'd want a place of her own but I don't suppose Daddy would shell out for that and lose his hold over her.' Jack frowned. 'What did she do with herself once she left that fancy school?'

'She didn't go to university. She had a few jobs in PR that Hammond probably fixed for her but none of them lasted for long.'

'That would explain why she had no option but to live at home and why she was so pleased to discover Dean's existence.'

'I guess.' Alexi shrugged. 'She had quite a list of boyfriends, I gather from remarks made at the hotel, but I don't think we need to look at them. None of them could have got into Hopgood Hall to kill her, and are unlikely to have had a reason to. No one benefits from her death, other than Dean, who becomes the only child whether he wants to or not. And we know he didn't do it.'

'Right.' Jack looked through the drawer full of DVD's beneath the huge television. They told him nothing. 'Let's go back down and talk some more to Hammond.'

William Hammond managed a brief, humourless smile when they returned to his living room. 'Any help?' he asked.

'Some,' Jack replied. 'If you could let me have your contact details, I'll email you a contract for my services.' He told him what his daily rate was, adding fifty per cent to the normal figure. Hammond didn't bat an eyelid as he handed him his thick, embossed card.

'You will give me daily updates?'

'Absolutely.' Jack paused and, on a whim, sent out a request that tested a theory. 'Just one more thing. I'd like a copy of the notes you provided Juliette with regarding everyone connected to the show.'

Hammond looked astounded. 'How the devil did you know...'

'I didn't, but you just confirmed it for me. You like to win, Mr Hammond. You didn't want Juliette to compete in a cookery show on prime-time television but didn't try too hard to dissuade her when she seemed determined because you didn't think she'd get through the selection process. When she did, you knew you had no choice but to go along with it, so you had people find out every-thing there was to be found on the competition in an effort to give her an advantage.'

This time Hammond's smile was admiring. 'You're good,' he said. 'Just a moment.'

'I hate to say it,' Alexi said softly when they were left alone, 'but you are pretty impressive. That wouldn't have occurred to me.'

'Well, what can I say?' Jack flashed a rueful grin. 'Sometimes I surprise myself.'

Hammond returned with a sheaf of papers enclosed in a plastic folder. 'This is everything that I gave to Juliette.'

Jack flipped through it. There were brief notes on the Hopgoods, including their financial situation. Alexi wouldn't be happy about that. She'd be even less enthralled to know there was stuff about her. Backgrounds on Marcel and all the main players in the production team were included. But there were several pages devoted to each of Juliette's competitors.

'Hardly in the spirit of fair competition, Mr Hammond,' Jack said, raising a brow.

He shrugged. 'Like you just said, I play to win. No one ever remembers the person who came second.'

'Right. Did you give a copy of these notes to the police?'

'No. They didn't ask and I didn't volunteer.'

'I see.'

Jack and Alexi shook hands with Hammond and took their leave.

'Well,' Jack said, patting the file of papers Hammond had given him as they got back in his car. 'At least now we'll find out what Juliette had on Anton.'

11

'What!' The file of papers was now on Alexi's lap, but so was Cosmo. There wasn't room for both and it was clear Cosmo had no intention of budging. 'What did you read about Anton? You only glanced at the papers for a moment.'

'I'll buy you dinner and you can read it for yourself.'

'You don't have to do that.'

'It's the least I can do if you're giving me free board.'

'Is that what I'm doing?' Alexi had been wondering when the subject of his living arrangements would come up. 'Good to know.'

'Well, I suppose I kinda assumed... but, if it's not convenient I'm sure Fay would—'

'You *can* have my spare room, Jack, but it would have been nice if you'd asked instead of just taking me for granted.'

'Has it occurred to you that I didn't ask earlier in case you said no?' He sent her a supplicating smile that threatened her resistance. 'I figured that if I left it until it was dark and cold outside, you'd take pity on me.'

'I'd be half convinced, but for the fact that the insecurity act doesn't jibe with the Jack I know and find so infuriating.'

He chuckled. 'Ah, but you love me anyway.'

'Don't push your luck, Maddox.'

'I'm housetrained.'

'Speaking of which, we'd best eat at home. For some obscure reason, Cosmo isn't welcome at most of the eateries around these parts.'

'I know a place halfway between here and Newbury that does takeaway.' He turned the car in that direction. 'Won't take five minutes to get there.'

'Afraid to sample my cooking?'

'I didn't think you *could* cook.'

'It's been a case of having to learn since I moved here. As you just pointed out, takeaways and home deliveries are few and far between. I can manage pasta and... well, okay I'll 'fess up, Marks and Sparks idiot-proof ready meals.'

Jack laughed. 'Glad you're not a completely reformed character. I like you fine just the way you are.'

'Hold the compliments, Maddox.' Alexi warded him off with a raised hand. 'I've already said you can have the spare room.'

'That'll do.' He removed one hand from the wheel and placed it on hers. 'To start with.'

'Don't pressure me, Jack. You just hit me with this relationship stuff yesterday and we've had a few other things to think about since then.'

'You're right and I'm sorry.'

'You mentioned Fay just now,' Alexi said to alleviate the loaded silence.

'How's she doing?'

'Better than I thought possible,' Alexi replied, referring to Natalie Parker's adoptive mother who had inherited Natalie's cottage. When she discovered her husband had been responsible for Natalie running away as a girl, Fay had left him, moved to

Lambourn and took over Natalie's floristry business. She seemed to find solace in surrounding herself with her murdered daughter's possessions. 'She designed the landscaping around the annexe at Hopgood Hall and has settled well into local life. I see her once a week. She insists on cooking for me and then giving me enough leftovers to last Cosmo and me for another two days.'

'Ah, so you exaggerated these new cooking skills of yours.'

'Do you want a bed or not?' Even in the dim interior of the car, she could see him waggle his brows. 'Mind out of the gutter, Maddox.'

'Gutter-thinking has a lot going for it.'

Alexi shook her head. 'As well as running the business and taking a few landscaping assignments that she picked up after doing so well with the annexe, Fay also spends time with Darren Walker.' Alexi was referring to a retired civil servant who'd recently moved to the area and whom Fay's daughter had met on a dating website.

'Really?'

'Yeah, they're both lonely so it works well. She's trying to interest him in doing something creative with his garden. He's teaching her to play golf.'

'All those years she was married to a golfer and he never tried to get her interested.'

'It's probably not the game that attracts Fay but the teacher. They go out to dinner once a week, I gather, plus Fay has plunged herself wholeheartedly into all aspects of village life. She has a busier social life than I do.'

'We'll definitely have to do something about that.'

'Anyway, I told Fay you were around and we have an open invitation to go and eat with her whenever we have the time.'

'We'll be sure and do that.' His hand landed on her knee. 'Will it be a date?'

Alexi sighed. 'You don't give up, do you?'

'Nope.' He pulled into the car park of a small restaurant that Alexi had passed several times but never set foot in. 'Stay put, I won't be long. You happy to let me choose for you and Cosmo?'

'Sure. And get dessert. Cosmo likes lots of cream.'

'Of course he does.' Jack sent her a sexy grin and scratched Cosmo's chin. 'Read those notes on Anton while I'm gone. They cast up a whole new raft of possibilities.'

Alexi *did* want to know what they said but didn't immediately look at them after Jack left the car. Instead, she stroked Cosmo and thought about the whirlwind that was Jack Maddox; a man who appeared to want a permanent place in her life. But for how long? And how permanent? He hadn't exactly beat a regular path to her door since the Parker case wrapped up. Was that an example of out of sight, out of mind, or had he told her the truth when he said he wanted to give her some space?

Patrick *had* been relentless in his determination to win her back. He was too up himself, too convinced he knew her better than to believe that she had put her London life, and him, behind her. But she had. He had betrayed her in the worst possible way and their relationship could never recover from that. The only reason why she didn't sever all ties was because she still freelanced for Patrick's paper.

She liked Jack. More than liked him. It would be way too easy to fall for him, but what if he shafted her in the same way that Patrick had? Better to be alone, without expectations, than to be used and then cast aside.

Alexi sighed. For a woman of the world she was... well, unworldly when it came to men. The permissive society had passed her by, which meant she spent a lot of time feeling frustrated. Jack could do something about that. She didn't imagine he'd need a map to find his way around a woman's body but... oh, hell. She threw up her hands, causing Cosmo to mewl a protest.

Alexi turned her mind off from Jack and switched on the car's interior light. She awkwardly flipped through the papers, her arms aching as she held them out over Cosmo's body since he still refused to move off her lap.

'You are going to have to go on a diet,' she told the cat. His weight was causing her to lose all feeling in her knees and he was so large that he was slipping over the sides of her lap. 'Sorry, baby, but facts have to be faced.'

Cosmo retaliated by getting up, turning in several tight circles that required him to dig his claws into her denim-clad thighs, and finally settled down again.

Alexi started to read, swearing when she saw the bits about her and the Hopgoods. Even though there was nothing there that wasn't in the public domain, it still felt like a violation of their privacy. She rummaged until she found Anton's profile, which was detailed. He'd been born in Trinidad and raised there by his grandmother. Been in the UK for a few years. Nothing surprising there. She already knew all that about him, so what had got Jack so excited?

She found it on the second page.

Anton was in debt to the tune of over twenty grand. He'd borrowed heavily from the sort of loan sharks you don't mess with; the type that don't advertise on TV, charge criminal rates of interest and have persuasive methods of dealing with late payers.

'You stupid idiot!' Alexi muttered.

It wasn't illegal to impose such extortionate terms but it was unethical. Chances were that if the television station knew about this, he wouldn't have been selected. He'd obviously gone out of his way to keep it quiet for that reason, so how had Hammond managed to find out?

'Why do you need that sort of money, Anton?' she asked aloud.

'Gambling debts is my bet,' Jack said, returning to the car with bags full of food. The smell made Alexi salivate. Cosmo also stirred himself and took an interest.

'You scared the life out of me!' Alexi slapped a hand over her heart. 'I didn't hear you coming.'

'You should have locked the doors. I could have been anyone.'

'No need,' she said, pointing to Cosmo.

'Ah yeah, I forgot about your bodyguard.'

'So,' Alexi said as Jack turned his car towards her cottage. 'Anton was in debt to some heavy types who probably aren't on the local constabulary's Christmas card list. There's a note here in what I assume is Hammond's handwriting, suggesting Anton's less than savoury connections might be a way to put paid to his challenge.'

'I told you Anton was holding something back.'

Alexi frowned. 'Would it be enough to get him thrown off the show?'

'Not sure, but if the press somehow got wind of it, it might make him look dubious and influence the outcome of the contest. And I dare say Juliette wouldn't have had sleepless nights about ratting on him. Marcel wouldn't be swayed, of course, but don't forget that the public get to vote, too. His financial irresponsibility would definitely harm his chances with viewers who struggle to live within their means.'

'And yet if he gave way to Juliette's blackmail, always assuming she was trying to blackmail him, he'd have to give less than his best and would lose anyway.' Alexi scowled. 'If it's so important to him to win, and it must be because it would be his way out of debt, he wouldn't take kindly to being threatened. I mean, there's a big cash prize at stake and almost guaranteed financial security through work with a top chef for the winner.' Alexi sighed. 'Anyway, it gives Anton a motive.'

'Yeah, it does.' Jack pulled his car into the driveway of Alexi's cottage. 'Come on, let's eat and we can talk about it some more in the warm.'

Jack opened the bottle of red he'd bought at the restaurant while Alexi busied herself with plates and cutlery. Cosmo wound his way around her legs until she fed him some of his dried food. He didn't seem impressed but cleared his bowl anyway; then meowed for more. Laughing, Jack produced a small container of cream from the takeaway bags.

'Well, you're obviously in with Cosmo,' Alexi said, laughing at the cream on her cat's whiskers. 'But it'll take more than that to... oh God!' She sighed. 'Perhaps it won't.'

Slices of beef wellington, aromatic gravy, garlic mash and buttery vegetables had Alexi's taste buds doing a happy dance. She sat at the kitchen table while Jack poured wine for them both. Eyes closed, she savoured the food and expelled another appreciative sigh.

'Okay,' she conceded. 'You just scored more brownie points.'

He smiled. 'Glad you approve. I like to see you enjoying your food; why deprive yourself one of life's sensual pleasures?'

'About my only sensual pleasure.' Damn, she hadn't meant to say that aloud. 'I did a feature once about the effectiveness of slimming clubs, or lack thereof. I'll always remember one lady saying that she'd been going to the club for over ten years but was about to resign. I asked her why and she said that during that time she'd lost over two hundred pounds, and gained them all back again. Her net weight loss after ten years of depriving herself stood at two and a half pounds. She felt guilty whenever she ate the things that gave her pleasure so decided she would eat whatever she liked, in moderation, and learn to love herself the way she was.'

'There you go. Junk food, convenience food, call it what you will, has a lot to answer for. Well, that and the fact that no one walks anywhere any more.' He topped up her glass and smiled at her. Cosmo, busy washing his face, watched them closely, presumably hoping for leftovers. 'Anyway, what was your take on Hammond?'

Alexi took a moment to consider the question. 'Everything we'd heard about him rings true. He's definitely a manipulator and assumes his money will get him anything he wants.' She paused. 'But it lost him the woman he loves—'

'Loves? He threw her out and hasn't had anything to do with her for twenty years.'

'Because he'd convinced himself she cheated on him. I'll bet you any money you like that she was a susceptible virgin when Hammond met her. If he thought another man had laid a finger on her then she would be damaged goods in his eyes and he wouldn't want her around. He knew she was vulnerable, even if he didn't know she was mentally unwell at that point, and used his money and influence to ensure his daughter stayed with him and never saw her mother. At least he could control how she turned out.'

'Or not.'

'Quite.' Alexi nodded her agreement. 'But the reason why I say he still loves her is that he hasn't married again, and has no permanent live-in significant other. And, did you notice that the only photographs in the soulless lounge were of his daughter... and his wife?'

'Yeah, I did, as a matter of fact. But if he still carries a torch for her, why the initial reluctance to accept that Dean's his son?'

'Because he would have to admit that he'd got it wrong, misjudged her. I don't think he's been truly happy since he threw Melody out of his life and to acknowledge that it needn't have been that way is a big ask of a man with his issues.'

'You're observant, Ms Ellis. Your theory is sound and would also explain why he's so willing to support his former wife and acknowledge the possibility that Dean might be his son. But even though he can't have failed to notice the similarity in their appearances, it's significant that he's not prepared to accept the fact until he has scientific proof that Dean actually *is* his biological son.' Jack pushed his empty plate aside and leaned back in his chair. 'Hammond only deals in certainties.'

'Do you think he'll try to get Melody to move back in with him?'

'Absolutely. He'll read up on her condition and know it's manageable with the right medication. And, of course, managing is what Hammond does best. Remember, Melody held down a job for two years while she was on her meds. Of course, whether Dean would go along with them getting back together is another matter. If it made his mother happy and if he was sure she'd get the care she needed, then my guess is that he'd accept it.'

'Oh lordy, I think I've died and gone to heaven.' Alexi pushed her plate aside and rubbed her belly. 'That was delicious.'

'We have dessert to go yet.'

Alexi blinked. 'You're kidding me.'

'Come on, Ellis, don't wimp out on me now.' Jack got up, cleared the table and then sliced generous portions of strawberry cheesecake oozing cream onto two plates. He placed one before her and grinned. 'I defy you to resist.'

'No contest.' She picked up her fork and took a sinful bite. 'Some things are easier to resist than others.'

Jack shot her a look, probably aware that she was referring to him. Hopefully not also aware that she'd choose him over the cheesecake any day, despite her reservations about getting her heart trampled on.

'I won't be able to move for a week,' she said, having cleared her plate while Jack was still only halfway through his.

'Stagger into the other room and make sure the fire's still happy. I'll clear up here.'

She did as he suggested and when he joined her with the remainder of their wine, she had a blaze dancing up the chimney. He sat on the couch next to her and handed her a refilled glass. She thanked her, shy suddenly, unsure if she was more apprehensive or excited by his close proximity. Telling herself not to behave like a lovesick teenager, she took control of the situation.

'Let's recap on what we know about the case,' she said. 'Seems to me the more corners we turn, the more suspects we fall over and I'm starting to lose track. The entire world and its dog seem to have reasons to want Juliette dead.'

'She wasn't a nice person.' Jack's arm was negligently draped across the back of the couch, his fingers occasionally touching her shoulder. 'Not entirely her fault. Her father expected perfection but also gave her every material benefit so she had no need to strive for it.'

'Exactly. In my experience those who succeed in any field are the ones who are the hungriest.'

Alexi shifted sideways in her seat, dislodging Jack's fingers from her shoulder.

'Marcel is obviously the police's number one suspect. He admitted having sex with Juliette and she was killed a short time later right outside his apartment.'

'But why take her back to her room and pose her there? Always assuming he did, he can't have known the cameras were out, unless he decommissioned them first. And if he risked doing that, who's to say how quickly someone might have come to fix them?' Alexi shook her head. 'You say the posing was symbolic. Well, in my experience, people who want to be *symbolic* in such a gruesome way are mentally unbalanced, and that sure ain't Marcel.'

'Nor was it Melody Davis. People suffering with bipolar disorder can be highly manipulative but... well, Hammond was right. She'd never have got into that part of the hotel undetected, or had the strength to carry Juliette. Besides, why would she?'

'I guess that means we're looking for a man then,' Alexi said. 'I'd always assumed that we were, but you mentioning the strength needed to move and then pose her bears that out. Greta looks strong but Juliette would have literally been a dead weight and I don't think she could have managed it.'

'Two people working together?'

'That's a stretch.'

'You're right, it is, but keep it in mind.' Jack rubbed his stubbled chin. 'The posing bit has got me stumped. What the hell is it supposed to mean? Anyway, hopefully the police will be as puzzled as we are, which should keep Marcel out of clink.'

'For now.'

'Right. So, to continue with our list of suspects, next we have the three contestants.'

Alexi flipped through Hammond's notes on them. 'John Shelton is a forty-year-old bachelor and Hammond discovered he's registered with several dating agencies. Obviously he wants to find true love but hasn't had much luck. Juliette played on that knowledge by... well, playing up to him.'

'She humiliated the poor sod,' Jack growled.

'But surely that isn't sufficient motive for murder?'

'His ego took a bashing.' Jack shrugged. 'People have killed for less. And you know what they say about still waters.'

'Yes okay, he's on our list of suspects. That means Greta has to be as well, even though her dispute with Juliette dates back to their school days. She hadn't expected to see Juliette again and had put it behind her. But when they finished up competing together and Juliette stole that show with her feminine antics, it brought it all back again. You referred to still waters. In return, I'd refer you to revenge and the best temperature at which to serve it.'

'Right, duly noted. We also have to think about Paul Dakin. I really want it to be him.'

'You and me both,' Alexi agreed, smiling as she watched Cosmo squirming in front of the fire, all four paws pointing skywards as he allowed the blaze to warm his belly.

'I think Juliette inspired the same sort of possessive desire in him as her mother did in Hammond and he was prepared to risk his career, his marriage, everything, for an hour or two in her company. Imagine how he felt when he arrived and found her sneaking out of Marcel's apartment.'

'And we know they argued.'

Jack nodded. 'He might also be the father of the baby she was carrying, if their affair started during the heats. Dakin was involved in those so they must have met weeks ago and I don't suppose Juliette would have let the grass grow under her feet when it came to... well, getting an unfair advantage with the movers and shakers.'

'We should certainly add the baby's father, whoever he is, to the list of suspects. Will they be able to find out?'

'Yeah, they can take a DNA sample from the foetus, will have done already I should think, but if the father isn't one of our suspects, or not on the DNA register, then obviously we won't get a match.'

They both fell momentarily silent. Alexi's thoughts dwelt upon the poor little baby who hadn't stood a chance.

'You okay?' Jack asked, squeezing her hand.

Alexi sighed. 'Let's think about Anton. We need to talk to him tomorrow. Ask him about his debts and if Juliette confronted him. He'll say no, of course, but we still have to ask. Anyway, your bullshit detector will tell you if he's lying.'

Jack grinned. 'It never fails.'

'Shall we give copies of Hammond's notes to Vickery?'

'Yes, they are vital to his case. It would be withholding relevant information. We also need to talk to Gerry Salter,' Jack said pensively. 'Whoever killed her, I don't think it was spur of the moment.'

'Because of the cameras being out at a time when someone just happened to kill Juliette and then posed her in her room?'

'Right. Anyone could have disabled the cameras but Salter should have noticed.'

'Unless he did it.'

'Good point.'

'So, we have six suspects, five of whom possibly had good reason to want to see her out of the way. Gerry Salter is our sixth suspect but we have no idea if Juliette pissed him off sufficiently to make him resort to murder.'

'Marcel looks the guiltiest on paper but he doesn't really have a motive either,' Jack pointed out.

'Good, because I don't want it to be him. The hotel would never recover.'

'Don't you just love detective work?' Jack sent her a devilish grin. 'Unfortunately, it's not nearly as glamorous as they make out on the telly. I have yet to confront a suspect with evidence and have them conveniently confess all in front of a room full of people. They still try to lie their way out of it and I doubt if this case will be any different.'

'Then it's a good job we don't have to extract a confession. It's Vickery's job to make sure he has the evidence to get a conviction.'

'Talking of whom, I need to go and see him in the morning, hand over the papers Hammond gave us and see if there's anything else he wants to share with us. But first I'll stop by at Cash Out and let my client know the case has been solved.'

'Make damned sure he doesn't prosecute Dean,' Alexi said hotly.

He took her hand and squeezed it. 'Don't worry. If he talks that way, I'll remind him how bad the publicity could get.'

'And how damaging would that be if the press got wind of it?' Alexi asked mischievously.

'Behave yourself!'

'Oh, I was.'

'Hmm, anyway, I'm sure he won't want to prosecute. He hasn't been keen on making a fuss from the word go, which is why he hasn't involved the police. Besides, if I tell him Hammond will refund his losses, I'm sure that will be the end of it.'

'Good!' Alexi stretched her arms above her head and yawned. 'What will I be doing while you're in Newbury?'

'See if you can have a quiet word with Gerry about the cameras. Find out what he's told the police and where he was when Juliette died. The usual stuff. We'll tackle Anton together when I get back. That should be before lunch.'

Alexi stifled another yawn. 'Oh lord, all that food and wine has me dead on my feet.'

'Then go to bed. It's late anyway.' Jack stood, took her hand and pulled her to her feet. 'Now go, before I forget that I'm a gentleman.' He kissed her cheek a little too chastely and was a little too willing to let her go for Alexi's liking. 'Sleep well.'

'You too.' She put the fireguard in place and headed for the stairs. 'Night,' she called over her shoulder.

12

The following morning, Alexi and Jack left her cottage together and headed for their respective vehicles.

'I'll see you at Hopgood Hall in a few hours,' he said, pecking her on the cheek.

'Yeah, later.'

She opened her car door so Cosmo could jump in. She and Jack were like an old married couple but without the fringe benefits, she thought as she waited for her car's heater to defrost the windscreen. They'd breakfasted together but only because Jack got up early enough to make them something, even clearing up after himself. He seemed intent upon proving to her that he really was well and truly housetrained.

'What's wrong with me, Cosmo?' She peered through the rapidly widening clear spot on the windscreen, shivering as she waited for the heater to blow out warm air. 'Why can't I just go with the flow?'

She reversed out of her driveway and took the narrow lane, brittle with frost, at a slower pace than Jack had just deemed judicious.

'I mean,' she added, flexing her gloved hands on the wheel. 'He's handsome, sexy, intelligent, makes me laugh *and* he can cook. All I have to do is give him the green light and it'll be game on.' Alexi shook her head. 'You know, I think there must be something wrong with my wiring, Cosmo. Most women would kill to have a shot at Jack Maddox.'

She was still conducting a one-sided conversation with Cosmo when she arrived at Hopgood Hall. There was no longer a police presence and the press contingent had dwindled to a few hardy souls. The majority would most likely take up residence in the bar, Alexi thought with a wry smile, as soon as it opened for the lunchtime trade. Her old colleagues were nothing if not diligent in pursuit of a story, especially *if* they could wait it out in warmth and an alcoholic fug.

'Morning,' Alexi said as she and Cosmo made their way into Cheryl's kitchen.

'Morning, sweetheart.' Cheryl was seated at the kitchen table, rocking baby Verity in her arms while Drew watched on with a doting expression. 'Where's Jack?'

Cosmo headed for Toby's basket, while the little dog all but danced on his hind legs by way of greeting.

'Gone into Newbury.'

Alexi removed her coat and gloves and then took the baby from Cheryl. She cooed and cuddled the precious little bundle while she updated her friends on their progress, such as it was.

'Poor Melody Davis.' Cheryl's eyes glistened. 'And poor Dean. That's just so sad. Hammond sounds really horrible. I'm starting to understand why Juliette was the way she turned out to be. With a dictatorial father like him, she didn't stand a chance.'

Alexi nodded. 'No arguments from me on that one.'

'Coffee?' Drew asked.

'You're a mind-reader.'

'Well, our news is that the show goes on,' Cheryl said. 'The cameras are switched back on and Marcel gets to swagger his stuff in the restaurant's kitchen with the contestants today.'

'I'm glad, but I don't suppose his heart will be in it.'

'Hey.' The door opened and Patrick came in. Cosmo hissed. 'I thought I heard your voice.' He leaned over Alexi, who was still cradling the baby, and kissed her forehead. 'You okay?'

'Apart from the fact that there's a murderer on the loose, people I care about are under suspicion, and the business I have invested in could well suffer because of it, I'm just fine and dandy, thanks.'

'Sorry.' Patrick held up his hands. 'Stupid question. I should have asked if you were hanging in there.'

'Yeah.' Alexi sighed. 'Kind of.'

'Have the police made any progress?' Patrick asked.

Alexi sat a little straighter, barely conscious of Patrick's question, as a thought struck her.

'What is it, hon?' Cheryl asked. 'You look like you just had a lightbulb moment.'

'Oh, it's nothing.' Alexi wasn't ready to share her fledgling idea just yet.

'Well, if it's any consolation,' Patrick said, 'the finest legal brains in the boss's empire think the killer is someone with an axe to grind against Juliette, not a serial killer starting out on a spree because he has a grudge against racehorses, cooking contests, or alien spacecraft.'

'Alien spacecraft?'

Patrick grinned. 'Just trying to lighten the mood.'

Alexi sent him a droll glance. 'Very comforting.'

Patrick took the seat beside Alexi and nodded his thanks when Drew placed a mug of coffee in front of him. Verity started to grizzle, so Cheryl took her back.

'She needs changing,' she said, disappearing through the door
to their living quarters.

Drew mumbled something about having things to do, and left
the room as well. *Thanks a bunch, guys!* Silence stretched between
her and Patrick, taut and uncomfortable. Alexi made no effort to
break it and concentrated her attention on her coffee.

'You know, if I could have my time over, I'd do things very differently.' Patrick had her full attention. Alexi had seldom heard him
sounding so unsure of himself. He almost never apologised about
anything because in his opinion he was never in the wrong. 'I was
so wound up with the paper's business, trying to juggle so many
balls at once, that I lost sight of what was really important to me. I
tried so hard not to discriminate in your favour that I finished up
doing the precise opposite. I was a damned fool!'

No question, Alexi thought but didn't bother to say. They'd
been here before and nothing had changed from her perspective.
Besides, having him close made her uncomfortable and she wanted
rid of him as quickly as possible rather than getting into an in-
depth discussion about her feelings for him, or lack thereof.

He paused, holding her captive with an intense gaze. 'I loved
you absolutely. I still do.' He shook his head, looking bereft and full
of self-disgust. 'But I blew it and I know you won't come back to
London.'

'No, I won't. Despite the fact that this sleepy little town appears
to be murder central right now, I like it here. The pace is slower and
I'm less likely to burn out. I have the book commission to keep me
occupied, I can pick and choose the stories I pitch to you and other
editors, and a business interest in this place to keep me motivated.'
She smiled. 'I also have friends who care about me and a social life
of sorts that doesn't revolve around the next big story. There's something to be said for that.'

'I get the attraction.' Patrick flashed a self-deprecating smile. 'Who would have guessed?'

'The pace of city life gets to everyone in the end so you did me a favour in some respects. If you'd fought my corner more vigorously, I'd still be slaving away on the *Sentinel*, not realising that I was running on empty.'

'And loving it.'

'Yeah, until I came down here and discovered there's more to life than scooping the opposition.' Alexi relaxed a little, even though she wasn't entirely comfortable with the soul-searching nature of their conversation. 'But you would miss the cut and thrust of the newspaper after a week, no question.'

'Is that why you won't consider taking me back? Because you're no longer comfortable in my world?'

'No, Patrick, what we had is beyond life support.' She spoke firmly because it was true. 'It worked but we've changed, or I have, and so now it won't.'

'It could.' He trapped her hand beneath his on the surface of the table. 'London isn't a long drive. I could come down a couple of days a week...' He shook his head. 'You're going to say no, aren't you?'

She nodded. 'It's over, Patrick. Move on. You won't have any trouble finding someone else.'

'Is it Maddox?' His frown emphasised the fine lines between his brows. 'I know he's staying at your place.'

She snatched her hand from beneath his. 'Have you been stalking me?'

'I drove over your way yesterday evening, hoping we could talk away from this place, but his car was there.'

'It's got nothing to do with anyone else. It's just that I'll never be able to get past the fact that you put the interests of the paper ahead of our relationship.'

'I know that.' He lowered his head and shook it slowly from side to side. 'Now.'

He sounded so desolate that Alexi almost relented. Just for a moment, she saw in him the certain something that had first attracted her to the dynamic editor. But she held firm, knowing that if she let him back into her life, she'd eventually finish up being lured back to London. She was surprised just how adamantly she didn't want to go.

'Go back to London, Patrick. The show's back on course here and hopefully Vickery will catch the murderer soon.'

'I will go, but only because I have to and because I don't believe you're in danger.' He skewered her with a determined look. The look she'd seen him adopt when he took it into his head that the *Sentinel* was going to scoop the opposition, no matter what it took. 'But know this,' he said, absently pushing a thick lock of hair away from his eyes. 'I'm not giving up on you. I'll give you some space and time but it is *not* over between us.'

Alexi let out a frustrated breath. She thought she'd convinced him but knew now that the game was far from over.

He stood up, squeezed her shoulders and headed for the door.

'Take care,' he said, turning to briefly look at her.

Then he was gone.

'Phew!' Alexi leaned back in her chair, and expelled an extravagant breath.

Determined not to dwell on the ashes of her relationship with Patrick, Alexi finished her cooling coffee and tried to decide what to do next. It was still only ten in the morning. The contestants would be in the annexe, talking recipes, going over what they'd be doing that day. Marcel would be there with them, once again the complete Frenchman, no doubt. If Gerry Salter wasn't monitoring the cameras, he'd be around somewhere. He always was. Alexi knew he'd been questioned by the police but she had yet to question him herself. She pulled her sheepskin jacket on, and headed for the back door.

'Not you,' she said when Cosmo got up to follow her. 'You'll only cause mayhem.'

Cosmo gave an indignant mewl, turned his back on her and curled up around Toby, looking as though he was about to smother the life out of the poor little dog. Laughing, Alexi opened the door to a blast of frigid air. Head bowed, she almost collided with someone coming the other way.

'Sorry!' She glanced up. 'Oh hello, Mike. I didn't know you were here today. No school?'

'Teacher training day, or something. Drew said he needed some heavy lifting done, so here I am.'

'He'll be back in a mo.' Alexi stepped back into the kitchen and closed the door again. 'Help yourself to coffee.'

'Thanks, I will.'

Mike took a handful of biscuits and slouched in a chair in the universally gangly pose of teenagers everywhere. The kid lived locally and helped out with the donkey work in return for pin money. Today, Alexi imagined, his appearance had less to do with Drew's need for help and more to do with Mike's curiosity.

'Any developments?' he asked, confirming Alexi's suspicion. 'The whole village is talking about it and I told Mum I'd see what was what.'

'It's early days.' Alexi didn't want to get held up or reveal anything she shouldn't. Cosmo didn't object to Mike so it was safe to leave the two of them alone. 'Have to go. Catch you later.'

Mike dunked his third biscuit in his coffee. 'Yeah, later.'

With hands thrust into her pockets, Alexi made her way to the annexe. The crime scene tape had been removed from the court-yard but she had to steel herself to walk through the area she had once loved. She couldn't shake the knowledge that less than two days previously, a woman had lost her life in the haven of tranquil calm that Fay had created out of nothing. The water feature that Juliette had collapsed against looked stark, almost sinister, in the brittle, winter sunshine. The water that in summer would fountain into the air and tumble down the man-made water slide was turned off and the focal point of the courtyard had a neglected air about it. Alexi had been delighted with Fay's design but would never again be able to look on it with the same pleasure.

'Gives you the creeps, doesn't it?'

Alexi jumped at the sound of another voice. She'd thought she was alone, but turned to see Gerry Salter leaning against the outside wall of the annexe. He wasn't wearing a coat and had obviously just nipped out for a smoke, as evidenced by the cigarette between the fingers of his right hand, burned down almost to the filter.

'Yeah, it does.' She was glad to have met Gerry by accident as opposed to making it obvious she'd come to track him down. 'I gather this is where she was killed.'

Gerry straightened up and ground out his cigarette beneath the heel of his boot. 'So they say.'

'You working right now?'

'Not for another hour until they move into the kitchen.'

'The coffee's on in our kitchen if you're interested,' she said, aware that Gerry couldn't help himself from the contestants' supply if Marcel was in there and the cameras were recording. She'd also just seen Drew and Mike disappearing into one of the storerooms so she knew the coast was as clear as it would ever be.

Gerry grinned. 'Lead the way.'

'Have you been grilled by the police yet?' Alexi asked as they sat across from one another with their coffees and Gerry clearly struggled to overcome the urge to light up again.

'Yeah. They seemed to think I must know something about the

cameras in Juliette's room going down. Kept on at me, they did, wanting to know how it could have happened, if anyone had asked me to do it, and stuff like that.' He shuddered. 'Talk about the third degree. If I told them once, I told them twenty times. Everyone on these fly-on-the-wall shows gets cabin fever sooner or later and—'

'You've worked on shows like this before?'

'Several times. I was contracted in for that reason.'

Alexi permitted her surprise to show. 'You're employed by Far Reach Productions?' She hadn't known that and if Hammond's investigators did, they hadn't seen fit to mention it.

'Nah. I'm a qualified sound engineer.' Gerry leaned back in his chair, apparently settling in for a good old natter. That was fine with Alexi. It would give her an opportunity to try and figure him out. She was usually good at assessing character – it was a necessary skill for any half-decent reporter – but Gerry was a bit of an enigma and she couldn't get a handle on him. 'Worked for a while at Elstree,' he said, referring to the British film studios. 'Got to know my stuff there, made some connections and then went freelance.'

'If your forte is sound, how come you finished up monitoring the cameras?'

He sniffed. 'It's called multi-tasking or, put another way, the bosses being tight-fisted.' Gerry waved a hand from side to side. 'Well actually, that's not fair. With the advances in technology, not as many people are needed on these sorts of locations. So those of us that want to stay in the business have to move with the times. I know what I'm doing when it comes to sound, but have to do the grunt work as well.'

Alexi studied him as he rambled on. In his early thirties, short and slightly overweight, with thin, sandy hair that was already receding and eyes that were set a little too close together, he was no oil painting. But he was friendly enough and, from what Alexi had seen over the past few weeks, seemed to get along with everyone.

'You don't mind living out of a suitcase all the time?' Alexi asked. 'Must play havoc with your home life.'

'Nah, free spirit, that's me. I go where the work takes me.'

'How did you land this job then?'

'I have an agency that touts my credentials but, on this occasion, I asked them to put me forward for it.'

Alexi blinked. 'Why? What's so special about this show?'

'I'm a local man. Born and brought up in Reading, so I do get to see my own bed occasionally. Of course, I knew from the buzz around the industry that *What's for Dinner?* was likely to be a winning formula. The gossip mill seldom gets these things wrong. So I thought, why not?' He slouched back in his chair, both hands clutching his coffee mug. 'Won't do the old CV any harm to be in on the ground floor with a Far Reach Productions winner.'

'Glad you think it's going to top the ratings. I had my doubts. I mean, cooking shows and *Big Brother* type scenarios have been done to death.' Alexi clapped a hand over her mouth. 'Perhaps I could have chosen my words more carefully.'

Gerry didn't respond. He helped himself to another biscuit, dropping crumbs down his sweatshirt as he demolished it in two bites.

'You weren't involved with the heats, then?' Alexi asked, aware that the conversation was in danger of stalling.

'Nah, I wasn't needed for them.'

'What did you tell the police about the cameras?' Alexi expected him to get suspicious and ask why she wanted to know. Instead, he leaned forward and looked as though he was about to give her chapter and verse. Alexi refilled his coffee cup and pushed the plate of Cheryl's homemade biscuits closer to him.

'It's like I said earlier. No one can live constantly in the lime-light.' He sniffed. 'Everyone thinks they can, until they try it. There're hours and hours of boring film but no one's free to be themselves, to really relax, because the one time a person does something the slightest bit oddball, naturally the entire nation sees it. These artificial situations are deliberately created because the producers know people will blow a fuse eventually. Stands to reason the contestants will want a few minutes now and then to be themselves.'

Alexi folded her arms on the table in front of her and fixed Gerry with a penetrating look. 'Are you saying that the contestants often disconnect their own cameras?'

'All the time. Officially, I'm supposed to go and check on them the moment they go on the blink.'

'You get a warning light on your console?'

'Yeah. Unofficially, I cut them some slack and leave it half an hour or so. If, for example, someone wants a little privacy for... well, whatever someone wants to do in private in a bedroom, alone or otherwise, we don't judge. But they certainly don't want the entire nation to know about it.'

'So Juliette's cameras going down wasn't that unusual?'

'Nah, they all get told, off the record, that the occasional short respite is in order, just so long as they don't abuse the privilege. I showed them all how to disconnect and reconnect the camera feed myself. Saves a lot of damage that way. Anyway, they can get away with doing it now and then, provided it's not at a time when Dakin's throwing his weight... sorry, I mean in-depth questions at them. And obviously, he wouldn't be doing that in the bedrooms.' Gerry treated Alexi to another grin. 'Well, not on camera.'

Alexi sat a little straighter. 'You think he and Juliette had something going?'

Gerry shrugged. 'He followed her around like a lap dog, so it wouldn't surprise me.'

'Had Juliette disconnected her cameras before?'

'Actually, no. She's the only one who hadn't. I think she enjoyed being caught in indiscretions.' One side of his mouth lifted. 'There's always one.'

'None of the others mentioned anything about disconnecting the cameras to me,' Alexi said, almost to herself.

'Well, they wouldn't.' He flapped a hand. 'Technically, it's against the rules and they were all warned by me when I showed them how to do it, not to let on. I said I'd lose my job if they did. Not that I would, of course, but the production company like to keep the illusion going that the contestants have no respite.'

'But someone died! The fact that her camera outage happened at the same time could change the entire course of the investigation.'

'Yeah well, I don't think any of the others are shedding too many tears over Juliette's demise. Heartless though it sounds, she was a right little madam and didn't do anything to make herself popular.'

'Hmm, so what do you think really happened to her?'

Gerry simply shrugged one shoulder.

'Come on, you must have a theory.'

'I dunno, but I reckon it has to be a crime of passion of some sort. Why else dump her in her room and stick that knife in her... well, in her enhanced bits?'

'Who do you suspect?'

'I don't think it was Marcel. He isn't stupid enough to leave evidence that points straight to him. Besides, far as I can tell, a chef's knives are his Holy Grail. I don't know whether or not Marcel had reason to kill Juliette but I do know he wouldn't desecrate one of his knives by using it on her.'

'Which leaves Dakin,' Alexi said pensively.

'He was here and he was heard arguing with her, right in the spot where she was killed.'

'By you?' Alexi asked, acting on a hunch. She had only been

told it was a member of the crew who'd seen them arguing but no one was saying which member.

'Yeah, actually.' Gerry looked mildly surprised. 'How did you know?'

'It's my job to officially snoop.'

'Yeah well, he was here but he doesn't know I saw him. He thought he'd evaded the cameras, which goes against the grain for a narcissist like him. And he did avoid them, but I happened to see and hear him.'

'Any idea what they were arguing about?'

'Nope. Didn't hear what was actually said and only saw them for a moment. I got distracted by a problem with one of the other feeds and didn't think much about it. Juliette was always at logger-heads with someone.' Another negligent shrug. 'Still, all I know is that I didn't kill Juliette and I dare say the police will find out who did.'

'Let's hope so.'

'And the show goes on.' Gerry rolled his eyes. 'Viewer numbers guaranteed to go through the stratosphere now this has happened and sponsors will be queuing up to back the next series.' He flashed a wry smile. 'Perhaps Evan Southgate did it.'

'Don't tell me Juliette was sleeping with him, too?'

'He's the producer. The man with the ultimate power to make anything happen. Of course she would have tried it on with him. But he wasn't here the night she was killed.' Gerry rolled his shoulders. 'Anyway, the others have got over the shock and are focused on the contest again. RIP Ms Hammond, but the show goes on.'

'Did you tell the police what you just told me about her using sex to influence the outcome of the vote and about the cameras sometimes being disconnected?'

'Sure. I wasn't having them suspect me, which is what they seemed to be doing for a while. Anyway, I talked it through with

Grenville Scott first and he agreed that I should tell the complete truth.' He snorted. 'Truth and lawyers aren't two words that sit well in the same sentence, if you ask me. Anyway, Grenville sat beside me all the time, making sure I didn't spill any more of Far Reach's grubby little secrets.'

Alexi shuddered. 'I hardly dare ask.'

Gerry grinned. 'Probably best.' He checked his watch, drained his coffee mug and stood up. 'Ah well, I best be getting back to work. There's no peace for the wicked.'

'Nice chatting with you,' Alexi said, absently.

'You too.'

Gerry snagged another biscuit and disappeared out the back door. She saw him stop to light up the moment he closed it behind him.

Alexi remained at the table, pondering on Gerry's revelations. It wasn't looking good for Marcel, she conceded. If he knew that the cameras going down wouldn't induce immediate panic, it was a game-changer. If he *had* killed Juliette and wanted, for some reason, to pose her in her room then he could easily have sneaked in and disconnected the feed, aware that no one would come running for at least half an hour. Thank God he still didn't have an obvious motive. Besides, if he'd been careful enough to disconnect the cameras, it beggared belief that he would thrust his own knife into her surgically enhanced breast and leave it there to be found.

'Hey, you were quick,' Alexi said, looking up when the door opened. A spontaneous smile sprang to her lips when she saw Jack standing there. 'How did it go?'

'Not so good.'

Alexi noticed his harried expression and felt anxious. 'What's happened?'

'Vickery's on his way over here,' he replied tersely. 'They're gonna haul Marcel in for another grilling.'

Alexi gasped. 'Why? What reason do they have?'

'He told me as a courtesy, but I can't warn Marcel and neither can you.' Jack ran a hand distractedly through his hair. 'The fingerprint evidence from Juliette's room came back while I was talking with Vickery, so he couldn't avoid sharing with me that Marcel's prints were found on a glass on her bedside table—'

'That doesn't mean a thing,' Alexi protested hotly. 'Anyone could have put that there.'

'Yeah, but his print was also found on the underside of the table itself.'

13

'Shit!' Alexi gaped at Jack, her entire premise regarding Marcel's honesty thrown into question. 'So he lied to us.'

'That was my first reaction.' Jack shed his leather jacket and threw it over the back of a chair. He turned another chair around and straddled it, leaning his arms on its back. 'But I've had time to think about it on the way back and it seems too clumsy to be believable.'

'Because we don't want to believe it?'

Jack shrugged. 'Perhaps.'

'Leaving that aside for a moment, let me tell you what Gerry Salter just told me about the camera feeds.'

'Ah,' Jack said, when she'd finished explaining. 'That changes everything.'

'That's what I thought. But we don't know that Marcel was aware the contestants could switch them off. They'd been told to keep it to themselves on pain of disqualification. I don't think Cheryl and Drew had any idea.'

'But Dakin would have known?'

'Probably.' Alexi scowled. 'Jack, it's the worst fit-up in the history of crime.' She stood up and paced the length of the kitchen, almost tripping over when Cosmo wound himself between her legs. She picked the big cat up and threw him over her shoulder. Cosmo purred loudly in her ear. 'Think about it for a moment. For Marcel to have done it, he would have had to follow Juliette for some reason after she left his apartment and after she'd argued with Dakin. But why?'

'Perhaps the police will say he saw her with Dakin and called her on it,' Jack said. 'Or they will suggest that it wasn't Dakin and Juliette arguing but Marcel and Juliette.'

'They can't say that if Dakin has admitted to being here and arguing with her.'

Jack waved a hand. 'I'm just playing devil's advocate. Whichever way they paint the picture, they will find a way to put Marcel in that courtyard with Juliette, either instead of Dakin or after he left. They'll say his famous temper got the better of him when he realised she'd been sleeping with Dakin as well as him. He pushed Juliette and... I don't know, she hit her head on the water feature and died. It was all a terrible accident.'

'And he then tried to disguise what he'd done. In a state of advanced panic when it could reasonably be assumed he wasn't thinking straight, he calmly let himself into her room, even though he knew the cameras would still be running. In spite of that, without leaving a single print or scrap of trace evidence apart from on the glass and table for some reason, he managed to disconnect the camera feed.' Alexi frowned.

'Anyway, let's go back to our hypothetical situation. Marcel's in Juliette's room and has disconnected the camera feed. Without knowing how long he had before someone came to investigate, he calmly went back outside, threw Juliette's dead body over his shoulder and, for some reason known only to him, arranged her on her bed. Then, he went back to the restaurant's kitchen, took one of his own precious knives and stabbed her with it. Having done that, he took a drink from the glass beside the bed because, obviously, pointing the finger of blame in your own direction is thirsty work. But he left no prints anywhere else because he was wearing gloves? Juliette's prints were all over the place so the killer definitely wore gloves.'

'So how could Marcel have left a print on the bedside table?'

'No idea,' Jack responded, 'but I dare say Vickery will have theories. But what we are saying here is that Marcel, if he is our killer, wore gloves but left his knife and a glass with his prints on it, but didn't leave prints anywhere else. Come on!'

'You've made me feel a whole lot better,' Alexi said. 'A decent defence barrister will drive a horse and cart through that hypothesis.'

'My theory is the killer created a spur-of-the-moment decoy and Marcel just happened to be it.'

'That implies a crime of passion, or Juliette saw or heard something that made her a liability. It doesn't have to be a premeditated murder. The killer had to think on his feet.' Alexi resumed her seat at the table and leaned her elbows on it. 'Will they arrest Marcel? I can't see him remaining passive if he's unjustly accused. He really does have a short fuse, you know.'

'Vickery will have to talk to him about this latest development but I hope he will see reason and not jump the gun. The fact that he doesn't plan to actually arrest him is a good sign. We need to talk to Grenville Scott, lay out the theory we just came up with to show how ridiculous it would be to accuse Marcel. Where is he, by the way?'

'Marcel? They resumed filming today. He'll be in the restaurant kitchen for another hour at least.' Alexi scowled. 'Vickery won't go and haul him out of there in front of the cameras, will he? I suspect Marcel really would lose it if he was humiliated in that way.'

'I doubt that he will.' Jack sighed. 'We're lucky that we drew him as senior investigating officer. He's fair-minded and even though he's under pressure to get a result, he won't be bullied into making an arrest unless he has solid evidence to back it up.'

'Well, that's something, I suppose.'

'Of course, you're partly responsible for that.'

'Me!' Alexi widened her eyes. 'What did I do?'

'Your reputation precedes you,' he said with a broad smile. 'Journalists are not always a copper's best friend; trust me on this. You have a reputation for being firm but fair and are usually on the side of the angels. But, you're also known for going in all guns blazing if you think there's been a miscarriage of justice. Vickery's bosses are very media savvy and won't want a Rottweiler of an investigative journalist giving them grief if they can help it.'

'Glad to be of service. Woof, woof!'

Jack laughed. 'They'll need a watertight case or the CPS won't proceed with it and I'm pretty sure, as things stand, that they can't pin it on Marcel. They'd be laughed out of court.'

'Is Grenville Scott still around?' Alexi asked. 'Patrick went back to London this morning and I got the impression that Grenville was going with him.'

'One way to find out.'

Jack pulled his mobile from his pocket and dialled the lawyer's number.

'Mr Maddox,' a cultured voice answered. 'What can I do for you?'

There was a deafening silence after Jack explained Marcel's predicament.

'Are you still there?' Jack asked.

'I am, but unfortunately I'm on my way back to London. I have to be in court this afternoon.'

'Can you send someone else to look after Marcel until you're free?'

'Well, that's not likely to be possible. Marcel Gasquet isn't actually a client of Far Reach Productions, you see, so isn't my responsibility.'

Jack shouldn't have been surprised. 'So you intend to hang him out to dry?' His voice vibrated with barely controlled anger. 'A convenient scapegoat upon whom Far Reach can turn their collective backs?'

'It would be a conflict of interest, dear boy,' Scott said calmly. 'If, as you contest, Gasquet is innocent, then in all probability someone connected to my client's organisation is guilty. It would be my job to represent that person if and when charges were brought. In defending Gasquet it might be necessary to point the finger of suspicion at someone connected to my client's company. I wouldn't be doing my job effectively if I didn't take that into consideration and they know it.'

'Yes, but Marcel isn't—'

'They have given me my instructions and I am duty bound to follow them. I'm sorry. I like Gasquet and, for what it's worth, I don't think he killed the poor girl. Anyway, there are plenty of other good solicitors available. Would you like me to recommend one?'

Jack hung up and flung his phone across the table. It skidded to a halt on the other side where Alexi caught it before it crashed onto the tiled floor and fell apart.

'Bastards!' he muttered.

'Calm down, Jack.' Alexi touched his arm. 'You can't be surprised by that, surely?'

'No, I guess I saw it coming but the way these big organisations cover their backs no matter what and... well, it gets my own back up.'

'He must know that Dakin is the most likely suspect and they're closing ranks to protect him.'

'Yeah, it stinks,' Jack said disgustedly.

'What annoys me is that Scott was probably in Patrick's car. That would be the same Patrick who assured me that he would do anything and everything to protect this hotel and everyone who works here.' Alexi blew air through her lips. 'So much for *I'll do anything to prove to you how much you mean to me*. He was so convincing, he almost had me fooled.'

'If you've seen your ex in his true colours then something good has come out of this.' Jack squeezed her hand, feeling a little calmer as he tried to figure out their next move. 'And it just so happens I know exactly the right person to represent Marcel. An old friend of mine: a one-man band working out of Newbury. He used to be with a big organisation but got fed up with office politics.'

Alexi nodded emphatically. 'I know the feeling.'

Jack reached for his phone and scrolled through his numbers. 'Ben Avery has worked with Cassie and me on a few cases and I know he'll bite our hands off to get involved with this one.'

He called, was put through to Ben, and they exchanged a few pleasantries. Jack explained the situation. A short time later, he hung up again with a smile on his face.

'By the time Marcel comes out of the kitchen, Ben will be here. I feel better already because Ben's loyalties definitely won't be in question.'

'What did Vickery make of Hammond's notes on the main players?' Alexi asked.

'He thought it was weird. The work of an overzealous parent. He's met Hammond, don't forget, and has got the measure of him, so wasn't that surprised.'

'And your client? Cash Out. What did Mike Bailey have to say when you told him you'd cracked the case?'

'He was horrified about Melody Davis's dismissal. He remembered her being on reception, even though he'd only exchanged a word or two with her in passing.'

'It's hardly surprising that she stuck in his memory. She's a striking woman. Once seen, not easily forgotten.'

'Yeah well, Bailey knew nothing about her getting the push. He doesn't get involved with the day-to-day hiring and firing and plans to have a few choice words with the person who does. He also understands why the son did what he did and won't be pressing charges or looking for restitution of the cash.'

'I should think not!'

'I spoke to Dean after I saw Bailey and told him the good news. He took the day off today, not sure if he would have a job to go to if Bailey pressed charges so was mightily relieved. But he was more concerned about his mother. He's told her about Juliette but said she didn't seem to absorb the enormity of what he was saying. She was, in his words, "way too calm about it".'

'It will hit her later.'

'Most likely. DC Hogan was going round to talk to them both, which is another reason why Dean wanted to be there.'

'Did you mention to Dean what Hammond said about taking care of them both?'

'No, that's a matter between them. I don't want to get involved.'

'That's probably wise.' Alexi sighed. 'God, what a day.'

'What did you make of Gerry Salter?' Jack asked. 'Did you believe him?'

'I didn't see any reason not to. I'm not as good as you are at judging when someone's lying to me, but I do have a lot of experience of evasiveness from all the interviews I've done over the years. Gerry answered my questions without hesitation and didn't give off any vibes that made me suspicious.' Alexi propped one elbow on the table and rested her cheek in her splayed hand as she relived their conversation in her mind. 'He also has no motive, other than that Juliette didn't come on to him like she did with the other men who could make a difference for her.'

'Do you think that bothered him?'

Alexi took a moment to consider the question. 'Actually, I don't. His ego might have taken a bashing but not to the extent that he'd commit murder over it.'

'No, most likely not,' Jack agreed.

'He's a local man, you know, Reading born and bred.'

'No, I didn't know that.'

'According to him, he has a good reputation and gets plenty of work. It finds him as a rule but he had his agent put out feelers because he wanted to work on this show.'

'Why was Salter so keen to work on this production?'

She shrugged. 'Says the inside word was that it would be big.'

Jack frowned. 'How could anyone be sure of that before an episode had even aired?'

'No idea, but he says the grapevine seldom gets it wrong. Don't they do audience surveys and stuff?'

'You tell me. That's more your area than mine.' Jack stood up and poured himself some coffee. 'The thing is, unless we find out who did kill Juliette, there's always going to be a question mark hanging over Marcel's head.'

'And the reputation of this establishment.'

Jack waved the coffee pot in Alexi's direction but she shook her head. 'We haven't spoken with Anton again yet, or John either. I was hoping we could get to them both this afternoon.'

'We'll try.' Jack leaned against the wall, sipping his coffee as he thought about it. 'What we really need is a plausible reason for Marcel's print being on that bedside table. That is the one sticking point that worries me. It puts Marcel in that room when he's maintained all along that he never set foot in it. That, in turn, casts doubt over his entire statement.'

'We need an alternative suspect just as much.'

'I'll get Cassie to delve a little deeper into Dakin's background. There might be text messages or even emails between him and Juliette if we're really lucky. People are impossibly careless about that sort of stuff.'

'That would prove they had something going, but Dakin's already admitted that to me. I assume he's told the police as well. He'd be a fool not to.'

'Even so, I'll have Cassie work that angle.'

'What angle?' Drew asked as he and Cheryl appeared together from their private apartment.

'We have bad news.'

Alexi brought them up to date on the Marcel situation and explained why they didn't think he'd actually be arrested.

'Have you warned him?'

'No,' Jack replied, 'and we can't. Vickery will be here any moment, probably before Marcel finishes in the kitchen. So will the solicitor I've engaged to represent him.'

'Well, I'm glad he won't have to rely on that Grenville fellow,' Cheryl said. 'Pompous and condescending doesn't come close to describing his attitude.'

Drew sat at the table next to his wife and threw an arm around her shoulders. 'Don't look so glum, love. It'll all work out. You'll see.'

'It had better or we'll be on the dole.'

'Talking of which,' Alexi said. 'I did wonder if we're coming at this the wrong way.'

'What do you mean?' Jack and Drew asked together.

'Well, think about it. We're all assuming that Juliette died because she severely pissed off someone connected to the contest. But, what if it's nothing to do with that? Jack and I trod on a few toes when we exposed Graham Fuller for the murdering scumbag that he is. Even though our proof was irrefutable and he finished up admitting killing his own daughter, some people around here still blame us for depriving the area of one of the country's best trainers. They took it as an insult to Lambourn.' She shared a look between them. 'What if someone was out for revenge against me? What better way than to attack the reputation of this hotel and its star chef? Marcel's name ensures that the restaurant is booked solid and keeps us solvent... just about.'

Drew and Jack exchanged a prolonged look. 'It's possible, I suppose,' Jack said, 'but extremely risky, what with all the cameras everywhere.'

'And who would care enough to take the chance?' Cheryl asked.

'Fuller's son is trying to hold his father's business together but most of the owners with decent horses have taken them away,' Alexi replied. 'He thought he would be stepping into his father's shoes, relying on his reputation to take over a thriving business. Instead he's left with third-rate horses and must feel resentful, especially since his mother, who held the purse strings, has legged it back to the States and left him in the lurch. Young Fuller might want to blame someone and we would be convenient.'

'How would he gain access to the annexe?' Jack asked.

'Easy if you're a local and know the lie of the land,' Cheryl replied. 'There's a shortcut across the paddocks we back onto. They're privately owned but who's going to be looking out for someone crossing them in the dark on a freezing November night?'

'And if Fuller, for the sake of argument, was dressed in dark clothing and had his face covered, even if he was caught on camera, he wouldn't be recognisable,' Alexi reasoned.

'How would he know Juliette would be obligingly hanging about in the courtyard?' Jack asked. 'Like Cheryl just said, it wasn't a night for lingering outside.'

'Pure luck,' Alexi replied. 'Juliette wouldn't necessarily have been his target. Anyone would have done. And that needn't have been his first try.'

'But how would he have got into the kitchen and got hold of Marcel's knife?' Drew asked. 'The door only opens if you know the code. All the contestants and kitchen staff know that code, of course, so it doesn't narrow it down that much, but it does exclude outsiders gaining access.'

'I'm working on that part.' Alexi wandered up and down, pondering.

'Someone could slip in and out unnoticed at the lunchtime height of service, I suppose,' Drew said. 'The door is open then and provided they were dressed in chef's whites and kept their head down, no one would realise they didn't belong. It gets hectic, everyone's concentrating on what they have to do and no one takes much notice of anyone else.'

'So, if you're right, the knife would have been stolen *before* the crime was committed?' Jack blinked. 'That would make it premeditated, pre-planned or whatever as opposed to the result of... I don't know, an argument that got out of hand, say.'

'It's unlikely, I know that,' Alexi said, sighing. 'But still, it's worth putting it to Vickery as another lead to follow. And if we get nowhere, Jack, we could make a few enquiries along those lines too. It's another area of doubt that would help to clear Marcel's name, if it comes to it.'

'Clear my name how?' Marcel asked, joining them and throwing himself into the nearest seat. 'God, I wish I hadn't agreed to do this.'

'Think of the fame and glory,' Alexi said, trying and failing to appear cheerful.

'What is it?' he asked, appearing to pick up on Jack and Alexi's discomfort.

Right on cue, Vickery walked into the kitchen with DC Logan and asked Marcel to accompany him to the station.

14

Ben Avery arrived just after Vickery. He was a tall man in his mid-thirties, with an open, friendly face that had deceived more than one opponent into underestimating his fierce intelligence. He had a mop of unruly, red hair, the freckles to match, and long, gangly limbs that made him look a bit like a praying mantis.

'Thanks for coming so fast,' Jack said, shaking his hand.

'Glad to oblige.'

'This is Marcel Gasquet and Alexi Ellis. Drew and Cheryl Hopgood.' More handshakes were exchanged. 'Inspector Vickery and DC Hogan you probably already know.'

'Welcome aboard,' Vickery said with a droll smile.

'Wouldn't miss it.'

'Marcel, Grenville Scott has gone back to London,' Jack explained. 'So, if it's okay with you, Ben will take care of your interests from now on.'

'Sure, but I still don't know what's going on.' Marcel looked bemused. 'Why do I need to go to the nick? I've already given a statement.'

'There's new information we need to talk to you about,' Vickery said.

Marcel blinked. 'Give me a clue.'

'All in good time, sir.'

'Can I have five minutes with Ben?' Jack asked.

Vickery nodded. 'We'll take Mr Gasquet back with us. Mr Avery can follow when he's ready. We won't start the interview without him.'

'Fair enough,' Jack replied.

'Don't say a word until I get there,' Ben warned Marcel as he stood up, muttering beneath his breath about the police wasting his time. But Jack could sense that beneath the bluster, he was frightened. He hoped the charismatic chef had told them everything and that there was no foundation for that fear.

Once the police had left with a very unhappy-looking Marcel, Jack lost no time in explaining the developments to Ben. He took no notes. He didn't need to because Jack knew he had a sharp mind and near photographic memory. Jack and Alexi between them, with occasional contributions from Drew and Cheryl, laid out all the reasons why it had to be a clumsy set-up. When they ran out of words, Ben nodded.

'I agree and Vickery obviously knows it too, otherwise he'd have arrested Marcel. It would help, though, if we had an explanation for that fingerprint.' He pulled a face. 'And it would help even more in a high-profile case like this one if we had an alternative suspect.'

'We do,' Alexi replied. 'Paul Dakin. He had means, motive and opportunity. But the studio's lawyers have cut Marcel loose and circled their wagons around Paul instead.'

'We'll keep digging,' Jack said. 'If we knew who the father of her baby is, it would help. That definitely can't be Marcel. He wasn't involved with the qualifying heats and didn't meet Juliette until she came here.'

'If he's telling the truth about that,' Alexi added.

'He is,' Cheryl said. 'I can vouch for that. I know when they took place. Being local, everyone was talking about them and Marcel was working here the entire time. We didn't even know at that point that this hotel would be used to film the actual contest.'

'That helps,' Jack said, 'in that it gives Marcel less of a motive.'

'Juliette seemed to have issues with all the other contestants,' Alexi added. 'We haven't spoken with John at all yet and need to do a follow up with Anton.' She explained about his financial situation and the large loan he'd taken from a dubious source. 'Juliette might have been using that against him. If it was construed as an illegal activity, it could have got him thrown off the show, which gives him a motive. And he would know how to disconnect the cameras. Anyway, we'll try and pin him down this afternoon.'

'Juliette didn't exactly make friends and influence people. And no one other than her father appears to mourn her death.' Jack slapped Ben's shoulder. 'Anyway, you'd better get off to the nick and stop Marcel from blowing a fuse. We'll keep digging into Juliette's background.'

Ben waved to them all and took himself off. The four of them watched out of the window as his gangly legs carried him across the car park and he climbed into an old Volvo.

'Now what do we do?' Cheryl asked.

'Lunch,' Drew replied. 'Starving ourselves won't fix anything.'

* * *

'That fingerprint,' Jack said as they tucked into the platter of smoked salmon and avocado sandwiches Drew had knocked up.

'What about it?' Alexi asked, wiping mayonnaise from the corner of her mouth with a napkin.

'I'd really like to know, just for my own peace of mind, how it came to be there. Is all the furniture in the annexe new?'

'Yes,' Cheryl said. 'We wanted everything to match.'

'So it's interchangeable?'

'All the bedrooms have the same furniture, but Marcel is adamant that he hasn't set foot in any of them.' Cheryl shrugged.

'I don't suppose he helped set it all up?' Jack asked, more in hope than expectation. 'I gather it was all hands on deck to get ready in time.'

Cheryl was so shocked by the suggestion that she almost choked on her sandwich. She took a hasty sip of tea to clear her throat.

'It was a manic time,' Drew said, patting his wife's back. 'All of us pitched in but it didn't occur to us to ask God's gift to culinary excellence to get his precious hands dirty.'

'Ah well, it was just a thought.'

'So, what next?' Alexi asked, pushing her empty plate aside and looking at Jack.

'We need to try and speak with Anton and find out more about his interaction with Juliette.'

'You can't do that yet,' Drew replied. 'They're about to have a session with Paul on camera.'

'That ought to be interesting,' Cheryl remarked. 'I mean, they'll have to bring up the subject of Juliette and the others won't be able to say what they really thought of her.'

'No one ever does when a person dies unexpectedly,' Alexi said. 'At least not in public.'

'I've just thought of something.' All heads turned towards Drew. 'I'm not sure if it means anything, but Marcel had a falling out recently with the guy he worked with in London before he came here. I heard him yelling at him on the phone. Something about a dispute over money, he told me. It got pretty heated.'

'That's right,' Cheryl agreed pensively. 'Marcel and a guy called David Rowe, another French-trained chef, opened a restaurant together in Chelsea but it didn't work out. There's such a thing as too many cooks—'

'Especially when they have egos the size of small independent countries,' Drew added. 'I gather they fell out all the time over signature dishes, sourcing their ingredients, pricing... You name it, they fought over it. They used to have bust ups in the middle of the restaurant apparently and the customers came in the hope of witnessing one of those as much as for the food. Marcel said he got sick of all the fighting, that it wasn't possible to have two stars in the same kitchen, so he cut his losses and came to work here.'

'It's the first I've heard about Marcel's previous life,' Alexi said.

'And off the top of my head, I can't see that it's relevant to this murder,' Jack added.

'Why did Marcel settle here in Lambourn?' Alexi asked. 'No offence, but it's not exactly the last word in trendiness and if he was used to London...'

Drew shrugged. 'A lot of well-known chefs are setting themselves up in restaurants attached to country hotels. Marcel likes horse racing, so Lambourn would have seemed attractive to him for that reason, I guess. Tips direct from the horses' mouths, so to speak. Besides, he was hurting financially; that much I do know. He had to buy his way out of his commitment with David and the place hadn't been running long enough for him to see a profit from it. His ego had also taken a bashing, which is why he was so excited about this chance to star on the box.'

'How bad is the situation between him and David Rowe?' Alexi asked.

'Not sure.' It was Cheryl who replied. 'I know they used to be tight but now there's a lot of bad feeling. David couldn't keep the restaurant going without Marcel. Marcel was the main draw for the customers, which wouldn't have done much for David's self-esteem. I think David's on the point of taking legal action against Marcel. He claims he defaulted on their agreement, which is why the business failed, costing David everything he had, and then some. Marcel says not.' Cheryl shrugged. 'Who do you believe?'

'Could it be relevant, given that David is so hell bent on revenge?' Drew asked, sounding hopeful. 'We should have thought to mention it before but it honestly didn't occur to me.'

'Has David ever been down here to confront Marcel?' Alexi asked. 'Would he know the lie of the land, in other words?'

Cheryl and Drew exchanged a look and both shook their heads. 'Not so far as I know,' Drew said. 'But if you're thinking he might have had a hand in Juliette's death—'

'Sounds as though their fight has become acrimonious. If David's lost everything, been boxed into a corner, then he might figure he has nothing left to lose and come out all guns blazing, looking for revenge,' Jack said.

'Sabotaging the show that's making Marcel a star and implicating him in a murder would be a great way to go about it, but there's no way he could have done it that I can think of,' Drew said. 'Far too complicated with the annexe being locked to outsiders, disconnecting the cameras and everything else. I just don't buy it. Besides, would someone with a grievance really be prepared to commit murder in order to come out on top *and* do all that staging?' He shook his head. 'Can't see it myself.'

'Perhaps not,' Alexi said, 'but it's another area to explore.'

Gerry sauntered into the kitchen, taking a shortcut from his room to the annexe.

'Did I just hear you talking about David Rowe?' he asked.

'Yes,' Alexi replied, sharing a mystified glance with her friends, all of whom looked as intrigued as she herself felt. 'Do you know him?'

'Not personally, but I do know he was shortlisted to be the chef on *What's for Dinner?* before it was decided to shoot it at this hotel.' He grabbed an apple from the bowl on the table and made for the back door. 'Have to dash. Our star presenter is about to work his smarm on the contestants. Can't miss recording that piece of television legend. See ya.'

'Oh dear,' Alexi said into the ensuing silence. 'Sounds like I might be indirectly responsible for David Rowe suffering another setback.'

'How?' Cheryl asked.

'Well, as you know, Patrick suggested they shoot the show here and use Marcel as a favour to me. He knew we were trying to reinvent the hotel and... well, my point is, David might have got his opportunity to shine on the small screen if it weren't for that.'

'Don't beat yourself up about it,' Jack said. 'None of this is your fault but I can see that if David and Marcel fell out over their restaurant and then he lost out on the show to Marcel, he would have one massive motive to set Marcel up. Arranging a murder to make it happen no longer seems like quite such a stretch.'

'You'll figure it out, Jack,' Cheryl said. 'I have every faith in your abilities.'

'That makes one of us,' Jack replied with an affable grin.

Cheryl went off to deal with the baby. Drew had chores elsewhere in the hotel and needed to check on the work young Mike was doing for him inventorying supplies. Alexi and Jack headed for the residents' lounge upstairs and Jack fired up his laptop.

'What are you looking for?' Alexi asked.

'Anything on record about Marcel's fight with David Rowe. You'd have thought he would have mentioned it. I mean, if he was threatening to sue, that implies a huge load of animosity. Someone with a grudge who'd go that extra mile to get revenge.'

'I agree, but Marcel's been poleaxed by this business and probably isn't thinking straight.'

Jack pored through pages of stuff while Alexi caught up with her personal email. 'Here we go,' he said, sitting back so she could read over his shoulder. 'There's a hearing in four weeks' time in London.' Jack let out a low whistle. 'David's suing Marcel for breach of contract, loss of revenue and damage to his reputation. He's asking for a million quid.'

Alexi laughed. 'In that case, Marcel ought to kill him.'

'He's obviously short of readies, or not too sure that he'll prevail, because he's using a no-win no-fee outfit to represent him.'

'They must think he has a good chance of success then, or they wouldn't have taken the case. They only take sure bets and try to settle out of court. I hear a lot of organisations, insurance companies and the like, prefer it that way. Saves the time and expense of court appearances and any negative publicity.'

Jack shrugged. 'Perhaps they see this one as an opportunity to make a name for themselves; to publicly flex their muscles and show what they can do. The case is bound to hit the headlines. I'm surprised it hasn't already, given what went down here.'

'It'll only be a matter of time. Still, Marcel should have mentioned it.' She sighed. 'I still don't think he realises quite how deep in it he is, otherwise he would have.'

'I think we ought to track Mr Rowe down and go have a little chat with him.'

'You think he'll tell us anything when he finds out we're in Marcel's corner?'

Jack shrugged. 'People with grievances can't help mouthing off if they think they have a captive audience, no matter how hostile.'

'Well, I can see he's got serious issues with Marcel. First, there's the failed restaurant which left him broke, his reputation in tatters. Then losing out on the TV show. If he'd got that, it would have bolstered his bank balance and got him back in the public eye. Losing it would have hurt, but losing it to Marcel, his former friend and deadly rival... Yeah, perhaps it would have made him desperate enough to try and get even.' Alexi scowled. 'I really wish I could see a way for him to have done it but someone unfamiliar with this hotel wouldn't stand a hope in hell.'

'I can't think how he could have pulled it off either, unless your theory about Fuller's son is on the money. David could have done his research when he heard Marcel had got the starring role and was working from here. There's stuff all over the net about Fuller and it wouldn't be hard to figure out his son must have one hell of a grievance against this place.' Jack shrugged. 'I know it's a reach, but stranger things have been known to happen. Fuller's son and this David character are both hurting financially *and* out for revenge. Compelling motives. Anyway, we've got sod all else to chase up at the moment.'

It surprised Jack how easy it was to find people's personal details online. They soon had all the information they needed. David Rowe was currently working the party scene, catering for society events from his home kitchen, the address of which he obligingly plastered all over his website. It was a big come down from being a celebrity chef with his own restaurant, Jack thought. No one could blame him if he was bitter.

'He lives in Kensal Green,' Jack said. 'Come on, we can be there in a little over an hour at this time of day.'

Cosmo, who'd followed them upstairs and was curled up on the window seat, stirred himself, like he knew a car journey was in the offing. He followed them back down and was first out the front door. No way was he being left behind. Toby whined but knew better than to follow. Laughing at their symbiotic relationship, Alexi climbed into the passenger seat of Jack's car and closed her eyes as he reversed out of his parking space.

'Tired?' he asked.

'Not sleeping well.' She opened her eyes again. 'I'm worried, Jack, and I feel guilty. I persuaded Drew and Cheryl to expand, to be more ambitious. What if I've cost them their business, to say nothing of their reputation?'

'Hey, you didn't do anything wrong.' He removed one hand from the wheel and placed it on her thigh. 'You were trying to help. You *have* helped. Marcel didn't do this, I'd stake my reputation on the fact, and we'll prove it, one way or another. Apart from anything else, I've seldom seen a more obvious fit-up. The knife, the glass with the fingerprint... the fingerprint on the table is still the only stumbling block. But Marcel wouldn't have been so adamant that he hadn't been in Juliette's bedroom if he had. Like you keep pointing out, he isn't stupid.' Jack grinned. 'Just arrogant.'

'Thanks, that's what I needed to hear.'

'My pleasure. And I'm pretty good value because if your insomnia continues, I have a solution for that problem, too.'

'I'll just bet you do.' Alexi sent him a wry smile but didn't worry too much when Jack left his hand on her thigh.

Once Jack hit the motorway, the motion of the car lulled her to sleep. Jack cast frequent sideways glances at her as he drove, liking what he saw, hoping she would decide to take their relationship further. No pressure. He could be a patient man when he needed to be and Alexi was worth exercising patience for.

She jerked awake again as they hit the outskirts of London and the car stopped and started in the heavy traffic.

'Sorry,' she said, yawning and stretching her arms above her head. 'Not very good company, am I?'

'You'll do.' He listened to the disembodied voice issuing instructions from his GPS and took a left turn. 'This is the road.'

'What if he's not home?'

'I'm banking on the fact that he will be. If he caters evening parties, he'd have to do the prep in the afternoons. I'd rather take the chance anyway than give him advance warning of our coming. Besides, if he knows beforehand that we're connected to Marcel, he might not agree to see us. If we're on his doorstep, it'll be harder to get rid of us.' He slowed, looking for a parking spot. 'That's his,' he said, nodding towards a nondescript semi in a dreary, residential road.

Cosmo remained in the car, comfortably sprawled across the back seat, while Jack and Alexi traipsed up the front path and rang the doorbell.

'About damned time.' A short man with dark hair and attitude, wearing an enveloping white apron, yanked the door open. 'I expect you... Who the hell are you?'

'Not who you were expecting, obviously,' Alexi replied. 'You must be David Rowe. I'm Alexi Ellis. This is Jack Maddox. We wondered if you could spare us a moment.'

'Yeah, I'm Rowe. What's this about?' David asked suspiciously.

'Marcel Gasquet.'

David narrowed his eyes. 'I have absolutely nothing to say about that bastard.'

He tried to shut the door but he was no match for Jack's arm strength.

'Even if he's suspected of murder?'

A broad smile broke across David's face. 'Couldn't have happened to a nicer guy.' He opened the door wider. 'Since you're not my suppliers and since I can't get on with anything until my order arrives, you might as well come in.'

Alexi and Jack followed David directly into a small lounge. An open archway led to the back of the house, the entirety of which had been converted into a huge, professional kitchen. Two young men wearing chef's whites were working away at one side.

'Take a break, guys,' David said.

They both pulled packets of cigarettes from their pockets and disappeared without a word.

'Okay, so how can I help you to convict the weasel?' David asked, leaning against an island and folding his arms across his chest.

'How did you two get to be so antagonistic?' Jack already knew but wanted to see what spin David put on it. 'I gather you ran a restaurant together and I know it failed but surely that's—'

'It didn't fail, or wouldn't have if Marcel had been prepared to compromise.' David's entire body vibrated with anger. It was clearly still a very sore subject. 'Everything had to be on his terms. I'm as good a chef as him but he would never accept any of my suggestions because he knew better.'

Jack nodded, going for a sympathetic look. 'Perhaps it wasn't possible for two leaders to... well, share the lead.'

'We discussed that at length. Had it all figured out. We were financially committed to that place but Marcel didn't stick to his side of the bargain, thinking he was better than me, arguing that the customers wanted *his* dishes, not mine. Saying I played it too safe, blah, blah. Who made him the boss? Anyway, now I'm reduced to this.' He scowled as he waved his arm around the large kitchen with its gleaming, stainless-steel appliances and plethora of utensils hanging neatly from ceiling racks. 'My reputation will never recover and that sod has to pay.'

'Did he actually break the terms of your business agreement?' Alexi asked.

'My lawyers seem to think so.' David scowled. 'Who are you two anyway? What's your interest in this?'

Jack explained their connection to Lambourn and the TV show. 'Ah, I heard about that girl getting killed. Marcel has got quite a temper on him but even I wouldn't have thought him capable of assassinating anything other than a soufflé.'

'He isn't,' Alexi replied, somewhat surprised when David didn't jump on the opportunity to talk up Marcel's potential guilt. It was a golden opportunity for a man with a massive grudge to bear to make life difficult for his nemesis. 'But someone's trying to make it look that way.'

'Well, it ain't me but if you find out who it is, let me know so I can shake his hand.'

'How did you and Marcel meet?' Alexi asked.

'In Paris. We'd both won positions as trainee chefs under M Mason.' Alexi nodded, as though she knew who David was talking about. Presumably someone with a prestigious reputation in the culinary world. Jack would take her word for it. 'We got on well, especially since he'd grown up in France and spoke the lingo. I didn't have a clue what people were saying most of the time so he helped me out in that respect; I'll give him that. Anyway, we roomed together, worked and played together and decided that when the time was right, we'd run a restaurant together. Damned stupid idea but then hindsight can be infuriating. Anyway, at least I was prepared to work at it, give it my best shot and try to make it successful. All Marcel wanted was the glory.'

Jack doubted if that was true. Marcel *was* a tyrant in his kitchen, mainly because he expected perfection, but he didn't think he'd try to do his partner down.

'I hear you were under consideration as the resident chef on the show,' Alexi said casually.

His eyes shot daggers at her. 'Yeah, briefly. Then wonder boy's name got thrown into the ring and that was that.'

'Did you meet with the producers?' Jack asked.

'We had a couple of exploratory meetings,' David said, sounding evasive. 'But I didn't build my hopes up.'

'Who did you see?' Alexi asked. 'And where?'

'What is this? Twenty questions?' He threw his hands up. 'I met a couple of suits for lunch in London, then had a second meeting at their offices. Can't remember the names of the people involved.'

You're lying, Jack thought. A six-week run on national prime time television was manna from heaven for someone in David's position. Of course he remembered who he'd spoken to but he obviously wasn't about to say. David had just elevated himself in Jack's mind from unlikely-to-be-involved to prime suspect.

'You didn't file your breach of contract case against Marcel until after you lost the show,' Jack said casually. 'Are the two connected?'

'Nah.' He flapped a hand. 'I'd spoken to the legal people weeks before but they needed to collect all the necessary facts before proceeding.' He examined his fingernails as though he found them fascinating. 'The timing's nothing more than coincidence. Besides, I didn't lose the show. You can't lose something that didn't belong to you in the first place. Am I pissed off that Marcel got it instead of me? You bet your life I am. Salt and raw wounds spring to mind. Still, on the bright side, he'll have enough money to settle my claim when I win in court now, won't he?'

'Not if this murder gets pinned on him.'

David's eyes flashed with malice. 'If that means he gets banged up and spends the next twenty years cooking sausage and mash for half the country's prison population, then I'll drop my case in the blink of an eye and laugh myself silly.'

'Very charitable of you,' Alexi said drolly.

'Yeah well, after what he did to me, it would take a better person than I'll ever be to feel sorry for him.' The doorbell rang and David looked relieved. 'That'll be my supplies. You'll have to go now. I'm running behind.'

'Thanks for your time.' Jack offered his hand, which David took.

'Glad to have helped bury him, if that's what I've done. A guy can live in hope,' he replied, shaking Alexi's hand and taking his time releasing it again.

'What did you make of him?' Alexi asked as they walked back to Jack's car.

'He's bitter, resents Marcel's success and, I'm betting, isn't as good a chef as Marcel. Whether Marcel actually screwed him over is yet to be established but somehow I doubt it.'

'He's carrying a load of resentment. Jealousy, bitterness and losing face are a lethal combination.'

'They are indeed.' Jack fastened his seatbelt and started the engine. 'And, for what it's worth, I think he did meet someone at the production company who might have been persuaded to set Marcel up for him. Just don't ask me who it was though because I don't have the faintest idea.'

15

By the time they got back to Hopgood Hall, a very pale and
subdued Marcel was back in the kitchen with Cheryl and Drew. He
rested his elbows on the table with his head in his hands, looking
close to the edge.

'How did it go?' Alexi asked, patting his shoulder.

'Talk about an inquisition.' Marcel looked up and sighed expan-
sively. 'They think I did it. I know they do. They're building a case
against me brick by brick, and there's nothing I can do to fight
back.'

'If they thought you'd done it and could prove it, they would
have arrested you,' Jack said reassuringly. 'Nothing they have so far
is sufficient to secure a conviction. Trust me on this. It's too convenient, too circumstantial.'

'Yeah well, it's only a matter of time.'

Drew glanced at the clock. 'Talking of time, the sun's over the
yardarm, more or less. Besides, you look a bit peaky, Marcel, which
makes this a medical emergency.' He pulled the cork on a bottle of
decent red and handed Marcel a glass. 'Get that inside of you, mate,
and the world will seem like a rosier place.'

Drew poured more moderate measures for the rest of them, excluding Cheryl.

'Was Ben a help?' Jack asked.

'Yeah.' Bleary-eyed and morose, Marcel nodded. 'I meant to say thanks for arranging that. At least I felt he was on my side, which is more than Grenville Scott ever was. And he stopped me from blowing a fuse at their inane questions.'

'They have to ask them,' Jack replied. 'And the goading is quite deliberate. That way, you're more likely to put your foot in your mouth.'

'Or punch their lights out.'

'You definitely needed Ben's services, by the sound of things,' Cheryl said, sipping at her orange juice.

'Let's consider what they have against you. You had sex with Juliette and have admitted it,' Alexi said. 'No law against that. She was in your apartment shortly before she died but left it in perfect health. She was then overheard arguing with Dakin, which makes him look like the more likely suspect.'

'Ah, but she was apparently seen in the annexe after that, alive and well.'

Jack and Alexi jerked upright.

'That's the first I've heard of it,' Jack said. 'Who saw her?'

Marcel shook his head. 'They won't say.'

'Doesn't matter, though, does it?' Jack said. 'If she was seen by Dakin and then someone else after she left you, the chances are you're innocent.'

'Vickery keeps implying that I saw her with Dakin and went looking for her again later to find out what they'd been arguing about.'

'Which they can't prove that you did,' Jack replied. 'So far, they're clutching at straws. And the most convenient straw they have is you.'

'And that bloody fingerprint!' Marcel swallowed the rest of his drink. 'How the hell did that get there?'

'There has to be a logical explanation,' Cheryl said stubbornly.

'It's not enough for them to get the cuffs out,' Jack assured him. 'But it doesn't help.'

Marcel snorted. 'Tell me something I don't know.' He ran a hand through his hair, looking beleaguered: a shadow of the confident, forthright chef Alexi had often locked horns with over the alterations to Hopgood Hall. 'Christ, how am I supposed to go on with this programme, pretending that my world isn't falling apart?'

'Bear in mind,' Alexi said, 'that there's a killer out there. Someone we probably know and speak to every day. We need to be careful. If we get too close then... well—'

Cheryl shuddered. 'Hell, I hadn't thought about it that way.'

'The killer's probably having a grand old time of it,' Jack told Marcel, 'watching you squirm, which is obviously his or her intention...'

'Very likely.' Marcel rubbed his chin. 'I've made my share of enemies but no one hates me that much.' He suddenly looked unsure. 'Do they?'

'Only you can answer that one,' Alexi replied.

'Can't think of a single person.'

'Well, someone's out to get you,' Jack reminded him. 'They wouldn't have gone to the trouble of setting you up if they didn't want to watch the fun and tell themself how clever they'd been.'

Marcel sat a little straighter and a glimmer of fire returned to his eye. 'Then the scumbag's in for a disappointment.'

Alexi flashed an encouraging smile. 'That's the spirit!'

'We've just been up to town to have a chat with your ex-partner,' Jack said.

Marcel's scowl returned. 'I'm sure he sent me his very best wishes.'

'Well, something like that,' Jack replied, waggling one hand back and forth.

'Things have reached quite an impasse between the two of you,' Alexi said. 'Surely it occurred to you that he could be behind all this.'

'Nah! He doesn't have the nous or local knowledge to set it up.'

'You're not making allowances for the hurt feelings of a very bitter and resentful individual.'

That comment merited a one-shouldered shrug. 'He seems to think I'm to blame because our restaurant didn't work. Truth is, it was a stupid idea in the first place. It's impossible to have two bosses, two prima donnas if you like, and we fought about the direction we wanted to go in all the time. David wanted to stick to a tried-and-tested menu; I wanted to be creative. It was my creative dishes that dragged the punters in. Plus, David wanted to hide away in the kitchen and have nothing to do with the customers. Unfortunately, it doesn't work that way any more. If you want to charge the kind of prices we were getting away with, you have to sell yourself right along with your truffled noisettes. See and be seen. Schmooze with the punters.'

'And behave badly?' Cheryl suggested with the ghost of a smile.

'Yeah, that too.' Marcel's lips quirked as he leaned back in his chair and stretched his arms above his head. 'The truth is, David dealt with all the paperwork, sorted out the lease and legal stuff and I just signed where he told me to. But I insisted that we not take more than a year's lease initially with the option to renew for a further two. I needed to be sure the venture would work before sinking more dosh into it. He agreed with me, then signed up for another two years without telling me.'

'Could he do that?' Jack asked.

'Yeah, I trusted him with all that crap, which is the only mistake I made. He had the authority to sign on behalf of us both.'

'Then you're probably liable,' Alexi said.

'Nah, I have a series of emails between David and myself confirming in writing the stuff we'd already agreed verbally. I insisted on that.' He shrugged. 'Perhaps I sensed even then that there might be trouble in paradise. Anyway, I stated quite clearly that I didn't want to extend our initial commitment until much closer to the renewal date because we were losing money. Unless we could turn that situation around, it seemed pointless going on.'

'Then why did he go ahead and do it?' Jack asked.

'I've often asked myself the same question.' He waved an arm through the air. 'Things were already fraught between us at that time and I think David knew that if we split up then he wouldn't be able to make it alone.'

'He tried to force you into staying the distance?' Drew suggested.

'Yeah, but I don't respond well to blackmail. Anyway, that was the beginning of the end. We had a big falling out and I said I was quitting at the end of the initial year. Cutting my losses, if you like. That's when I decided to come here. David threatened legal action, but I didn't take him seriously, simply because I didn't think he had a case. Then he got some ambulance-chasing lawyers on board who thought our email exchanges wouldn't stand up in court. Personally, I think they're just in it for the glory. David and I are both well-known and they want to cash in.'

'How can they cash in if you were losing money? Jack asked.

'The restaurant was losing but I still had funds of my own. I'm not daft enough to put all my eggs in one basket. David knew that and must have told his lawyers I was worth going after.' He spread his hands. 'Truth is, David's a decent, run-of-the-mill chef but he doesn't have the flair, the secret ingredient if you like, to stand out in an increasingly crowded marketplace. With all due modesty—'

'Which is not your style,' Cheryl reminded him, grinning.

'Right, so I'll say it straight.' They were treated to a brief glimpse of the old, cocky Marcel as he winked at Cheryl. 'I know how to make a statement, both with my food and with my behaviour, that keeps people coming back for more. They either love me or hate me. What they can't do is ignore me.' He sighed. 'Anyway, what made you go to see David?'

'We figured the animosity between the two of you had reached the stage where David might be desperate enough to want the final word,' Alexi explained. 'Did you know he was in line to be the chef on *What's for Dinner?* until they decided upon you instead?'

'Hell, no I didn't!' Marcel sat a little straighter. 'That really would have pissed him off.'

'More to the point,' Jack added, 'he had two meetings with the production team. Who's to say he might not have hooked up with one of them and concocted this scheme? Or even with Graham Fuller's son?'

'To murder a contestant just to get back at me?' Marcel's eyebrows disappeared beneath his hairline. 'Blimey, that possibility never even occurred to me, which is why I never brought David's name up. He's angry and bitter but even so, I can't see him going that far. He doesn't have the balls. Besides, even if he did, it's a pretty extreme way to exact revenge.'

'He said the same thing about you,' Alexi replied. 'Not the angry and bitter part. He chose other adjectives to describe your behaviour—'

Marcel chuckled. 'I can well imagine.'

'He did say that he didn't think you'd resort to murder, especially when you had so much going for you.'

'He's right about that.' Marcel shook his head. 'If I wanted to kill someone, I'm hardly likely to frame myself.'

'The point is,' Jack explained, 'until we can expose the real killer, it's in your best interests if we present the police with as many alternative possibilities as we can. Far Reach Productions are closing ranks around their nearest and dearest. We need to do the same with you. Vickery must know about your dispute with David Rowe but since he hasn't been in touch with David yet, he probably doesn't think it's relevant. I'll have a word or two in his shell-like and see if I can change his mind. I might even throw Fuller's son's name into the ring while I'm at it.'

'I really appreciate what you're doing for me,' Marcel said, encompassing Jack and Alexi with one gaze. 'And you two for standing by me,' he added to Cheryl and Drew.

'We're only doing that because you draw the customers in with your appalling behaviour,' Drew assured him.

'Yeah, don't go all soft on us when this is over,' Cheryl warned. 'We've got used to your tantrums and might even miss them.'

Marcel smiled, obviously touched.

'Do we have any other viable alternative suspects?' Cheryl asked.

'Our money's on Dakin,' Alexi replied. 'He had means, motive and opportunity but so far, we haven't got a hope in hell of getting him to incriminate himself, especially now that the production company's big guns have his back.'

'Anyway, my business partner's digging into his background, finances, stuff like that to see what pops up,' Jack said. 'We'll know more, if there's anything to know, when she gets back to me.'

'We still need to talk to Anton and John,' Alexi said. 'Anton especially. We know he borrowed a massive sum from a loan shark who charges 1000 per cent interest.'

'Bloody hell!' Drew breathed.

'Would that really get him thrown off the show?' Cheryl asked. 'If Hammond's people found out about the loan, I reckon the studio must have done their homework too and decided that Anton's looks and personality were more important than a questionable financial decision. Dakin might even ask him questions about it live on air. A lot of people get themselves into similar pickles and would sympathise. If I'm right about that, Juliette couldn't blackmail him to perform badly in exchange for keeping his secret.'

'Look at the broader picture,' Jack said. 'The guys that do the lending aren't in the charity business and wouldn't lend so much to someone with no means of making repayments. Threats, intimidation, broken limbs won't see them get their dosh back. So why lend to someone like Anton in the first place?'

'Because he can be of help to them in some way,' Alexi suggested, catching on to where Jack was going with this.

'Right, that's my bet. Repayment suspended in lieu of services rendered. And you can bet your last penny that the type of services blokes like that need are on the dark side of the law. Anton's young, fit and intimidating, I would imagine, if he wants to be. Just the sort of person to persuade people to pay up. All Juliette would have had to do was threaten to drop a word or two in the right ear about Anton's suspicious activities and it *would* be enough to have him thrown off the show.'

Alexi nodded. 'And would leave Anton with no alternative but to keep Juliette quiet. Permanently.'

'Where does he say he was when she was killed?' Cheryl asked.

'In his room,' Jack replied. 'The cameras prove that he was most of the time but he left it for varying periods. Now John *was* in his room, no question, so talking to him is really just a formality. With regard to Anton, as we don't know the actual time of the killing to within a few minutes, any one of his absences would have been enough to get the job done.'

'You'd best leave speaking with him until the morning,' Drew said. 'This evening is one of the periods when they all have to hang out in the lounge and the cameras keep rolling. He can't leave.'

'Tomorrow will be fine,' Jack replied.

Alexi's mobile rang and she moved to the side of the kitchen to take the call. 'Hey, Fay,' she said. 'How are you?'

Fay was full of questions about the case, most of which Alexi couldn't answer. 'We're taking one step forward and two back right now,' she said.

'Would you and Jack like to tell me all about it this evening over one of my beef stews?'

'Hold on, I'll ask him.'

Jack agreed at once. 'I look forward to it, Fay,' he shouted so she'd hear him.

'Okay, we'll see you in about an hour,' Alexi said, ending the call. 'Fay sends you her love,' she told Marcel. 'Although how anyone could love you when you make no effort to play nice is beyond me.'

Marcel treated her to a heated smile. 'I might be prepared to make an exception in your case.'

Jack frowned at him, making everyone laugh and lightening the mood.

'Go and take your frustration out in the kitchen, Marcel,' Jack said, standing. 'Alexi and I are off out to dinner.'

Alexi needed to stop off at home for a shower and to change. She raised a brow but made no comment when Jack extracted a holdall from the car that contained clean clothes and toiletries. When they were both spruced up, they travelled the short distance to Fay's in Jack's car, stopping at the local off-licence to pick up some wine. Naturally, Cosmo tagged along.

'It's been too long,' Fay said, engulfing Jack in an expansive hug the moment she opened her door. She then repeated the process with Alexi. Cosmo didn't wait to be hugged but shot through the door ahead of everyone.

'It's great to see you too, Fay,' Jack said.

'Sorry about Cosmo's manners,' Alexi said as she watched her cat head straight for the kitchen. 'But given how good those smells are, I can't really blame him.'

Alexi handed her the flowers that Jack had picked up along with the wine. 'It seems a bit like coals to Newcastle,' she said.

'Nonsense, the garden is barren at this time of year so flowers for the house are especially welcome. Thank you. I shall put them in water at once.'

'And I'll open one of these,' Jack said, pointing to the carrier with two bottles of wine in it. 'I think we could all use a drink.'

Alexi still had trouble entering this cottage without shuddering. It was the place where Graham Fuller had cornered her and almost strangled her to death. But at least it had happened upstairs and Alexi didn't plan on going anywhere near the room in question. The lounge, on the other hand, was toasty, with a roaring log fire and thick curtains closed against the cold, winter's night. A table had been laid for three and Fay suggested eating at once.

'You could give Marcel a run for his money,' Alexi said, closing her eyes as Fay's wonderfully rich beef stew literally melted in her mouth.

'Nonsense! I can cook for a few people. But trying to juggle it so that a whole restaurant gets different things all at the same time is my idea of a nightmare. I can't imagine why anyone would willingly put themselves through that torture.'

'Me neither,' Alexi agreed. 'But then, there's no accounting for taste.'

They talked about general things while they ate, mostly Fay's new life and burgeoning business.

'With Christmas just around the corner,' she said, smiling, 'I'm getting lots of pre-orders for table arrangements and so forth. It's very kind of local people to give me the business.'

'But you've thrown yourself into village life,' Alexi said. 'Unlike me. Of course they'll support you.'

'The WI, flower-arranging clubs and church charities aren't your sort of thing,' Fay replied. 'Leave that to us oldies who have nothing better to amuse ourselves with.' She sent Jack a sparkling smile, as though she thought she knew precisely how he and Alexi were amusing themselves. Alexi shook her head at her.

'You're a wicked old matchmaker,' she said. 'Jack and I are simply friends.'

'Of course you are, dear,' she said, standing up to clear the plates. 'Who's for homemade strawberry shortcake?'

Cosmo meowed, even though he'd just consumed his own very large portion of stew. Alexi groaned. 'I think I love you, Fay.'

'Ah ha!' Jack flashed a wicked smile. 'Now I know where I'm going wrong.'

Fay laughed. 'Don't suppose you're used to rejection, Jack. It will do you good.'

Alexi shook a finger at her. 'Go and get the dessert and stop interfering, you annoying woman!'

While Fay was out of the room, Jack reached across the table and captured Alexi's hand. 'See,' he said smugly. 'Even Fay thinks we should be together.'

'You paid her to say that.'

'Actually, I didn't, but now that you mention it... ouch!'

Alexi, who'd just kicked him under the table, smiled serenely and said nothing. Now wasn't the time to tell Jack that she'd made her mind up.

'So, tell me all about the goings-on at Hopgood Hall.' Fay said later as they sat beside the fire with their coffee. 'I feel so sorry for poor Drew and Cheryl. They don't deserve this.'

'That's true,' Alexi replied.

She proceeded to tell Fay everything they knew and who they suspected.

'So poor Marcel is being made a scapegoat,' Fay said thoughtfully. 'How very unpleasant for him.'

'He's worried, Fay,' Alexi said, 'and frankly, so am I. For him, and for the future of Hopgood Hall. Tainted by association and all that. It's only a matter of time before details of Marcel's possible involvement leak out. These things always do and even if the police don't have enough to bring charges, it could be enough to kill off Marcel's career.'

'Yes, I can quite see that. It might help when they get the results of the DNA test on Juliette's foetus. The father is the most likely suspect, I should have thought.'

'We think Dakin killed her,' Alexi said, 'but haven't got a hope in hell of proving it, unless Cassie comes up with something incriminating in her background checks. Or, of course, if he proves to be the father of the baby.'

'Have all the men been asked to give DNA samples anyway?' Fay asked.

'A very good question,' Jack replied. 'And one that I didn't think to ask Vickery. I assume that they have but I'll make sure. And if anyone declined, it will arouse my suspicions.'

'What about the other contestants?' Fay asked. 'It sounds as though Juliette rubbed them all up the wrong way.'

'John is pretty much in the clear. He was in his room, on camera, for the entire period when Juliette was killed,' Jack explained. 'Greta was in the lounge, also on camera. Anton, on the other hand, was in and out.'

'We're going to try and talk to Anton sometime tomorrow,' Alexi said.

'We're going back to school as well,' Jack added.

'We are?' Alexi permitted her surprise to show. 'First I heard of it.'

'I meant to say. I rang the headmistress of Eversham School

today. She's been following the show and remembers both Greta and Juliette when they were pupils there. I thought she might be able to shed further light on the animosity between the two of them.'

'Doubt it,' Alexi replied. 'Teachers are usually the last ones to know what issues the kids have. Besides, Greta was under the camera's eye the entire time. She couldn't have done it.'

'Even so, there's something about their early relationship that's bugging me,' Jack said pensively. 'I've learned to follow my instincts, especially when I have bugger all else to go on. Mrs Bagshaw, the headmistress, can spare me fifteen minutes at eight-thirty in the morning.' He glanced at Alexi. 'Like you say, it's probably a waste of time, but do you fancy tagging along?'

'Sure. If nothing else, it might throw up more doubt about Marcel's involvement, which is what we're trying to do.' Alexi yawned, then apologised. 'It's been a long day.'

'Then get yourselves home. Sounds like you have an early start in the morning.'

'I hate to eat and run,' Alexi protested. 'At least let me help with the dishes.'

'Nonsense.' Cosmo, stretched full length in front of the fire, got up and stalked to the front door. 'How does he do that?'

'He's clever,' Alexi said in a proud tone that made Jack and Fay laugh.

'There's no denying that,' Fay agreed.

It took just a few minutes to drive back to Alexi's cottage. The temperature had dropped to zero and she huddled deeper into her sheepskin jacket, aware that the car's heater wouldn't get up to speed before they reached home.

As soon as she unlocked the door, Jack set to work banking up the fire. He must have been a pyromaniac in a previous life, Alexi decided, because he had it crackling away in no time flat.

'You're wasting your time,' she said.

'I thought I did a pretty decent job, all things considered.'

'Oh, you did.' She threw off her jacket and walked towards him in a deliberately provocative fashion. 'But it seems to me that since everyone, including Fay, thinks we're an item, we shouldn't miss out on the benefits.'

Hope flared in his eyes. 'You've decided?'

'Looks that way.'

Jack skewered her with a look. 'You sure?'

'Changed your mind, Maddox?'

'Hell no, but I don't want you to feel pressured.'

'Stop prevaricating. It's time to live up to the hype.'

With another of his devastating smiles, he closed the distance between them, pulled her into his arms and kissed her like a man with a point to prove.

'Do you know how often I've dreamed about doing that?' he asked in a husky voice when he finally let her up for air.

'Is that all you've dreamed of doing?'

'Hmm, it's a start.'

His hands roved up her sides, cupped the edges of her breasts and then travelled down again, finishing up on her backside as he pulled her against his erection.

'Come on,' he said, sounding suddenly like he was in a tearing hurry. 'Let's take this somewhere more comfortable.'

16

Jack woke early with a naked Alexis draped over his body. The wait had been beyond worth it. Having decided to take their relationship on a stage, Alexi didn't hold back and let him know what she wanted. Jack was more than happy to deliver.

He watched her as she slept, head rested on his shoulder, hair fanning out over his chest. Jack would have watched her indefinitely and then thought of an inventive way to wake her up if he'd had the luxury of time on his side. Unfortunately, he didn't. They needed to go into Reading and meet with Juliette's former headmistress. Mrs Bagshaw had, Jack suspected, only agreed to see him out of a morbid sense of curiosity and, perhaps, because she wanted to protect the reputation of her school. Jack was fairly sure it would be a waste of time and was tempted to cancel in favour of a prolonged lie-in. But lingering doubts about Juliette and Greta's early days endured, thus making the decision for him.

Sighing, he gently dislodged his shoulder from beneath Alexi's face. She mumbled something incoherent, turned over and continued to sleep. He'd take a quick shower, then wake her up with breakfast in bed. But first he had to remove the other obstacle preventing him from doing so.

Cosmo had taken issue with Jack usurping his usual spot next to Alexi and it was a while before Jack was able to establish the pecking order. Cosmo took umbrage, having been repeatedly ejected from the bed, and stalked off. Eventually, when they settled down to sleep, Cosmo deigned to join them, installing himself on Jack's feet and not moving.

'Come on, big guy.' Jack gently agitating the cat with his feet. 'Time to start the day.'

Half an hour later Jack, fresh from the shower and Cosmo, who had also just completed his morning ablutions, returned to the bedroom with Alexi's breakfast. She sat up when the door opened, adorably dishevelled as she blinked sleep from her eyes. She pushed tangled hair off her face and stroked Cosmo, who had jumped onto the bed and nudged her with his big head.

'Morning, sleepyhead.' Jack put the tray on the side table and leaned in for a prolonged kiss.

'Morning yourself. What time is it?'

'Half seven.'

'You're lying. We only just went to bed.'

Jack chortled. 'Time flies when you're having fun.'

'You smell all fresh and nice.' She made it sound like an accusation. 'How long have you been up?'

'A while.' He examined her face, trying to read her expression, but it gave nothing away. 'You okay?'

She sent him a somnolent smile. 'Feeling pretty good, for someone who's had no sleep.'

'No regrets?' Jack smiled at her. 'Just so you know, I don't do one-night stands. Last night was, I hope, the first of many that we'll spend together.'

She nodded, looking relieved. 'Let's talk about it after we've found Juliette's killer.'

He tweaked her nose. 'It's a date.'

She stifled a yawn with the back of her hand. 'Is that coffee I can smell?'

'And scrambled eggs and bacon.'

She shuffled into a sitting position. 'Carry on this way and I'll have to turn sideways to walk through the door.'

'Do you always talk so much first thing?' he asked, chuckling and pinching a piece of her bacon. She slapped his fingers.

'Only when I'm nervous.'

'Darling, you have absolutely nothing to be nervous about. Now come on, eat up. Then hit the shower. We need to get going.'

By eight o'clock they were on the road but got caught up in the inevitable morning traffic. They made it to Arborfield with a couple of minutes to spare before their appointment with Mrs Bagshaw.

'Some place,' Alexi remarked as Jack drove slowly through tall, wrought-iron gates with the name of the school emblazoned above them in a high arch. 'Must cost parents a few bob to send their little darlings here.'

'If you need to ask, you can't afford it.'

'Kids are an expensive luxury, especially if you want them to have the best of everything. Makes you wonder why people have so many of them.'

'Not thinking in terms of motherhood yourself?'

'I never have but I will admit that being around little Verity has made me a bit broody. Don't worry, the mood will pass.'

Jack sent her a prolonged sideways look before returning his attention to the road. 'I wasn't worried. Just curious.'

'Anyway, let's think about Mrs Bagshaw and what we plan to ask her.'

Jack glanced at the bare, frost-covered branches of trees leading to the banks of the river; a boat house visible, a few hardy aquatic fowl paddling miserably about in the shallows. Why did he imagine they were miserable? They were ducks. Paddling about in freezing water was what they did. He chuckled to himself at the quixotic nature of his thoughts as they drove on past manicured playing fields, tennis courts and what was obviously a gymnasium. A few track-suited girls were doing circuits of the running track. The whole school took up a fraction of what used to be one family's private estate. A steady stream of expensive cars, some driven by chauffeurs no less, came the other way, presumably having dropped kids off.

'They don't board here?' Alexi asked.

'Nope. It's a girls' day school.'

Jack found the car park and slotted his vehicle into a vacant spot. Cosmo barely stirred, knowing, as he always seemed to, that he wouldn't be getting out with them. He opened one eye just long enough to watch them leave the car, then continued sleeping off his breakfast.

Jack asked directions from the teacher at the door who was checking the kids in and was pointed in the direction of Mrs Bagshaw's office. They made their way down a long corridor, passing gaggles of girls in uniform who talked and giggled, swapping secrets and details of personal dramas in the manner of girls the world over.

When they arrived at their destination, they were told by the head mistress's secretary that they were expected and could go straight in.

Mrs Bagshaw was an elegant woman in her fifties or older, wearing a grey, tailored suit, her hair styled in a neat bob. She stood up from behind an imposing desk and came around it to offer them her hand. Jack made the introductions.

'Thank you for seeing us,' he said.

'I'll admit that curiosity got the better of me.' She turned her attention to Alexi. 'And I had an ulterior motive. I wanted to meet Ms Ellis. I admire your work. It's a refreshing change nowadays to meet a journalist who bothers to check her facts and doesn't compromise her standards.'

'Thank you.'

'I was rather hoping that I could persuade you, Ms Ellis, to come and talk to some of our sixth form about the challenges and rewards in your profession.' she said, motioning them to a comfortable arrangement of upholstered chairs in one corner of her spacious office.

'Please call me Alexi, and I'd be glad to do that,' Alexi replied, looking to Jack as though she shared his initial impression of Mrs Bagshaw, which was favourable. 'But I ought to warn you, I won't sugar coat it, and will possibly deter any wannabe journalists by telling it like it is. The industry has changed beyond recognition, and not necessarily for the better.'

'I think they'd prefer to know the truth.' Mrs Bagshaw smiled at them both and then sat a little straighter, all business again. 'Now, how can I help you? You said this was about Juliette Hammond and Greta Reid. I was horrified to hear about what happened to Juliette.'

'We all were,' Alexi replied with feeling.

'She was not always easy to handle, not even as a child, but she didn't deserve that.'

'No,' Jack agreed, nodding. 'Nobody does.'

'I've been watching the show and have to say I was surprised to see not one but two of my former pupils taking part. I assumed it would only be a matter of time before the girls started talking on camera about their time here. I don't mind admitting that I was anxious about what they might have to say.'

'I gather there was some animosity between them when they were here,' Jack said. 'That would account for your anxiety.'

Mrs Bagshaw took a moment to consider her response. '90 per cent of our girls come from families who can afford the fees, which means we get a pretty mixed bag of abilities. Greta won a scholarship and remains in my memory as one of *the* most intelligent girls it has been my pleasure to teach. My career spans over thirty years so that's saying something. But there was something special about Greta. Not only did she have a sharp mind and retentive memory, but she also *wanted* to learn everything we could teach her. It was as though she knew what an opportunity she'd been given and had no intention of squandering it.'

'I imagine the scholarship kids don't speak the same language as the majority of pupils here,' Alexi said.

'Same language, different accent,' Mrs Bagshaw replied.

Jack smiled. He already knew that much, having overheard the upper-class accents in that corridor.

'Several of our scholarship students have left because they couldn't settle, preferring the local comprehensive where they fit in better. We have a no bullying policy here but I'm not so naïve as to imagine it doesn't take place. Think back to your own school days. Anyone who didn't fit in was a victim of some sort of discrimination. Greta was different, though. She didn't seem to mind that she didn't go to hunt balls or get into the members' enclosure at Royal Ascot—'

'You're joking,' Jack muttered.

'Barely.' Mrs Bagshaw sighed. 'Anyway, Greta was keen to learn and made no effort to ingratiate herself with the wealthier students. Juliette, I believe, befriended her, not the other way around.'

'Because she wanted something from her?' Alexi suggested.

'Almost certainly. Juliette, and many others like her who pass through this establishment, are adept at using charm and guile to get what they want. Anyway, I'm absolutely certain that Greta helped Juliette with her home assignments in return for being accepted by Juliette's inner circle.'

'You didn't try to stop Juliette getting outside help with her work?' Jack asked.

Mrs Bagshaw looked amused by the suggestion. 'It would be like trying to halt a tidal wave. If they don't crib from other students, they rely on the internet. Such are the times we live in. Fortunately, when it comes to exams, they have to rely on their own brainpower, or lack thereof.' Mrs Bagshaw paused, appearing to measure her words. 'You must understand that students who attend this establishment and others like it expect, if you like, to obtain a certain degree of proficiency in whatever skills they happen to possess. Juliette adored cooking and was very good at it. She was also a good sportswoman; tennis, hockey and skiing were her forte. But when it came to intellectual pursuits... Well, let's just say that Oxbridge wasn't likely to come knocking at her door any time soon.'

'It must sometimes be dispiriting, being aware the parents don't expect you to push your charges.'

'Every so often one like Greta comes along, which makes it worthwhile. As for girls like Juliette, she would get preferential treatment in the job market, if she applied for something within her capabilities like reception work or in the PR field, simply because of her background.' Mrs Bagshaw was clearly pragmatic, Jack thought. 'That's simply the way the world works. Unfair perhaps, but we have to do the best we can, working within the limitations of the system.'

'You say Greta and Juliette were tight. When did that situation change?' Alexi asked.

'During Greta's final year with us. Juliette was one year below. And before you ask, I have absolutely no idea why.'

Jack nodded, thinking of their fight over the gardener's assistant; not something they were likely to share with their headmistress. Even in an establishment where money appeared to purchase a fair degree of behavioural latitude, having sex with the hired help would most likely be frowned upon and result in expulsion.

'Greta was reasonably nice looking when she was here,' Mrs Bagshaw remarked.

She picked up a year book and showed them a head and shoulders shot of Greta. Her face was a lot thinner than now, her optimistic expression typical of the young and idealistic who were convinced they could change the world. Her hair was arguably her best feature, Jack thought, as he studied her image. It was held back in a ponytail which she'd dragged over one shoulder when the picture had been taken. There was a class shot as well. Jack picked out Greta immediately.

'Yes, she was a nice-looking girl,' Alexi agreed. 'She still is.'

'Juliette was a class apart, of course.' Mrs Bagshaw swapped to another year book and showed them Juliette's picture. 'And she knew it,' she added, screwing up her nose.

'You didn't like her?' Jack asked.

'Most of my fee-paying students have a high opinion of themselves. They're brought up to think themselves better than their company, so to speak. Juliette was an extreme example of that attitude. Life definitely owed her a living.'

'Wow!' Alexi shook her head as she looked at the picture of a young Juliette. 'Such a waste.'

'I agree. I might not have liked her attitude but she didn't deserve to die.' Mrs Bagshaw sighed. 'Who does? Especially that young.'

'All we can do for her now is to try and find out who killed her, and why,' Jack said.

Mrs Bagshaw looked startled. 'Surely that's a job for the police.'

'Alexi has a business interest in the hotel where the competition is being filmed. Naturally, she doesn't want a stigma attaching to the place, especially since it's owned by friends of hers.'

'I understand.' Mrs Bagshaw nodded. 'If the police don't find the killer, rumours start and word of mouth could kill the hotel's trade.'

'Precisely.' It was Alexi's turn to nod. 'With that in mind, can you think of anything between Greta and Juliette when they were here that might have come to a head when they were unexpectedly thrown together on that show?'

Mrs Bagshaw shook her head. 'Even if there was, Greta isn't capable of murder.'

'I'm sure she isn't,' Jack said smoothly, thinking that anyone was capable of killing, given sufficient provocation. 'We're simply trying to build up a better picture of Juliette. We need to understand her and what was going on in her life.'

'I have been thinking about both girls ever since I saw they were in the competition.' Mrs Bagshaw said. 'There was an incident, shortly before Greta left, although I can't see what help it would be to you. Anyway, Greta appeared at school with her hair shorn to within an inch of her scalp. All her teachers were astounded. She was inordinately proud of her hair and it was obvious the alteration wasn't something she'd decided upon herself.' She frowned pensively. 'I tried hard to get to the bottom of her problem since it was obvious something was amiss but she wouldn't talk to me about it. I always felt it was something to do with her and Juliette. They were at daggers drawn after that. They couldn't be in the same room without the most awful atmosphere prevailing. I've never known hostility like it. Needless to say, Juliette had most of the school on her side in whatever the dispute was about and poor Greta was left friendless.'

'What did you do about it?' Alexi asked.

'What could I do?' Mrs Bagshaw's expression became stoic. 'Greta hadn't lodged a complaint and wouldn't have thanked me for stepping in. That would make it appear as though she'd come tattling to me, which would have made matters worse for her. I tried asking a few discreet questions but was met with a wall of silence. Other matters took my attention and in the end, I gave up. There is only so much I can do without seeming like an interfering busybody.'

'I see.' Jack thought of something else. 'You had a team of people caring for the grounds back then. Can you remember the name of the company?'

'Good heavens, whatever does that have to do with anything?'

'It probably doesn't but Greta mentioned them in passing. I just wondered if—'

'Well, if it's important, I can tell you they're called Wright Land-scaping. We still use them. They're based in Reading and are in the phone book, or my secretary can give you their number, if you want to talk to them. I can't think why you should but...'

They talked for a little longer but other than reinforcing her admiration for Greta's intelligence and barely concealing her contempt for Juliette, Mrs Bagshaw had nothing more of interest to tell them.

'It's been very pleasant meeting you both,' she said, glancing at her watch and standing up. 'But now you really must excuse me. I don't think I can tell you anything else that will help you and I have another meeting.'

'Of course,' Jack replied. 'Thanks for making time for us.'

'Here's my card,' Alexi said, producing one from her bag and handing it to Mrs Bagshaw. 'Give me a call if you're serious about that talk and we'll fix something up.'

'That's very kind of you.' Mrs Bagshaw walked them to the door.

'Do let me know if anything develops; especially if it has any bearing on this establishment. Not that I can see how it would, but I have my governors to answer to.'

Jack and Alexi said their goodbyes and made their way back to Jack's car. When they climbed into it, Cosmo fixed them with an accusatory look, a bit like a peeved father demanding to know what had taken so long. Alexi reached across to smooth his head, which Cosmo took as an invitation to jump over the back of her seat and land on her lap with, given his size, a surprisingly soft thud.

'I wonder what happened to Greta's hair,' Alexi said pensively a short time later. 'Could it be significant, do you suppose? It's clear to me that she's proud of her hair today, so she would have been back then too and was hardly like to chop it all off.'

'That is a very good question,' Jack replied, subsiding into deep thought. 'I suppose we could ask her.'

'We could, but would she give us an honest answer? Besides, she'll know that we've been here asking questions and that might put her back up.'

'True enough.' Jack paused to let a gaggle of girls cross the road in front of him. 'Let's play it by ear.'

'You think Mrs Bagshaw thought the incident with the hair was important?'

'I do. She mentioned it to us for a reason. It's clearly been bugging her. I liked Mrs Bagshaw. She seems genuinely invested in her students' wellbeing, as well as for the reputation of her school, obviously. Anyway, let's get back and see what developments there have been.'

17

Alexi's head was full of unanswered questions, and not just about their interview with Mrs Bagshaw. She really shouldn't be thinking about her night of passion with Jack at such a time. But, selfish, shallow creature that she was, she couldn't seem to focus her mind on much else. Alexi was hooked, her lingering doubts well and truly eradicated and she wanted to know where they went from there.

But now wasn't the time to ask. They had a murderer to expose first or, at the very least, the interests of Hopgood Hall and its temperamental chef to protect. Besides, Jack had been unnaturally quiet for the drive back to Lambourn. Her head told her he was deep in thought about something Mrs Bagshaw had said. Something that hadn't registered with her but had lodged itself in his quick brain.

'What next?' she asked, as Jack turned his car into Hopgood Hall's car park.

Jack glanced at the dashboard clock. 'It might be a good moment to catch Anton.' Alexi checked the time too. It was ten-thirty.

'Yeah, that ought to work.' She released her seatbelt. Cosmo leapt from her lap the moment she opened the door and disappeared around the side of the hotel to patrol his territory. 'They're not due in the kitchen for another half-hour.'

'I'll catch you up in a minute,' Jack said, branching off for the stairs. 'I need to check in with Cassie and make a couple of calls. I'll only be a few minutes.' He touched her backside briefly and dropped a kiss on the top of her head. 'Don't start without me,' he said in a provocative drawl.

'I'll see if I can get Anton to come up to the house,' she said. 'He'll never open up if we talk to him in the annexe with the cameras rolling.'

'Good thinking.'

Cheryl was in the kitchen alone, rocking the baby in her arms. She took one look at Alexi and her face broke out with a broad smile.

'About time,' she said smugly.

'For what?' Alexi asked, feigning ignorance as she headed straight for the coffee pot.

'Ha, like your face doesn't tell its own story. You look like a lady who's been lit up from inside and there's only one activity I know of that creates that sort of look. How was it?'

Alexi took a seat and couldn't help grinning right back. 'Well worth waiting for.'

'But?' Cheryl peered at her intently. 'You're having doubts.'

'Not doubts precisely.' Alexi blew on the surface of her coffee and took a cautious sip.

'I'm well aware that you're wary but Jack isn't another Patrick. Not all men are selfish jerks. Anyway, we don't live in the dark ages any more. If it proves to have been a mistake, you could just go your separate ways and chalk it up to experience. Might be a bit awkward, what with you working this case together, but still—'

'Yeah, you're right. I'm overanalysing, as usual.' Alexi grinned. 'Blame it on my occupation. I never take anything at face value because things are seldom that straightforward. I'm always on the lookout for hidden agendas.'

'Jack's not-so-hidden agenda has been to get it on with you. It was obvious when you worked the Parker case. You were the only one who didn't seem to notice.' Cheryl smoothed the now sleeping baby's downy head. 'I'm glad you took the plunge. You've been a man-free zone for quite long enough and Jack is just the guy to break the drought with.'

'He's made a few oblique remarks about a relationship.'

'There you go.' Cheryl looked smug. 'Told you he had morals.'

'Who has?' Drew asked, coming in the back door and rubbing his hands together. If he didn't dress in T-shirts and go coatless as if it was the middle of summer, he might not feel so cold, Alexi thought.

'Just the man I was looking for,' Alexi said, adroitly changing the subject. 'Before you get warm, you wouldn't pop over to the annexe and ask Anton if he could spare me a moment, would you? Jack and I thought we'd take the opportunity to have a word with him about that money he borrowed.'

'I live to serve,' Drew said, sending her a little salute and disappearing again.

'How's Marcel?' Alexi asked while they waited.

'He's driving himself crazy, trying to think how his fingerprint got on that bedside cabinet. Some of the weird theories he's come up with defy belief.' Cheryl sighed. 'I never thought I'd say this but being subdued doesn't suit Marcel. I'd even welcome a few of his famous tantrums right now.'

'Don't give up hope yet,' Alexi said, realising how worried Cheryl must be about the future of the hotel. Alexi only had a small investment in it which she could afford to lose. To Drew and

Cheryl, it was their everything. 'We both know Marcel didn't do this and somehow we'll find a way to prove it.' Alexi wondered if she was making promises she wouldn't be in a position to keep. 'You'll see.'

'Did you learn anything at that school to help you?'

Alexi frowned. 'I think so, but I'm not sure what to make of it.'

Alexi told Cheryl all about the bad blood between the girls, brought on by Juliette stealing the gardener from Greta: something she hadn't shared with her before.

'Blimey,' Cheryl said, looking taken aback. 'What do you make of all that?'

'I'm not sure what to make of it, whether it's relevant to her death—'

Cheryl widened her eyes. 'You think Greta killed her?'

'I haven't ruled anyone out but if it was Greta then I don't see how it was done.' She sighed. 'Her camera feed wasn't switched off. It's so damned frustrating.'

'I have an ideal cure for frustration,' Jack said, grinning as he joined them.

'I'll just bet you have,' Cheryl replied, ignoring Alexi's scowl.

Anton and Drew came through the back door at that moment, rubbing their hands against the cold. Drew and Cheryl beat a hasty retreat whilst Anton took a seat at the table, looking uncomfortable.

'Are you about to get the thumbscrews out?' he asked.

'Actually, I was going to ask you both if you'd like coffee,' Alexi said, thinking how much she liked Anton and how much she hoped he wasn't the guilty party. She needed to keep an open mind but if he had a plausible explanation for the loan then she would give him the benefit of the doubt. 'But I can do thumbscrews if you'd prefer. With or without sugar?'

Anton chuckled. 'Coffee, mon.'

'How's the atmosphere over there?' Jack asked, pointing a thumb over his shoulder in the direction of the annexe.

'Pretty grim. None of our hearts are really in the competition any more but we all still want to win.' He waggled a hand from side to side. 'Kinda contradictory, I know, and it makes me mad as hell that I can't find the fire that got me this far. Juliette would laugh her head off if she thought her death had affected our commitment.'

'She would achieve in death that which she tried to do while breathing,' Alexi said. 'Which was to rig the result.'

'Other than winning it herself then yeah, she'd settle for upsetting the applecart.' Anton stretched his long legs out in front of him and laced his fingers behind his head. 'We have Paul Dakin all over us, overdoing the sentimental "let's make it work for Juliette" angle. It's sickening to see him. But do you know what the worst part about it is?'

Jack and Alexi shook their heads simultaneously.

'Well, I figure all the viewers will lap up that shit.'

'Very likely,' Jack agreed.

'Personally, I hate public outpourings of grief, so even if I was grieving, I'd do it in private.'

'What are you saying amongst yourselves?' Alexi asked. 'You, Greta and John. I know you do have moments when you can speak off camera and you wouldn't be human if you didn't have theories of your own about why Juliette died and at whose hand.'

'We have no idea who killed Juliette, and that's the God's honest truth. Trust me, if I had even a suspicion, I'd tell you or Vickery. Our problem is that too many people seemed to dislike her for us to be able to draw up a shortlist.' He straightened up in his chair and leaned forward on his elbows. 'But one thing we do know. It wasn't Marcel. He's been set up.'

'Agreed,' Alexi said. 'I know he's your hero but how can you be so sure?'

'His knife, that glass... it's all too obvious.'

'You disliked Juliette,' Jack pointed out. 'So your name would have to be on any shortlist. Greta's and John's too for that matter.'

'Yeah.' He raked a hand over his dreadlocks. 'Point taken.'

'Perhaps you all did it,' Jack said, not sounding as though he was joking.

'I almost wish we had, mon,' Anton replied. 'But if I went about bumping off everyone I disliked, I could patent my solution to world over-population.'

'In other words, you had no motive,' Jack said.

He flashed his teeth. 'Right.'

'Tell us about your run in with Juliette,' Alexi said softly.

'Incriminate myself, you mean?' Anton shook his head. 'I ain't stupid.'

'Look, the police know about all that money you borrowed,' Jack told him.

Alexi noticed tension ripple through Anton's previously relaxed pose. 'Shit!' he said softly.

'Juliette's father did background checks on all the opposition,' Jack said, 'presumably so Juliette would have leverage against them. Knowing what we do about her character, it's a stretch to believe she didn't use it. We had to pass that information on to the police.'

'They haven't talked to me about it yet,' Anton replied gloomily. 'But I guess I can expect to be hauled in again.'

Alexi was surprised it hadn't happened already. Did that mean they'd already decided they had their man in Marcel or were they busy working other leads?

'Talk to us about it,' Jack said. 'We don't think you killed her but there are gaps in the camera footage, which means you had the opportunity. Now the police might think you also had a motive. But we can help you if you tell us the truth. Why were you desperate enough to borrow money from such dodgy people?'

Anton sighed. 'Juliette was a right madam!' he said savagely. 'She was all over John, getting him so worked up he couldn't think straight, right before we had to cook off against each other. She knew precisely what she'd done to the poor guy. I tried to warn him but he told me I was jealous and to leave him be. Juliette appreciated his finer qualities and he had a date with her.' Anton shook his head. 'Like that was gonna happen, mon.'

'We know it didn't,' Alexi said, 'and that John feels like a prize fool. But we don't think he killed her over it.'

'Nah, he doesn't have it in him.'

'What about Greta?' Jack asked.

'She lived in fear about the scathing things Juliette would probably say on camera about their schooldays, putting Greta down and saying how she only fitted in thanks to Juliette. Greta was frustrated because she couldn't tell the truth. I dunno what the truth actually was, but I dare say Juliette's scheming somehow made life uncomfortable for Greta when she was no longer of use to Juliette. It's just the sort of thing a user like Juliette would do.'

'Did she talk to you about that loan?' Alexi asked.

'Oh yeah. Couldn't wait to tell me she knew all about it and that she'd make sure it got me thrown off the show if I didn't cock up my dishes.'

'How did you respond?' Jack asked.

'I laughed in her face. Told her to do her worst.'

'Not the reaction she was expecting,' Alexi said, thinking that she hadn't expected it either.

Anton shared a look between her and Jack. 'She couldn't do anything to hurt me. There's no law against borrowing from a loan shark and I was rather looking forward to her mentioning the subject on camera.'

'You were?' Alexi glanced at Jack. 'Why?'

'So I could put her in her place.' Anton rubbed his face in his hands. 'My grandma taught me good values, kept me on the straight and narrow. I owe her everything.'

'What happened to your parents?' Alexi asked.

He shrugged. 'My ma buggered off when I was little, left me with Gran, my father's mother. My dad was a musician. A calypso god in Trinidadian terms, especially at carnival time. He went off to America in search of fame and fortune but was killed in some gangland fight that he wasn't part of. Wrong place at the wrong time and all that. Gran was persuaded by a Miami-based lawyer to seek compensation for the loss of her son and received a decent sum when the case was settled out of court. Most of it is invested and she can't get her hands on it for another few months. But she needed to go to Miami for a hip replacement operation. She said she'd wait but I wasn't having that. She was in constant pain and I wasn't willing to let her suffer when I could do something to prevent it.'

'So you borrowed the money to pay for the operation, aware that you can repay it in full when her investments mature,' Jack said, his concerned expression clearing.

Anton nodded. 'Right, but I was damned if I'd tell Juliette that. Let her make a fool of herself.' He spread his hands. 'She didn't understand the concept of playing fair so why should I stop her?'

'What you did for your Gran,' Alexi said, reaching out to touch his hand. 'That's the nicest thing I've ever heard.'

Anton shrugged, looking uncomfortable with the praise. 'Gran is the only family I have left. Families look out for each other. It's what they do.'

'How did you finish up in this country?' Jack asked.

'I won an all-Caribbean cookery contest for young talent which meant I could come to England to train with a London chef. Ha!' He barked a bitter laugh. 'Act as underpaid dog's body is what my great opportunity turned out to be. That's why I was so keen to get accepted onto this show and let the viewing public see what I could really do. But, the thing is, I wouldn't have known how to boil an egg if it weren't for Gran. She's the best cook I've ever known and she doesn't possess a single cook book. She's just instinctive; loves experimenting and got me hooked from an early age. If it weren't for her, I'd never be where I am now. I owe her everything. More than I could ever repay.'

'Well,' Jack said. 'You obviously didn't have any reason to kill Juliette.'

Anton drained his coffee and stood up. 'Right, if there's nothing else, I'd best get back to the grindstone.'

'Thanks for telling us, Anton, and I hope your gran will be okay,' Alexi said.

He smiled. 'Oh, she's doing great. She had her operation last week and is already up on her feet again.'

'I'm glad.'

'Me too.'

Anton let himself out of the back door and they watched through the window as he sauntered back to the annexe with his gangly gait, head bobbing as though keeping time with music only he could hear.

'He told us the truth, didn't he?' Alexi asked.

'It would be easy enough to check his story but I'll leave that to Vickery. I didn't see any of the obvious signs that he was lying.'

'I think he really was looking forward to showing Juliette up on camera.' Alexi smiled up at Jack. 'I don't blame him for that and am glad he's not the killer.'

'Which leaves us with Dakin, or possibly Gerry Salter,' Jack said, 'and so far Cassie hasn't come up with anything that will help us to prove that either of them did it.'

'Then what—'

'Knock, knock.' Mike poked his head around the back door. 'Can I come in?'

'Sure, Mike.' Alexi smiled at Drew's part-time helper. 'I didn't know you were due in again today.'

'No classes for me today so I thought I'd see if Drew needed me. I can always do with the cash.'

'This is Jack Maddox. Jack, this is Mike. He helps out here sometimes.'

The men shook hands.

'Any progress on the case? It's all over school that Marcel did it.'

'Damn!' Alexi muttered. 'On what basis?'

'Oh, you know how it is. Marcel's known to be tetchy so it has to be him.'

Alexi pulled a face.

'Personally, I like Marcel,' Mike said. 'He's all right. Of course, he gets impatient and loses his rag sometimes. Like that time when his new wine coolers got mixed up with other stuff on a delivery lorry. The first time around, the wrong ones had been delivered and he was pissed off about that. Wouldn't wait for me to find the new ones and bring them to him. He had to plough into the back of the lorry himself and look for them.'

Alexi and Jack shared a look. 'When was this, Mike?' Alexi asked. 'And what else was on the lorry?'

'I dunno off hand.' He scratched his head. 'Does it matter?'

'It could be vital. Try to think.'

'Well, we'd just finished painting the annexe and most of it was furniture for the—'

'Marcel touched the furniture?' Jack asked, an edge to his voice.

'Well yeah, he had to move it out the way in order to get to the back of the van.'

'Was it bedroom furniture?' Alexi asked, holding her breath as Mike took his sweet time thinking about it.

'Yeah, the smaller bits. Night tables, and stuff—'

'But the furniture came wrapped in protective plastic, I seem to recall,' Alexi said, her excitement dwindling.

'Yeah, but that stuff is so thin it's worse than useless. Grab something too hard and you put a finger straight through it.'

'Thank you, Mike!' Alexi was sorely tempted to kiss him. 'You have just fitted the final piece of the puzzle into place.'

Mike looked bewildered. 'Have I?'

Jack nodded. 'It would explain why there was only one print. I'd been wondering about that. If Marcel had touched the table, he wouldn't have done it with just one finger.'

'But if his finger broke through the plastic cover...' Alexi nodded. 'Vickery needs to know about this.'

'Indeed he does. Mike, did anyone else other than you see Marcel in the back of that lorry, moving the contents about?'

'Yeah, the lorry driver and his mate. They seemed a bit surprised that a chef in his kitchen whites would lower himself to do the donkey work so they'd probably remember.'

Jack pulled out his phone, got put through to Vickery and said he had a new witness he would want to talk to.

'Come on, Mike,' he said. 'You and I are going to take a trip into Reading.'

'What can I do while you're gone?' Alexi asked, taking Jack aside. 'We've cleared Marcel and Anton. We're almost certain John couldn't have done it and I can't think why Gerry would. My money's still on Dakin but how the hell do I prove it? There must be something we're missing.'

'We have a copy of the camera footage during the vital time period but haven't looked at it ourselves yet. Go through it and see if anything strikes you as being out of place. We ought to have gotten to it before now.' He smiled at her. 'Oh, and you might want to let Marcel know that he's off the hook as far as the fingerprint goes.'

'That will be a pleasure.'

Jack planted a quick – far too quick – kiss on her lips and disappeared with Mike.

Alexi shrugged back into her coat and wandered outside at a more leisurely pace. Cosmo had been outside with Toby ever since they'd got back and he appeared now, trotting behind Alexi as she headed for the restaurant's kitchen.

'You know better than that,' she told him, bending to tug on one of his flat ears. 'If you set one paw in Marcel's kitchen, you'll probably finish up as dish of the day.'

Cosmo meowed indignantly and beat a hasty retreat.

Smiling, Alexi let herself in through the back door. Marcel was busy instructing his regular kitchen help and the contestants in what was required for that day's lunch service. Standing back to listen, he sounded lacklustre to Alexi and most unlike his usual, forceful self. It was obvious from the expressions on the faces of contestants and minions alike that he was not inspiring them.

Marcel saw her standing there, told his people to get to work and came across to join her.

'News?' he asked. 'I only want to know if it's good.'

'It is. Do you remember when your wine coolers weren't delivered and turned up later in—'

'Shit, of course!' He picked Alexi up, swung her around and, to the obvious astonishment of the workforce, all of whom had stopped what they were doing to watch them, planted a sound kiss on her cheek. 'I was steamed up about the mix-up and insisted on inspecting the coolers on the lorry. Didn't want the ones that wouldn't fit delivered for a second time.'

'And you moved some of the small items on the lorry out of the way in order to get to them?'

Marcel growled. 'How could I have forgotten that?'

'Fortunately for you, Mike remembered. He's gone into Reading now with Jack to tell Vickery.'

'So whoever tried to frame me with my knife and that glass caught a lucky break with that fingerprint.' He folded his arms, scowling, and shouted something across the kitchen to Greta who had obviously done something to displease him. Alexi wondered how he could tell from such a distance. 'Any closer to knowing who it was?'

'We're working on it. The main thing is, you are looking less and less like a suspect.'

'Thanks, Alexi.' He groaned when he saw another of the contestants commit a culinary travesty. 'I'd better sort this lot out before what's left of my reputation gets put through the shredder.'

'Rather them than me,' Alexi said, shuddering but also feeling as though a great weight had been lifted from her shoulders. The murder *had* happened at Hopgood Hall, there was no escaping that fact, but at least it hadn't been committed by their celebrity chef. The guilty party, whoever it was, had to be an outsider and so with a bit of luck, the hotel's reputation would escape unscathed.

Marcel winked at her, looking more like his old self already. 'They love me really.'

'If you say so. Catch you later.'

18

Cheryl and Drew were both in their kitchen when Alexi returned.

'You'll be pleased to hear that Marcel is back in full tantrum mode,' she told them, throwing herself into a chair.

'How come?' Drew asked.

Alexi explained. 'Jack's taken Mike into Reading nick so he can tell Vickery.'

'Thank heavens!' Cheryl sank into a chair. 'I knew there had to be a logical explanation. He must be beyond relieved.'

'I wasn't here when the furniture was delivered,' Drew added. 'Otherwise I would have remembered.' He grinned. 'I mean, anything as out of the ordinary as Marcel helping to unload a delivery truck would have stuck in my mind.'

'I had no idea he'd done it,' Cheryl said. 'I had Mike organise the delivery but he didn't mention it.'

'I don't think Marcel went so far as to do any heavy lifting,' Alexi pointed out. 'Anyway, it might help, Drew, if you dig out the name of the company who delivered that furniture, just in case Vickery wants to speak with the driver to confirm Mike's account.'

'That I can do.'

'I'm glad it looks as though Marcel's in the clear,' Cheryl said, 'but it doesn't get us any closer to unmasking the identity of the real killer. Speaking of which, I don't suppose Anton's the guilty party?'

'Far from it.'

Alexi repeated the gist of Anton's reason for borrowing all that money.

'Aw, that's so sweet of him to care about his granny,' Cheryl said. 'I knew there was a reason why I liked him.'

'Nothing to do with his good looks, hunky body and killer smile then?' Drew asked with a smile of his own.

'We're not all that shallow,' Cheryl replied, trying not to laugh.

'Still,' Alexi mused, tilting her head to one side. 'They *are* factors that need to be taken into consideration, if I can be permitted to say so.'

'*You* can, since, unlike some I could name,' Drew said, pinioning his wife with a look of mock disapproval, 'you're not spoken for. Whoops, sorry, that's all changed, hasn't it?'

Alexi pushed herself to her feet. 'A situation which isn't likely to endure if Jack keeps on giving me all the *best* jobs.'

'Since when did anyone get you to do anything you didn't want to?' Cheryl asked. 'She's obviously got it bad, Drew.'

'Ha, much you know! I have to go through all the footage for the time of the murder, see if I can spot any anomalies.' Alexi grimaced. 'Lucky me.'

'Good luck with that,' Drew said.

'Want some help?' Cheryl asked.

'Nah. There's no need for both of us to lose the will to live.' Alexi poured herself yet more coffee, snagged a couple of Cheryl's homemade biscuits and headed for the door. 'If I survive this mind-numbingly boring assignment, I'll catch you both later.'

Alexi took her coffee up to the residents' lounge, where her laptop was set up. She had the footage that Jack downloaded and, with a weary sigh, settled down to watch. She tried hard to concentrate but it wasn't long before her eyes started to droop. She'd not had much sleep and watching people trying to act normally when they knew they were in the spotlight was akin to watching paint dry. Even Cosmo hadn't come in to see what she was doing. Talk about a fair-weather feline. She'd left the lounge door open, hoping for distractions from passers-by, but for the hour she'd been working, not a soul had used the corridor.

'I can't take much more of this,' she said aloud. 'There has got to be something.'

But Alexi knew the police experts would have been crawling all over it and had a much better eye for these things than she did. Surely, if there was something there, they would have found it by now? This was a massive waste of time. Even so, she persevered, wondering why Jack had insisted she do it. She thought how preoccupied he'd been on the drive back from the school. She refused to believe that was because he was having second thoughts about getting involved with her so it could only mean that an alternative possibility had occurred to him. Something he was hoping she'd hit on and independently corroborate.

Alexi blinked to clear her vision and continued with her task. She noted down the times and durations of Anton's absences from his room, even though she was confident he hadn't killed Juliette. Still, she knew very well that a competent defence lawyer would use those absences to point the finger of guilt at him as an alternative suspect.

Having completed Anton's tape, she transferred her attention to John's. The time stamp at the corner of the screen confirmed what she already knew; he hadn't left his room for the entire time period when Juliette had been killed.

Alexi leaned back, placed both hands on the small of her back and leaned into them, more convinced than ever that this was a waste of time. Still, she moved onto the footage of the residents' lounge in the annexe, already knowing what she would see. Greta with her feet tucked beneath her bum, lounged in a corner of a settee, reading a book. Alexi yawned, surprised that anyone could sit that still for two entire hours. Alexi liked to read as much as the next person and knew how easy it was to get lost in a good book, but Greta had made an art form out of being a couch potato.

Her eyes fluttered to a close. She'd been fighting sleep all the time she'd been watching the footage, and the three coffees she'd had that morning weren't up to the job of keeping her awake.

She glanced at her watch after what felt like a minute or two and swore. Over half an hour had elapsed. Good job she'd pressed the pause button on the footage, even though she didn't recall doing so, otherwise she'd have to start all over again.

Except she hadn't pressed pause, she realised, sitting a little straighter. She was still watching Greta in the same pose she'd been in when she'd nodded off. She knew because at that point, she had removed a foot from beneath her backside and scratched at the sole. She was doing exactly the same thing again now, even though the time stamp in the corner of the frame confirmed thirty minutes had elapsed.

Wide awake, Alexi ran the footage back and confirmed what she already knew.

'Bloody hell!' she said aloud, when there could be no further doubt. 'Someone fixed the tape to make it—'

'I knew you'd figure it out eventually.'

Alexi nearly jumped out of her skin. She'd been so absorbed in watching the tape that she hadn't heard anyone enter the room. How long had Greta been there? She was like a statue, leaning against the door jamb, observing Alexi with unnerving stillness, and had probably heard her reaction when the truth dawned.

Greta pushed herself away from the door and loomed over Alexi, causing her to momentarily panic. What the hell should she do now?

Her first reaction was to yell for help, but it was unlikely to be forthcoming. No one had passed this room, at least while Alexi had been awake. Cheryl and Drew were in the bowels of the house somewhere and would never hear her. Cosmo was nowhere to be seen. The only alternative was to dial 999 but something held Alexi back. In spite of the fact that Greta might be a cold-blooded killer, Alexi didn't feel afraid of her. She examined Greta's face for clues as to her state of mind and got the impression that she was more nervous than dangerous.

Greta might or might not have killed Juliette but she definitely knew way more about the crime than she'd so far admitted. That much was obvious. So many things were. Now. Jack had almost certainly cottoned on to Greta while they'd been at the school, hence the reason for his introspection on the drive back. Nice of him to share. Alexi decided against calling the cavalry. An underlying need to hear the truth before it got muddied by aggressive police and protective defence lawyers won the day.

'What's going on, Greta?' Alexi asked, surprised by how composed she sounded.

'You know, don't you?'

Alexi saw no point in prevaricating. 'Some of it, but I'd like to hear your side.'

'Come on, pick up your bag, we're going for a little ride.'

Now fear did kick in and her hand moved towards her mobile, sitting beside her laptop. 'What's wrong with talking here?'

'There's something you need to see.'

'Look, Greta, you're obviously involved in some way with Juliette's death so why would I voluntarily go anywhere alone with you?'

'I did not murder Juliette.' She met Alexi's gaze unflinchingly and Alexi believed her.

'But you know who did.'

'I know why she died, yes.'

'But didn't tell the police.'

She sent Alexi a scathing look. 'They would never understand.'

'But you think I will?'

'You're a journalist, a damned good one. I think you will come with me because your curiosity has got the better of you and because you can sense I'm no threat to your wellbeing.' She sighed. 'I just need to make you understand and that conversation needs to take place somewhere that'll make you see the whole picture that much more clearly.'

The obvious thing to do would be to stand her ground but Greta was right about one thing; Alexi's journalistic antennae were twitching. This was potentially the story of a lifetime *and* an opportunity to make things right for the hotel. Of course, there was a very real possibility that Greta wanted to take her somewhere quiet to... well, keep her permanently quiet, but Alexi still didn't feel afraid. She was either very stupid, very trusting or had good instincts.

'Jack knows,' she said. 'He told me to look at this footage again and that I'd see it for myself.'

Greta briefly lowered her head. 'Then the police will be here soon. We don't have much time. Do you want to hear this or not?'

'Let me just tell Drew and Cheryl we're going out for a while.'

'There's no time but keep your phone with you if it makes you feel safer.'

Greta scooped Alexi's phone from the desk and threw it into Alexi's bag, which she handed to her. Well, unless Greta was taking her somewhere outside of mobile phone coverage, she'd be okay, wouldn't she? Of course, half the places around here had dodgy reception but she'd take a chance. Greta seemed calm, rational, resigned to being caught, but Alexi also sensed a mild desperation about her. She needed to find out what was going on with her, what she or someone else had done to Juliette and why. Besides, one of the few favours Patrick had done Alexi was to insist that she took self-defence classes, given some of the questionable areas her pursuit of a good story led her to. Unless Greta had a gun, which Alexi doubted, then Alexi was confident she could defend herself if it came to it.

Where the hell was Cosmo? She would feel safer if he came along wherever they were going, Damned poser of a cat was probably still showing his better profile to the cameras.

'We'll go in your car, Alexi,' Greta said, leading the way out of the hotel.

* * *

Jack and Vickery chatted in the inspector's office, the latter having just watched as Mike gave his statement.

'We never would have pressed charges against Gasquet, even without proof of how that fingerprint got there,' Vickery said. 'But I'm glad we've cleared it up.'

'Nice of you to let me know,' Jack replied with a wry smile.

Vickery spread his hands. 'You know how it is. We had to go through the motions. Dakin is still our number-one suspect but so far, we've got nothing to connect him to the crime.'

'Other than him being at the hotel when he wasn't supposed to be and arguing with Juliette.'

'Yeah, apart from those inconsequential matters that could be explained away by a sharp defence barrister. We're still waiting for the DNA results to come in on Juliette's foetus. The lab's backed up just like always. Urgent means two weeks if you're lucky. Anyway, if

Dakin turns out to be the father then his fancy lawyers won't be able to protect him.'

'Couldn't have happened to a nicer guy.'

Vickery nodded emphatically. 'I hear you.'

Jack explained to Vickery what Anton had told them that morning about his loan.

'We were getting around to him later today. We'll still have to but it sounds as though he's in the clear.'

'Thought you would have spoken to him before now.'

'We had a double murder last night here in Reading.' Vickery rolled his eyes and Jack noticed how gaunt and tired he looked. 'Guess who got landed with that one.'

Jack sympathised with the detective's predicament. He remembered all too well the frustration he'd felt when too many crimes prevented him from investigating any of them as thoroughly as he'd have liked. It would suit Far Reach Productions just fine if Juliette's file finished up gathering dust at the bottom of someone's in tray. Memories would fade and they'd be able to put a spin on it that left them smelling of roses. And Jack was well aware that in spite of Marcel's innocence, a good PR team would have a field day with the circumstantial evidence that implicated him. His reputation would be in tatters. So too would that of the hotel.

'Not on my watch,' Jack muttered to himself.

Mike reappeared, having just signed his statement. He looked excited rather than apprehensive now that it was all over. His sallow complexion had gained some colour and the hunch had left his shoulders. Jack figured his role would get blown up with each telling but couldn't resent the kid his moment of glory.

'All set?' Jack clapped him on the back. 'Ready to go?'

'Sure.'

'Thanks for your help,' Vickery said.

'Any time.'

Jack listened with half an ear to Mike's excited chatter as he drove them back to Lambourn. What he really wanted to hear was his ring tone. He was waiting for a call back from Wright Landscaping. It came when he was five minutes away from Hopgood Hall.

'Mr Maddox. Ben Wright, we spoke earlier.'

'Yeah, thanks for getting back to me. Did you have a chance to check your records from ten years back?'

'That's why I'm calling.' They were on the speakerphone, Mike listening to every word, his eyes wide with curiosity. 'We had two part-time workers during that period. Students making a bit extra in their off time.'

'Do you have their names?' Jack asked, trying to curb his impatience.

'One was Crispin Fuller.' *Crispin?* 'The other was a chap by the name of Gerry Salter.'

'Where are we going?'

The two women walked through the entrance hall and down the hotel's front steps. There wasn't a soul in sight. It was too early for the bar to be open for the lunchtime trade and everyone connected to the contest would be in the kitchen at this hour. Which, of course, was where Greta ought to be.

'Won't you be missed in the kitchen?' Alexi asked.

'That hardly seems important now,' Greta replied, a note of regret in her voice. 'But I called to say I was feeling unwell, in case you're wondering.'

Alexi opened her car and slid behind the wheel. Greta climbed into the passenger side as Alexi jammed the key into the ignition and turned it. She stalled the engine twice before managing to engage reverse and back out of her space.

'Where to?' she asked.

'We're heading for Reading.'

She followed Greta's instructions, giving up on trying to make conversation when she received only monosyllabic responses. Alexi almost smiled when she found herself wondering if there was a correct line of small talk when passing the time of day with a possible murderer.

'Turn left here, then second right,' Greta said when they approached the outskirts of Reading and stopped at a red light.

Alexi found herself driving deeper and deeper into a confusing rabbit warren of streets on a rundown council estate. Fortunately, Greta appeared to know precisely where she was going. There were gangs of kids loitering about, watching her car's progress with expressions of deep suspicion. A smattering of women pushed prams. They looked like little more than kids themselves.

'Nice place,' she said.

'You have no idea.' Greta pointed to a house. 'Turn into this driveway.'

Alexi did so and cut the engine. It was a house that looked a little better kept than its neighbours. At least there wasn't a car up on bricks in the drive and there was no rubbish in the front garden. Someone had tried to make something of that garden, as evidenced by a few hardy shrubs that struggled against the odds to survive.

Alexi followed Greta from the car. Greta opened the door to the house with her own key and stood back so Alexi could enter it ahead of her. She paused, wondering anew about the wisdom of coming here. Perhaps this time her journalistic curiosity really would be the death of her. And yet she still got the impression that Greta was more nervous than dangerous. Alexi remembered her phone in her bag, reassured by the knowledge that help was the press of a button away.

Thus encouraged, she stepped directly into a living room that made her blink back her surprise. It was spotlessly clean and expensively and tastefully furnished.

'Not what you were expecting?' Greta asked, a challenging note in her voice.

'I'm not sure what I expected, Greta, or what this house has to do with Juliette's death.'

'Come through to the kitchen and I'll try to explain,' Greta said.

* * *

'Shit!' Jack thumped the steering wheel. 'I should have told her who I suspected was behind it and warned her.'

'Told what? Who?' Mike asked.

Jack ignored the younger man as he pressed the speed dial for Alexi. It went straight to voice mail and Jack left a terse message, asking Alexi to call him immediately.

'Damn!'

Rather than waste time ringing Drew, Jack concentrated on getting to Hopgood Hall in record time by running red lights. Needless to say, he was held up by a string of racehorses that seemed to take forever to get out of his way. One of them shied sideways all the way across the road and its jockey almost came to grief. Finally, the road was clear and Jack floored the accelerator, mindless of the speed limit and the possibility of encountering more horses.

He pulled into Hopgood Hall's car park with a squeal of tyres and saw Alexi's space was empty. He swore as he leapt from his vehicle and took the three front steps in one stride.

'Where's Alexi?' he asked, bursting into the kitchen and startling Cheryl.

'Upstairs, working on her computer.'

'Her car's gone.'

'Oh, is it? She said nothing to me and I didn't see her go out.' Cheryl's face paled. 'Is something wrong? You're worrying me, Jack.'

'Sorry, no time to explain. Where's Greta?'

'She'll be in Marcel's kitchen.'

Jack went out through the backdoor at a run. Cosmo was

loitering there and followed behind Jack with a pathetic meow. Jack burst into the kitchen, where full lunchtime service was underway. His heart lurched when he saw that Greta was missing. Gerry Salter was there though, monitoring the cameras. They were fixed, set to automatic, but he needed to be on hand to keep an eye on the feed in case anything went wrong. Jack ignored Marcel's inquiring look and grabbed Gerry's arm.

'Greta's got Alexi,' he said tersely.

'Oh, shit! I wondered... I thought, when Marcel said she'd phoned to say she was ill, but I couldn't get away.'

'Come on, we have to find them.'

'What the hell's going on?' Marcel asked.

Jack ignored him, glad that he didn't have to drag Gerry along. He'd taken a chance on Gerry Salter and had read him right. If Gerry and Greta really were in this together then Gerry wouldn't still be hanging around the production if he thought Greta had kidnapped Alexi. Explanations as to why he'd got involved in covering up Greta's crime would have to wait until they found Alexi.

'Where would she have taken her?' Jack asked as he and Gerry ran to Jack's car. Cosmo hopped in the moment Jack opened the door and occupied the back seat. 'We'll check Alexi's place first but if she's not there—'

'I doubt they will be. Greta has a council house in Reading. She feels more in control when she's on familiar turf.'

Jack had a dozen questions, even though most of the pieces had fallen into place during the visit to the school when he learned just how seriously humiliated Greta had been by Juliette's spiteful actions. He'd bet his last penny that Juliette had cut Greta's hair in retaliation for something. Greta took great pride in her hair. People with low self-esteem or poor body image often latched onto one good aspect of their appearance that they liked about themselves. Juliette had shattered Greta's pride in her hair only because she was spoiled and vindictive.

Jack wondered why Greta's parents hadn't done something to protect their daughter when they'd seen how upset she must have been. Perhaps Greta hadn't told them what had really happened. If the falling out with Juliette that resulted in her hair being forcibly hacked off was the result of a tussle over Gerry Salter's affections, she probably wouldn't have. It wasn't the sort of detail to share with one's parents, Jack supposed, even in this so-called enlightened age.

Jack called himself all sorts of an arrogant fool for not having warned Alexi of his suspicions.

'The camera footage at the time of the murder. You doctored it.'

It wasn't a question and Gerry simply nodded. 'I don't expect you to understand but I owed Greta. Juliette's death was an accident but if... when their history came out, no one would have believed it. Greta was desperate and needed my help. I'd let her down once. I couldn't do it again.'

'You and Greta, in the school grounds?'

'Yeah, you figured it out.'

'It seemed like a stretch but I obviously got it right.'

'What were the chances of Greta, Juliette and me being thrown together on this show?'

Jack had wondered the exact same thing. Careful not to jump to a conclusion that would fit the growing evidence against Greta and Gerry, Jack had asked for the name of the landscapers. They'd checked their records and his suspicions were confirmed. The three of them had indeed been thrown together on this show a decade after the incident at the school and Greta didn't have a forgiving nature, especially since Juliette hadn't changed and wasn't playing fair in the contest.

As predicted, there was no sign of Alexi's car at her cottage.

'Do you know where Greta's house is?' Jack asked curtly.

'Yeah, head for Reading. I'll direct you.'

He thought about calling Vickery. It was what he ought to do but he'd wait until he got to Greta's house before he made a decision. Greta had to be nervous and unstable but Jack had his doubts about her being a cold-blooded killer, an assumption borne out by Gerry's insistence earlier that Juliette's death had been an accident. The result of a scuffle, perhaps. Jack would find out but for now, it seemed unimportant. All that mattered was finding Alexi alive and unharmed. A heavy police presence might spook Greta if she felt cornered and Alexi would be directly in the firing line. Not a chance he was prepared to take. He tried Alexi's mobile and it went straight to voicemail again.

'She didn't kill Juliette, did she?' Jack asked.

'No.' Gerry shook his head. 'They argued, a scuffle broke out and Juliette fell. She hit her head. That's what killed her. It was an accident and I can prove it. I have it all on film.'

Jack took his eyes off the road for a moment and shot him an incredulous look. 'Then why the hell didn't you come forward and—'

'I often used to film stuff in the courtyard, just in case the producers needed more background material. The contestants tend to be less guarded if they don't actually know they're being filmed. That's how I started getting so much footage of Cosmo, when I was playing around with camera settings. The producers love it and told me to keep on going with the ad hoc stuff, especially Cosmo.'

Jack blasted past a row of cars at just over ninety. 'So you and Greta were an item when you worked on the grounds at Eversham School.'

'Yeah, Greta knew you'd figure it out if you went to the school.

We talked about it last night.' Gerry exhaled slowly. 'Our relation-ship was more than a case of teenage hormones, if that's what you're thinking. We were in love. Planned to move in together as soon as she finished school.'

Jack elevated one brow. 'Some love if you cheated on her with Juliette.'

'Hell, that wasn't supposed to happen! I've spent the past ten years regretting it and paying the price.' Gerry sighed. 'I mean, look at me. I'm no oil painting and find it hard to talk to women in social situations. Okay, I was a few pounds lighter back then and had more hair, but still nothing to write home about. But Greta and I... well, we hit it off from the word go. Young as we were, we both knew the score. She was out of place in that school and I was never going to make it as a film producer. We kept one another grounded. You don't have to be beautiful and popular, we discovered, to be happy with what you are. Not if you have someone to share it with.'

'Juliette,' Jack reminded him.

'Did you see what she looked like?'

Jack nodded.

'She was all over me one day, making jokes about meeting me in the potting shed later. I didn't take her seriously but when I got there, she was waiting for me and... well, it wasn't my finest hour, I'll admit that. But I was young, flattered and had testosterone flooding my bloodstream, like you do at that age. I wasn't daft enough to think it was anything other than a one-off. I figured perhaps the other girls had dared her, or something. You know what teenage girls are like. Anyway, Greta wasn't supposed to know and wouldn't have, if Juliette hadn't taken pleasure in making sure she caught us in the act.'

'She set you up?'

'Oh yeah, and ruined things between Greta and me. Greta

wouldn't speak to me after that but I've never been able to forget her. I've never stopped feeling bad about what I did to her, and never found anyone to measure up to her. I could use my position working on live TV to impress women. A lot of the guys do, but that's not what I'm about. I want women to like me for myself, not for what they think I can do for them.'

'You put yourself forward for this show when you heard Greta and Juliette had made the finals, I assume. It wasn't the coincidence that you implied earlier.'

Gerry nodded.

'You also knew they had unfinished business and that it would be a good opportunity to plead your case with Greta.'

'Right.' Gerry curled his upper lip. 'Greta recognised me immediately. We talked, I explained and she finally forgave me. Juliette, on the other hand, breezed past me like I didn't exist. Well, why would I for her? There was nothing I could do to help her win the show. She didn't remember me or my name. I don't think she ever knew my surname and I was glad about that. I figured if she did know who I was, she'd find some way to use my relationship with Greta to put Greta down on camera.'

'But you jeopardised Greta's chances just by being on the show and trusting to luck that Juliette had a bad memory.'

'Nah, I knew the chances of Juliette knowing me were practically nil. It was a risk worth taking just to get back with Greta again.'

Jack slowed his breakneck speed when they turned into the road Gerry indicated and he saw Alexi's distinctive Mini parked in a driveway. Several kids loitered around it, eyeing the hubcaps. Jack was glad that Cosmo had hitched a ride with him.

Jack stopped behind Alexi's car and thought for a moment. 'Do I need reinforcements?'

'No, best not. I don't think she'll do anything stupid. Especially not if I'm there to reassure her.'

'I'm relying on you,' Jack said. 'If anything's happened to Alexi, then...'

Jack let Cosmo out of the car and the cat instinctively went into guard mode. He arched his back and hissed at the kids, who rapidly retreated. Dreading what they might find inside the house, Jack was about to ask Gerry's advice on the best way to approach the situation. But Gerry took matters into his own hands by simply ringing the doorbell.

To Jack's utter astonishment, the door was opened by Alexi.

'Come on in,' she said. 'We wondered when you two would show up.'

* * *

Jack squeezed her hand. 'You okay?' he asked.

'You knew,' she replied accusingly. 'You might have warned me.'

'Sorry, I didn't anticipate this. I thought you'd be safe. We'll talk about it later. Where's Greta?'

'In the kitchen.'

Jack looked surprised when he saw that the two of them had been drinking tea and sharing a packet of chocolate digestives. Gerry went straight to Greta and hugged her.

'What have you done now?' he asked, shaking his head at her. 'I can't leave you alone for five minutes.'

'I told you they'd figure it out,' she said, sobbing into Gerry's shoulder.

'We always knew it was possible and agreed if it happened we'd tell the truth. You didn't need to kidnap anyone.'

'I didn't. Alexi agreed to come here with me.' Jack sent Alexi a look that told her he thought she was out of her mind. 'I figured that if she saw this place, understood a bit about how I was brought up, it might help her to see things my way.'

Gerry stroked her hair, which appeared to calm Greta. 'No harm done.' He paused as his gaze fell upon the antiseptic ointment and plasters on the table. 'Is there?'

'Just a silly accident that I had,' Alexi said, lifting her hand. 'I dropped a mug and cut my finger when I picked up the pieces. Greta helped me clean it up.'

'Let's have some more tea,' Gerry said, reaching for the kettle. 'Then we'll tell them everything, love.'

Alexi had already heard some of it from Greta and assumed Jack had been similarly enlightened by Gerry. They waited in uneasy silence for the kettle to boil. Jack squeezed her hand but Alexi already knew him well enough to sense that she was in for a right tongue-lashing when he got her alone. *Bring it on!* They might be an item but she was still very much her own person and made her own decisions. Besides, she had been right; Greta hadn't done anything the least bit threatening.

'My parents lived in this house all their working life,' Greta said a short time later, nursing a fresh mug of tea between both hands. 'That's what I wanted Alexi to understand and why I brought her here. Imagining sink housing estates and actually setting foot in them are two very different animals. Anyway, the point I'm trying to make is that it was hardly the most prepossessing start but I rose above it and went to that posh school every day from this address.'

'That must have made you stand out,' Jack said.

'Yeah, and I loved being different. Loved thinking I'd bucked the trend, thanks to my intelligence. Not many people from around these parts did. But I would have done way better if it hadn't been for bloody Juliette. She had everything. I had bugger all. I knew why she wanted to be my friend; I wasn't stupid. That was okay until I made a mistake one day when she and a crowd of her friends invited me to play a game with them. We all had to say what two things we most liked and what two things we most disliked about our respective appearances. I was spoiled for choice when it came to the dislike part but the like question was easy. My hair and my boobs.'

'You revealed your weaknesses,' Alexi said sympathetically, well able to recall similar schoolgirl games in which she had embarrassed herself by being too honest.

'Yes. I should have realised when Juliette frowned that I'd said the wrong thing. She had nice enough hair, but it was thin and wispy. And, in spite of the services of a series of Wonderbras, she was flat-chested.'

'Ah,' Jack said softly. 'The knife through the implant. I knew it had to be symbolic.'

'I also made the mistake of telling her about Gerry and me. A lot of the girls in her year had never had sex, much less done it on the school grounds. That was the ultimate in daring and I was the centre of attention for a while. Of course, she wasn't about to let me usurp her in that respect so she went after Gerry, simply because she could.' Greta scowled. 'Not content with having him, she made a point of letting me catch them together and then telling me all about it in minute detail.' Greta shook her head, tears streaming down her face. 'I was devastated. The one thing I had that meant something to me and she had to ruin it.'

'What did you do?' Jack asked.

'I pretended not to care, then sabotaged her history project. I was still doing her homework and deliberately put wrong facts into an essay. She had to write it out in her own handwriting so the errors ought to have been obvious, even to someone with her limited abilities. Of course, she didn't spot them and as a result, failed an important exam her dad expected her to pass. She blamed me and—'

'And cut off your hair,' Alexi said.

'Right.' Greta shuddered. 'They cornered me in the cloakroom. Three of her friends held me down and she wielded the scissors. I'll never forget the humiliation, or the way the four of them laughed themselves silly.'

'That was beyond cruel,' Alexi said, reaching out to touch Greta's hand.

Greta sighed. 'It was a long time ago.'

'Not so long that you've got past it,' Jack said. 'So how did you feel when you knew the two of you would be on live TV?'

'My first reaction was to withdraw. Then I thought, why the hell should I? It was a cruel coincidence but the naïve part of my brain thought she might have improved and would play fair.' She threw up her hands. 'Ha, like that would ever happen.'

'When Greta saw I was on the production team, I managed to convince her that what had happened between Juliette and me hadn't entirely been my fault.' Gerry looked sheepish. 'Of course, it was. I could have said no and have spent the past ten years wishing that I had.'

'I knew that at the time, but just couldn't forgive him.' She reached for Gerry's hand. 'But ten years on, I was willing to give it another go.'

'We soon knew Juliette wouldn't play fair,' Gerry said, taking up the story, 'so I promised Greta that I would monitor her movements. I could do that. No one notices the cameraman, especially a quiet one like me who keeps himself to himself. I knew she'd sneaked into Paul Dakin's room in the hotel several times but we weren't too worried about that. He was just the host. He didn't get to vote. But Greta was convinced it would only be a matter of time before she went after Marcel. To get to his apartment, she had to go through the courtyard. Each time she left the annexe, Greta sent me a text and I watched her through my camera.'

Greta nodded. 'I was furious when I heard she'd stayed in Marcel's apartment for an hour. It didn't take a genius to figure out what they'd been up to and I was determined to have it out with her once and for all. But before I could, Dakin found her in the courtyard. I think he realised where she'd been and they started arguing. He stormed off and it was my turn to go out and confront her. She laughed in my face when I took her to task about her underhand tactics. She said I ought to have learned by then that it was every man for himself... or every man for her. I was that angry, I got up in her face and she pushed me away. I pushed back, she fell and didn't get up.'

'I ran out to see if I could help, to cool tempers before it got even more out of hand,' Gerry said. 'But Juliette was dead. There was no pulse. Nothing we could do.'

'Except call the emergency services and report an accident,' Jack pointed out.

Greta nodded. 'It's what I should have done, I know that now but... oh, I don't know what came over me. All I can think is that I suffered a temporary bout of insanity. Once again, she'd screwed up my life but I was no longer a teenager out of my depth and comfort zone. I saw red and wanted to make a statement that only I would understand, I suppose. Lay the ghost of my past that had held me back for too long.' She wiped tears from her eyes with the back of her hand. 'Still, I shouldn't have involved Gerry in my stupid quest for revenge.'

'I wanted to be involved, love.' He stroked the fingers of the hand he was holding. 'All I've wanted for the past ten years is to be a part of your life. To make amends for hurting you.'

'That was it, you see. I've never been able to get past Juliette and what she did to me, for no other reason than that she was vindictive. What kids turn out to be in their adult lives is shaped by traumatic events that occur during their most impressionable years, I've always thought.' Greta looked resigned. 'That's not an excuse, by the way. Just an observation.'

Alexi nodded. 'I tend to agree with you,' she said, thinking about Natalie Parker and how her personal demons had ultimately driven her to her death.

'Have you seen where Juliette lived?' Greta asked, looking angry again rather than pensive.

Alexi and Jack both nodded.

'My parents were good, hardworking folk who did their best for me. They were that proud when I got into Eversham and told anyone who'd listen that I'd make something of myself. But, as you can see, I'm still stuck here. Dad died five years ago. Mum went last year. I was able to take over the tenancy—'

'And keep it nice,' Alexi added.

'I try. It's not easy around these parts. Burglaries never get investigated. It's virtually a police-free zone.' She shook her head. 'I know I sound like I'm making excuses, and perhaps that's what I'm doing. My point is, Juliette could have been anything she wanted to be, with Daddy's money to ease her path. I had to do it the hard way. I was no competition to her, but she put me down when I was at such an impressionable age and... well, I figured when I knew we'd be on the show together that we were both adults and I'd finally get to put it behind me. I needed closure and thought I could handle being near her. That we could be civilised. But, of course, I was being naïve. Nothing had changed with her *modus operandi*.'

'I do understand how it must have been for you, Greta, to have to revisit all those horrible memories,' Alexi said. 'Schoolgirls can be downright vicious. But what I don't get is why you tried to frame Marcel.'

'Don't you see?' Greta spread her hands as though it ought to be obvious. 'It was history repeating itself. I'd been prepared to give her the benefit of the doubt and let bygones be bygones. But she was still manipulating men to get what she wanted and when I saw her come out of Marcel's apartment and knew she'd used her wiles on him, it felt like my head was going to explode with anger. I was that mad I actually saw spots dance before my eyes and thought I was going to pass out. I've always thought people exaggerated when they said things like that. Now I know differently.'

'But why go to so much trouble to set Marcel up?' Alexi asked.

'I actually liked Marcel,' Greta replied. 'He can be a bit of a prima donna, but he's a great chef, passionate about food. I thought he'd keep it professional and judge us on our ability to cook. I also thought he had more sense than to fall for Juliette's conniving ways.' She shrugged. 'You'd think I'd know better than that by now. Anyway, it was a spur of the moment decision to make him suffer. Juliette was dead and I had seconds to decide how to play it. I persuaded Gerry to help me stage her to make it look like Marcel had done it.'

Jack frowned. 'By sticking Marcel's knife through Juliette's breast?'

'Yeah, I know, viewed in the cold light of day when I'm no longer in shock, it does seem vindictive, I suppose.' Greta appeared contrite. 'It's just that I wanted the world to know it wasn't only her smile that was false. As soon as I started thinking rationally again, I knew I'd been stupid and ought to tell the truth but I just kept thinking how pathetic it would make me look if I did. I mean, we all carry emotional baggage, but we're supposed to get over childish hang-ups when we become adults. I knew our pictures, mine and Juliette's, would have been flashed up side by side on TV screens. I'd come off second best, just like always, and Juliette would be painted as a kind kid who tried to befriend me. I mean, no one ever talks ill of the dead. Not even when they deserve it. Anyway, it would look to the world as though I was jealous of her and took the opportunity to grab revenge. I wasn't jealous. It was just her methods that got me so damned mad.'

'And the glass with Marcel's fingerprint?' Jack asked.

'I saw it on the side in the kitchen when I took his knife,' Greta replied. 'I knew it had to be his. No one else would dare to leave a dirty glass in his domain. I also knew charges wouldn't stick because Marcel *had* never been in her room. He wouldn't do that, even if he was tempted, because he knew about the cameras always being on. Anyway... well, I just wanted him to suffer for a while...'

'Charges might well have stuck when they found Marcel's print on that bedside table,' Alexi pointed out.

'We would have spoken up if he'd been charged,' Gerry said. 'We just hoped it wouldn't come to that and the case would go cold for lack of leads. Then we'd be in the clear.'

'It was stupid,' Greta said. 'I didn't think it through properly and I'm prepared to face the consequences. But just so we're clear, it was all my idea. Gerry tried to talk me out of it and only helped me because he still feels guilty about going with Juliette all those years ago.'

'What I don't get is why you persuaded Alexi to come here,' Jack said.

'Like I already said, I wanted her to see where I came from and understand why I'm still here. Besides, pride took over. I knew she knew, and I didn't want to be carted out of Hopgood Hall in hand-cuffs, in full view of the cameras. She has her phone. She could have called for help at any time.'

'You might have answered my calls then,' Jack muttered. 'I was going crazy.'

Alexi blinked. 'My phone didn't ring.'

'Oh, I turned it off when I put it in your bag,' Greta said, looking sheepish. 'Sorry. I didn't want any interruptions.'

Alexi grabbed her phone from her bag and switched it on. There were four missed calls from Jack and two from Cheryl.

'What will happen to us?' Gerry asked.

'Well,' Jack replied. 'I suggest you turn yourselves in to Vickery, tell him what you've just told us. If you have the accident on camera then there will be no murder charges.'

'Especially if Juliette struck the first blow. Or push,' Alexi added.

'She did,' Gerry said. 'It's clear as day on the footage.'

'Okay. You'll be charged with staging a crime, withholding evidence and wasting police time, most likely.'

Greta swallowed, her complexion sallow, eyes moist. 'Will I go to prison?'

'There are no guarantees,' Jack said. 'I'll get Ben Avery, a local solicitor, to go with you when you turn yourselves in. If you tell him your story first, show him the footage, he'll put up a good case for probation. But you did try to frame Marcel. It might not be so easy to talk your way out of that one.'

'Unless I can persuade Marcel not to make an issue out of that,' Alexi said.

'It's more a case of what the police try to do about Greta's wasting their time by misleading them,' Jack said. 'But again, we'll have to wait and see.'

'Thank you,' Greta said meekly. 'I've been a fool. As wicked and vindictive as Juliette in many ways. God, how could I have stooped to her level?' She dropped her head into her hands. 'But, if I had the time over again, I doubt that I would do things differently. That's how badly Juliette screwed up my life. My only regret is involving Gerry.'

'Stop beating yourself up, love.' Gerry squeezed her hand. 'We're in this together and there's nothing more to be said.'

'Let's all go back to Hopwood Hall, get Ben over, look at that footage and decide how to proceed,' Jack said. 'Vickery can wait until tomorrow.'

'Hope our cars are okay out there,' Alexi said. 'No offence.'

'None taken,' Greta replied.

'Don't worry,' Jack said, a protective arm wrapped around her shoulders. 'Cosmo's on guard duty.'

Alexi lay stretched full length on her sofa in front of a roaring log fire, her head resting in Jack's lap. Now mid-December, with Christmas fever at epidemic proportions, it had been two weeks since Greta and Gerry admitted to what they'd done. The show was continuing with three contestants. The papers were full of speculation about Greta's involvement in Juliette's demise. The winner of the contest would be announced during a Christmas Eve, feature-length special. Alexi's money was on Anton. Viewing figures had broken all records, what with the real-life drama surrounding the show competing with the contrived situations on screen.

Dakin was no longer the host and was hiding under a rock somewhere until the media interest in him abated. The DNA on Juliette's foetus had come back, proving that he was the father and the station had fired him. His wife, so rumour had it, was divorcing him and it would be a long time before the man's insincere face graced the small screen again.

'Wonder how the media discovered that Dakin had been arguing with Juliette minutes before she died, trying to force her into aborting his baby,' Alexi mused, a mischievous smile flirting with her lips.

'Thank goodness Gerry got that all on camera. He picked up sound as well as visual of his argument with Juliette. She'd asked Paul to come down, not for a roll in the hay but so she could tell him the glad tidings about the baby. Unfortunately for her, Paul was thinking of number one and wasn't overjoyed at the thought of impending parenthood.'

Alexi sniffed. 'Well, at least Juliette's determination to have the baby was one aspect of her character that a gossip-hungry public couldn't hang her out to dry for.'

'Yeah, the kid had her good points. You just had to dig deep to find them.'

Alexi scrunched up her features. 'How's Juliette's dad doing with Melody, by the way?'

'I spoke to Dean just yesterday. He's not happy about it, but he says his mother's a changed woman since Hammond came back into her life.'

'And he has a life of his own now?'

'Right.' Jack nodded. 'It's early days but Melody is now spending more time with Hammond than she is at home with Dean. Dean has reluctantly agreed to spend Christmas with Hammond. He says the old man has aged since the death of his daughter and he's hopeful that he and Melody will help one another heal.'

'Older and wiser,' Alexi said, reaching up to touch Jack's face. 'They deserve another chance and Dean deserves the opportunity to get the education he didn't have time for when he was his mum's carer.'

'Right. Hammond's already offered and I don't think Dean will look a gift horse in the mouth. Mind you, if Hammond thinks he can replace a daughter he could manipulate with a son of the same ilk, then he's in for a rude awakening.'

'Well, I'm glad that Dean's getting his chance.'

'And they say no good deed goes unpunished. In Dean's case, a bad deed for good reasons. His stealing from Cash Out has changed his life for the better.'

'At least Hopgood Hall and Marcel are cleared,' Alexi said, 'which is all that really matters to me.'

'Another example of morbid curiosity.' Jack leaned over to kiss her. 'Cheryl and Drew tell me they're over-subscribed for the Christmas and New Year period and have bookings well into next year.'

'We also have lots of enquiries for bookings on the annexe.' She sent him a cherubic smile. 'Who am I to deny these ghouls their five minutes of reflected glory? Only problem is, a lot of them have mentioned *His Lordship*.' She nodded towards Cosmo, stretched full length in front of the fire. 'They want to know if there will be photo opportunities. Can you imagine how that would go down?' Alexi shuddered. 'Blood will be spilled.'

'I doubt it. He likes being a celebrity. My money's on him behaving impeccably.'

'I admire your optimism.' She pulled a doubtful face and wriggled into a more comfortable position. 'Anyway, Marcel has promised us the best Christmas lunch in living memory to thank us for clearing his name.'

'He's not still being nice to people, is he?' Jack asked, feigning alarm. 'That goes completely against the grain.'

Alexi chuckled. 'Don't worry, he's back to shouting and throwing his weight about.'

'Normal service resumed then. Thank heavens for that.'

'What about Greta and Gerry?' Alexi asked. 'Any news from the CPS yet?'

'It looks like it will be probation for them both,' Jack replied. 'Ben Avery has arranged for Greta to talk to a shrink about the scars left by Juliette's treatment of her during their school years. The shrink's report will weigh heavily with the judge when it comes to sentencing. There's also the small matter of them turning themselves in voluntarily only a couple of days into the investigation due to "guilty consciences".' Jack made quote marks round the last two words with his fingers. 'But I could still throttle you for voluntarily going with her when you knew she was involved with Juliette's death.'

'Yeah well, once a journalist...'

'Alexi!'

'Honestly, Jack, you're always talking about your instincts. Well, in this situation, I used mine. I had my phone with me and just didn't sense any hostility in Greta. Besides, I can defend myself, especially against another woman.'

Jack snorted. 'Come at it whichever way you like, she covered up a death and tried to frame someone for murder. I still have nightmares when I think what she could have done to you.'

'Well, she didn't. Cut the girl some slack, Jack. She's had some bad breaks. We all have our demons and Greta hadn't been able to get past hers, until now.'

'Yeah, you're right.' She sensed some of the fight drain out of Jack. 'Anyway, going back to Vickery, once he got over his annoyance at having his time wasted, he's been sympathetic to Greta's cause. Besides, it looks good for him that he solved such a high-profile case, even if technically it was us that did it for him.'

'Why didn't the police notice that the tape had been doctored?'

Jack shrugged. 'Reduced resources. Some civilian watched it all, made sure the time stamps looked genuine and that was all the urgency it was given. The tech guys would have got to it eventually but they had other priorities.'

'Well, at least Greta and Gerry found each other again and Greta can finally put the past behind her.'

'I still have trouble with the fact that she tried to frame Marcel. That was downright wicked.'

'Yeah, but he was a bad boy for overstepping the mark with Juliette. As for Greta and Gerry, the media are clamouring for their story and I've promised to write it for them once their case has gone to court.'

'Which means they'll get public sympathy.'

'And, just so that you're aware, I shall make my story balanced and paint Juliette in a not entirely bad light. Just because she was a poor little rich girl doesn't mean she had it easy. I mean, we've both met her father.'

'True.' Jack stroked her hair. 'But do Greta and Gerry deserve public acclaim after what they did?'

'They are not career criminals, Jack. I honestly believe Greta was not entirely of sound mind when she staged Juliette's death and I have some sympathy for her. I did a feature on the long-term effects of bullying once and you wouldn't believe the scars it leaves. Anyway, everyone deserves a second chance.'

'Right, so we've solved the case and fixed Greta and Gerry's futures. That means you have no further excuses to delay making a decision about us.'

'What do you have in mind?'

Jack's expression turned serious. 'I want to be a full-time presence in your life, Alexi. No half measures.'

Alexi sat up and sent him a look of genuine astonishment. She had wondered what he had planned but hadn't stopped to consider the live-in possibility. 'You want to move in with me?'

'She's pretty slow to catch on, isn't she, Cosmo?'

The cat opened one piercing hazel eye, regarded Jack lazily for a moment or two, and then closed it again.

Alexi laughed. 'He's sitting on the fence.'

'But I'm not. I never say anything I don't mean. I'm not Patrick and I won't hurt you.'

'Except that every time you come into my life, a dead body turns up.'

'Stop avoiding the issue. I'm in love with you, Alexi. There, I've said it.' He fixed her with an intent look. 'Don't you have anything to say to me in return?'

Oh yeah, she had plenty to say. She loved him right back, had known it for a while, but was way better with the written word than she'd ever be with the spoken one. Besides, she figured that actions spoke louder than words in any form so silenced him with a searing kiss.

ACKNOWLEDGMENTS

My grateful thanks as always to the wonderful Boldwood team and in particular, to my talented editor, Emily Ruston.

MORE FROM E.V. HUNTER

We hope you enjoyed reading *A Contest to Kill For*. If you did, please leave a review.

If you'd like to gift a copy, this book is also available as an ebook, large print, hardback, digital audio download and audiobook CD.

Sign up to E.V Hunter's mailing list for news, competitions and updates on future books.

https://bit.ly/EvieHunterNewsletter

A Date to Die For, the first of E.V. Hunter's Hopgood Hall Murder Mysteries, is available to buy now...

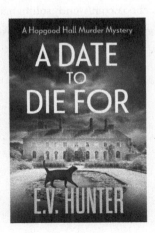

ABOUT THE AUTHOR

E.V. Hunter has written a great many successful regency romances as Wendy Soliman and revenge thrillers as Evie Hunter. She is now redirecting her talents to produce cosy murder mysteries. For the past twenty years she has lived the life of a nomad, roaming the world on interesting forms of transport, but has now settled back in the UK.

Follow E.V. Hunter on social media:

 twitter.com/wendyswriter

facebook.com/wendy.soliman.author

bookbub.com/authors/wendy-soliman

Poison
& Pens

POISON & PENS IS THE HOME OF
COZY MYSTERIES SO POUR YOURSELF
A CUP OF TEA & GET SLEUTHING!

DISCOVER PAGE-TURNING NOVELS FROM
YOUR FAVOURITE AUTHORS &
MEET NEW FRIENDS

JOIN OUR
FACEBOOK GROUP

BIT.LYPOISONANDPENSFB

SIGN UP TO OUR
NEWSLETTER

BIT.LY/POISONANDPENSNEWS

Boldwood

Boldwood Books is an award-winning fiction publishing company seeking out the best stories from around the world.

Find out more at www.boldwoodbooks.com

Join our reader community for brilliant books, competitions and offers!

Follow us
@BoldwoodBooks
@BookandTonic

Sign up to our weekly deals newsletter

https://bit.ly/BoldwoodBNewsletter